Get Your
Sexy On

Get Your Sexy On

Kimberly Kaye Terry

APHRODISIA

KENSINGTON BOOKS

http://www.kensingtonbooks.com

APHRODISIA BOOKS are published by

Kensington Publishing Corp.
850 Third Avenue
New York, NY 10022

All Kensington Titles, Imprints, and Distributed Lines are available at special quantity discounts for bulk purchases for sales promotions, premiums, fund-raising, and educational or institutional use.

Special book excerpts or customized printings can also be created to fit specific needs. For details, write or phone the office of the Kensington special sales manager: Kensington Publishing Corp., 850 Third Avenue, New York, NY 10022, attn: Special Sales Department, Phone: 1-800-221-2647.

Aphrodisia and the A logo Reg. U.S. Pat & TM Off.

ISBN-13: 978-0-7582-2250-3
ISBN-10: 0-7582-2250-5

First Kensington Trade Paperback Printing: October 2008

10 9 8 7 6 5 4 3 2 1

Printed in the United States of America

Get Your Sexy On

1

The Sweet Kitty Gentlemen's Club
Downtown Washington, DC

"Sin, it's showtime. Time to get your sexy on, girl."

After curling the mascara wand one last time over her naturally thick lashes, Sienna glanced away from the mirror.

She smiled at the woman who gave her the reminder and pushed the wand back inside the mascara tube and twisted it closed.

"Yeah, Kitty, I know," she murmured, throwing the woman a small affectionate smile. "I'll be ready in a sec. Gotta give 'em the best that I got, to get what I want," she quipped.

Deloris, aka Delatta Kitty, ran her hands down the sides of her thong-covered rounded hips. "Definitely, baby girl. And maybe after your last set, you and I can have a drink and you can show *me* the best that you got," the older woman murmured in her whisky-toned voice, and gave Sienna a small wink.

"I don't know if you can handle the best I've got. I may be too much for you." She rose from her chair and glanced at her reflection in the chipped oval mirror.

"Promises, promises. Why don't you let me be the judge of what I can handle, baby girl?"

"Yeah, right. I value my health too much, even if I were so inclined, Ms. D," she said, looking back in the mirror, checking her makeup. "Carmen lets it be known that if anyone, man or woman, ever tries to step to you, they will have to deal with her."

Deloris had been with her lover, Carmen Delgado, one of the other dancers, for more than a decade. Barely out of their teens, the two women had met at another club, dancing two in a cage. No matter how much Deloris flirted with other women, Sienna knew she would never cheat on Carmen. She loved Carmen as much as the woman loved her.

"Yeah, my woman can get a bit hot around the collar sometimes. But still, if you're ever lonely . . ." Deloris let the sentence dangle and Sienna released a groaning laugh. "Girl, you're going to get me in trouble. If your woman even *thinks* I'm trying to step to you, my ass is grass!"

Deloris returned the laugh and strolled away from Sienna, her full hips swaying.

Sienna shook her head and grinned as Deloris put more than a little bit of attitude in her walk as she strolled away. Sienna released a small chuckle before she turned her attention to the mirror for one final, critical assessment, pursing her crimson red lips.

She opened the tube of lip gloss on the vanity and ran the cotton tip over her full upper and lower rims.

Sinful lips. She had sinful lips.

That's what she'd been told on more than one occasion. Her foster father had told her that her lips were full of sin, just like she was. He had licked his thin lips; a nasty, lustful smile had crossed his pinched features while he watched her dress for school.

Sienna thought of the other crude things he'd said when no one else was around to hear.

When no one had been around to stop him.

She shoved the memories out of her mind of what he'd

forced her to do with her sinful lips. She focused her thoughts on her future, away from her painful past.

"Just one more night of this, and I'm done. Lord, just let me make it through one more night," she whispered out loud, closed her eyes, and sent the prayer heavenward.

She opened her eyes and smiled, determinedly, at her reflection. Using both hands, she fluffed the long, dark blond, curly wig around her face, making sure that none of her own dark, silky curls escaped.

Sienna turned from the mirror, leaving the dressing area as she heard the DJ start to mix in her signature song with the R&B tune bumping from the speakers.

As she walked, her sway became more pronounced, her body relaxed, her small breasts pushed out, her shoulders thrown back.

Sienna tossed her hair away from her face, licked her full lips, and smiled.

She was almost ready.

The closer she came to the long, black velvet curtain cloaking the stage, the more she shed her inhibitions.

The less she cared.

It was showtime, like Deloris said.

Time to get her sexy on.

The slow, hot heat from the rhythm invaded her limbs and she reached back and fluffed out the colorful feathers attached to her thong.

Her fingertips then ran lightly over her breasts, skimming her protruding nipples, making sure her sequined pasties were secure.

With a toss of her head and a smile, the transformation was complete. She was no longer Sienna Featherstone, part-time substitute grade-school teacher, full-time college student.

She was Sinful Feathers, headlining act at the Sweet Kitty Gentlemen's Club.

And for one final night, one final time, it was time to get her sexy on.

2

Garrett McAllister sat back in the high-backed wooden bar chair and raised the shot glass of whisky to his lips and took a healthy swallow. With a grimace, he placed the glass back on the small dented table in front of him, and turned bored eyes toward the gyrating woman on the main stage.

Her moves were the same as all the others before her.

She shimmied and danced, kicking her long legs out in front of her, gyrating for all she was worth. She worked her double-D cups, grabbing her breasts and squeezing them, dancing and twirling around the small stage for the throng of men standing in rapt attention.

When one of the men looked particularly animated, the dancer dropped down on all fours, slid on her back, throwing her legs in the air, and shimmied her ass in front of him.

At his vantage point, Mac could see the saliva practically oozing from the sides of the man's lips as the dancer slid one long, manicured finger inside her thong panties. She pushed the scrap of lace aside to give the man an extra peek at what else she had for sale.

It was no secret that some of the strippers at the Sweet Kitty offered more than a stage or lap dance to the men who frequented the club.

There were several rooms upstairs where, with the right price, a man—or a woman—could buy a "bed dance." According to club rules, all bed dances, although conducted on an actual bed, with the customer lying down and the dancer on top of him or her, were conducted fully clothed.

But what happened when the doors were closed in the bedrooms was a different matter altogether, Mac thought cynically.

The music ended, and with it, the dancer's set. The woman abruptly stopped dancing, midshimmy, and gathered the tossed bills before swiftly walking off the stage.

At the curtain separating the stage from the back room, she paused and glanced over her shoulder toward the customer she'd given a private viewing. She pointed to the back of the club with one of her long, talonlike fingernails, where a winding staircase, leading to the upper rooms, was located.

With nonchalance, Mac observed the exchange. He noted the man's head hastily bobbed up and down in affirmation and the woman left the stage area with a satisfied grin.

His gaze raked over the clientele at the Sweet Kitty. The clientele ranged from men in beat-up jeans, T-shirts, and yellow work boots, to businessmen wearing Brooks Brothers suits and Rolex watches.

"Mac, ain't nothing going on here tonight besides tits-and-ass shakin'. I don't think our guy is going to show," Kyle Hanley said, drawing his attention from the scene on the stage. His partner's gaze was on the women dancing on small round upraised stages, scattered throughout the dimly lit club.

"Patience, man. It's his club, he's bound to show. Besides, you have somewhere else you'd rather be?"

"Hell yes. The luscious Tawny and her sister, Tanya, and I have plans. I thought we'd be done with this case, and if ol' boy ain't showing, I can sure in hell find a better way to spend my time." Kyle's restless eyes scanned the room.

Mac released a grunt for a laugh. "He may still show. Don't want to take the chance on missing him. I'm sure you lovebirds can do whatever the hell you have planned, later."

Mac turned back to the stage, ignored his friend's glare, and did a quick scan of the room, hoping to find Damian in the crowd. Although he preferred one woman at a time, had only participated in one ménage à trois, which left him strangely unsatisfied, Mac had no problem with his friend's proclivity for multiple partners.

To each his own.

He didn't understand male/female relationships, much less a relationship involving *two* women—so what the hell did he know anyway? Although he'd been surprised when Kyle had disclosed his sexual preference—a *need* he'd said—for two women at once, that he couldn't find satisfaction with one woman, it hadn't altered his view of his friend.

Mac and Kyle had been friends as well as battle buddies throughout their career, from their first enlistment in their Special Forces unit in Heidelberg, Germany, to their last duty station in Afghanistan. Dating back over fifteen years, he was closer to Kyle than he was to anyone else in the world, besides his sister. Mac couldn't think of a better man, one he'd trust more to have his back, than Kyle.

Their latest case had been an easy one. They'd been hired to locate Larissa St. John, the missing daughter of a wealthy couple in New England. Larissa had left home the previous year, leaving behind a note that said she was tired of school and wanted to live her life the way she wanted.

Although she had been over the age of consent, twenty-one years old, her parents had hired Mac to go and find their daughter.

Mac and Kyle had tracked the wayward deb to DC and found her shaking her moneymaker like a seasoned pro. When they identified themselves to her, and explained that her family had sent them to bring her back home, she'd broken down in tears.

The life she envisioned "on her own" hadn't turned out to be the life of glamour she thought she'd have.

They'd finished the case in less than two weeks, after having placed her on the plane to go home. The men would have returned to their home base in Hampton, Virginia—had Mac not discovered something far more interesting than a runaway quasi adult thumbing her nose at conventionality, trying to prove she was grown by stripping.

He'd discovered the Sweet Kitty was a front for a money-laundering operation, among other criminal activities, all tied up with a Dominican named Carlos Medeiros. Mac had first come across Medeiros's name during a previous investigation, another runaway case. Medeiros ran a tight operation, and Mac hadn't been able to tie him into the disappearance of two young college-aged women, although the intel he'd gathered pointed to Medeiros being involved.

Medeiros surrounded himself with a bevy of guards, 24/7, and Mac hadn't been able to get close enough to him to gather the evidence he needed to take to the police. When he and Kyle found the young women in a Vegas brothel, they'd been so desperate to go home, they hadn't given him any substantial information about their involvement in the brothel. Either that, or they were too afraid to speak. Mac had been left frustrated, knowing there wasn't a damn thing he could do. His gut, however, told him Medeiros had been involved.

The owner of the brothel had been just as tight-lipped about how she'd "found" the girls.

Damian Marks, the owner of the Sweet Kitty, was nothing but a local hood. Trying to play with the big boys, Damian thought he'd hit gold when he'd hooked up with Medeiros. Mac had a feeling Marks had bitten off more than he could chew, dealing with Medeiros.

"Man, check *her* out. Shit, she's fine." Kyle had interrupted Mac's thoughts. Kyle nodded his head toward the stage, and Mac's glance fell on the new dancer.

Damn, it was *her*. His dick thumped against his zipper and Mac readjusted himself, his eyes glued on the woman on the stage.

The second reason Mac wasn't ready to leave DC yet was because of her. Sinful Feathers.

Damn, she was beautiful. And she stuck out like the peacock her feathered costume suggested—she was all bright color in a gray lackluster world.

He adjusted his seat, to see her better. He and Kyle were seated at one of the tables to the right of the stage. They'd picked a table giving them an optimal view of the entire club, but still protecting their backs, so no one could sneak up on them. Both men had trained for covert operations, where that was an essential part of any mission.

Still, they were angled and positioned close enough so Mac could catalog her beauty, along with the graceful way she moved. His eyes narrowed against the spiraling smoke from the cigarette he'd left burning, unnoticed, in the glass ashtray.

She wrapped both of her slim hands around the thick pole in the center of the stage with practiced dexterity. With fluid ease, she flipped her curvaceous, yet agile, body upside down and slipped one long, muscled cocoa-brown leg around the lower end of the pole. She wrapped the other leg higher up the pole.

Her torso dangled downward, one hand casually holding on to the pole keeping her balanced, the other arm thrown behind her. The ends of her long hair swept the stage floor as she arched her body away from the pole in time with the heavy beat of the music.

Mac blindly reached for his half-forgotten drink as he watched the beautiful dancer work the pole.

With a grimace, he took a swallow, his eyes never leaving the semi-nude dancer on the stage.

3

Unlike the other dancers, this one never looked at any of the men who whistled and called out to her. She wasn't dancing for the ogling men, but for herself.

Mac was intrigued by her casual, absentminded sexiness. As though she didn't give a damn what the ogling, horny bastards at the club thought as they watched her sinewy body wrap around the pole, dancing as though she were alone in the room.

Throughout the two-week investigation, Mac had witnessed several degrees of skill from the strippers at the Sweet Kitty. From the burgeoning, awkward attempts by the neophytes, much like the stuck-up heiress he'd rescued, to the jaded, yet proficient, skills of those who'd danced for years.

None he had seen were like this woman. None of them had played with his mind, had given him hot dreams at night, cold showers in the morning, like she had.

Everything about her was different, from her slow, hypnotic moves, to the sensual, rhythmic music she moved her body to, or the way she never glanced at anyone in the audience while she danced.

She danced to a slow rhythm that really had nothing to do with the music, a beat that only she could hear. It made a man long to be the only one she was dancing for. Made him long to have her wrap her beautiful body around his, have her look in his eyes, seeing him, no one else but him, as he stroked into her hot, creaming pussy, until she cried out his name.

Blindly Mac reached inside his jacket and pulled out his money clip, his eyes never leaving the stage.

At the end of what felt like an eternity, but was only the five-minute length of the song, Mac felt as though he were coming out of a fog.

Sinful glanced around once the song ended—as though she shared the same dim fog of unawareness with Mac as the music faded away, blending into the next song—and then slowly stood.

In that sexy backhanded way of hers, she casually scooped up the pile of bills scattered on the stage. She was hunched down, gathering the money, when her gaze connected with Mac's.

Mac's heart loudly thumped, audible to his ears, his nostrils flaring as she came close to him. One slender arm reached out, palm outstretched, and he looked down at his own hand, a twenty-dollar bill held between his fingers.

He hadn't been aware he'd taken the money out. When she came close, he inhaled deeply, picking up on her scent, despite the cloying perfume and smoke in the club, and closed his eyes briefly. He opened them when her fingertips touched his, and an electrical current passed from her to him.

He glanced at her face. In the dim light, he saw the red flush darken her smooth brown skin, her eyes widen in awareness.

Her small pink tongue darted out and laved the lower, full rim of her lips as they stared at one another.

When she noticed the new dancer on the stage ready to perform, she was the first to look away. With one final, hesitant look his way, she gracefully left the stage.

Mac felt inexplicably shaken, wondering what the hell had just happened between them. He shook his head, as though to clear it, and turned to see his partner, Kyle, staring at him, mouth slightly open, his expression puzzled.

"What the fuck was that all about?"

With a noncommittal shrug, Mac pretended nonchalance, picked up his shot glass, ignored the way his hand shook, and took a healthy swallow.

The fiery burn of the whisky easing down his throat didn't do a damn thing to ease the painful throb in his pants. Or erase the memory of the dancer's hot body working the pole the way he wanted her to work him. Nor did it erase the electric charge they had generated when her soft hand touched his.

Impatient and irritated, he glanced around the floor once again for a glimpse of Damian Marks or Carlos Medeiros.

"Let's get the hell out of here. They're not showing tonight."

As Mac stood to go, throwing down several bills to cover their tab, he noticed Marks enter the club. Mac slowly sat back down.

"Looks like one of them decided to make an appearance," Kyle said, and sat down as well.

Mac watched as Marks strolled through the club, stopping every so often to speak to a customer, before he walked closer, approaching a table to Mac's far left, where a group of four men dressed in business attire sat.

Mac signaled for a waitress to come and ordered a Coke.

"No more alcohol tonight," he told Kyle when he raised a brow at his choice of drink. "I need to keep my wits together."

"Yeah, I think they all flew south after that last dancer." Kyle laughed.

"Go to hell," Mac mumbled, his attention on Marks. Before, when he walked through the crowded club, stopping occasionally to speak, he'd had his normal swagger, arrogance clinging to his thin frame like the cheap suit he wore.

With this group, he was all smiles, grinning like a damn Cheshire cat as he spoke to the men, Mac thought. He didn't sit at the table with them, although there was an open seat. After several minutes, one of the men said something that wiped the smile off Marks's face.

"Damn, I wish I could hear what they were saying," Kyle said, watching the exchange as well.

"Whatever it was, it knocked that stupid-ass grin off Marks's face," Mac said, grunting.

"Think they're connected with Medeiros?"

"Probably. We'll follow them when they leave, get a make on their transportation and run a check."

"I gather we're not going home very soon, after all."

"No. I think we'll be sticking around for a while. We just may come up with something more interesting than returning a runaway."

"Man, we ain't making no money hanging around here," Kyle groused, but Mac ignored him.

The image of the dancer's sensual glides against the pole flashed in Mac's mind. Marks wasn't the only reason he wanted to stick around the Sweet Kitty for a few days more.

4

"What do you mean you're ready to quit? Who told you that was your choice, bitch?" Damian Marks walked closer to Sienna, crowding her, shoving her until her back touched the back of the door.

Sienna was so afraid she felt close to peeing on herself, but she knew if she backed down now, the asshole would never let her go. She swallowed her fear and tried to shove at his chest.

"Back up off me, Damian! What the hell is wrong with you? I've paid you the money I owe you, then some! And I'm done with this life! I want out. I finished school and I'm ready to take care of my brother now!"

A sharp crack split the air, forcing her head back and away when his hand connected with the side of her face.

"Take care of your brother? That retarded mother—"

"Don't! Don't you fucking say it! Don't you say anything about my brother!" Sienna cried, biting back the tears that sprang to her eyes. She raised her hand to hit Damian, and he caught her raised fist in a punishing grasp.

"Don't. Don't make the mistake of hitting me, Sin. I would hate to see something happen to Jacob."

Sienna's eyes widened in alarm and her heartbeat slammed against her chest. The flat expression in his soulless eyes scared her to death, and promised sure retribution if she hit him.

She could handle his retribution against her. That didn't scare her.

What made her back down was the knowledge that he'd carry out his ugly threat and hurt her helpless brother.

"Now get your ass out there and make me some money," he said.

She held his gaze for long moments, refusing to look away.

He broke first, turning away from her. The breath she'd been holding rushed out of her. She'd opened the door to leave, until his next words halted her in her tracks.

"Tonight I want you working the floor."

"What? You know I don't—"

"Tonight, and any other night I want you to, you will do what the hell I tell you to do. Now get your ass out of here, and get to work," he said, and turned away from her in cold dismissal. "And Sin?"

Sienna half-turned to face him. "What?" she asked in a low voice.

"If I were you, I'd be careful. Very careful. You owe me, and when *I* say the debt is collected, then the debt is collected. Don't make me have to remind you who's in control around here, again, bitch." The threat, along with the deadpan expression across his thin, pale face, sent chills racing down Sienna's spine.

"I think I have trouble."

"What trouble, Damian?" the low, deep voice asked, his tone calm, casual, conversational.

Immediately Damian raised his thumb to his mouth and began to chew nervously on his nail. He paced the length of his office. In disgust, he yanked his fingers out of his mouth, forcing himself to resist the urge to bite his nails to the skin.

A weakness he tried his damndest to overcome, but whenever he talked to Carlos—even on the phone—the old habit reared its ugly head.

"One of the dancers wants to quit."

"And?" the man drawled in his smooth, barely accented voice.

"It's Sienna," he said abruptly, and waited.

There was a heartbeat of silence.

As he waited for the response, the nerves in Damian's gut clenched to the point that he felt like hurling.

"What have you done?" The voice that was once smooth took on a sharper tone, the accent became thicker.

Damian nervously grabbed the expensive bottle of Glenfiddich single malt and poured it into one of the Waterford Crystal shot glasses set on the bar in his office.

"I have every confidence that you will do whatever it takes to make sure this doesn't happen, *sí*, Damian?"

"Uh, no. I mean, yes. She's not going anywhere. I'll make sure of it. You can count on me, sir."

"Good, Damian. That is good. Because I would hate for something *unfortunate* to happen, were she to leave. I've so enjoyed our association."

The dial tone on the other end signaled the end of the call.

Damian hung up the phone and sat down listlessly in his chair; fear and the consequences of what Carlos would do to him if Sienna left churned a hot path through his gut.

He looked around at the elegance of his office, at all the rare, expensive prints carefully hung on the wall, the expensive leather furniture, the wine rack with an assortment of high-priced wine— all of it represented how far he'd come from the poor snot-nosed kid from the wrong side of town who ran away.

He was no longer the picked-on street kid who was trying to make enough money to make rent because his strung-out whore of a mother was too fucked-up most times to give a damn if he ate, and mostly forgot he existed, nine times out of ten.

Not only did he own one of the most profitable strip clubs in downtown DC, but he was an associate of one of the most powerful men in the city. Even if the man didn't acknowledge him in public, had to keep a certain "distance," Damian knew that if he played his cards right, he'd score big.

And all those motherfuckers who made fun of his drunk-ass mother, and laughed at him for wearing torn-up clothes, begging for food when he was hungry, they would have to recognize.

Recognize that he had arrived. He was the damn man! If anybody felt the slightest urge to try anything stupid with him now, he had someone in his corner that none of them would dick with.

He poured another glass and tossed the drink down his throat, wiping his mouth with the back of his hand.

Now, to make sure the stupid cunt Sienna didn't fuck up his plans.

5

Sienna took a deep breath and slowly released the pent-up air in a small puff.

Damn.

She hadn't had to do a lap dance in a long time, but since Damian wanted to prove a point, that she was totally under his dominance, she had to swallow what little pride she had and do what she had to do. She'd do anything to keep her brother safe. She was all he had.

Her eyes searched the crowd for Damian, but she didn't see him. But she knew his eyes were on her, somewhere.

No doubt he was watching her across the room behind one of his "special" two-way mirrors, getting his laugh on, knowing how much she hated this.

She surveyed the crowded throng of men and slowly threaded her way through the club. She heard the murmurings from some of the club's regulars, surprised to see she was on the floor. She hadn't had to work it, hadn't had to do any lap dances for a long time.

She also caught the surprised—and mocking—glances of

several of the dancers in response to her arrival on the floor. She stiffened her back, plastered a purposeful half smile on her face, and lazily surveyed the men.

"Come on over here, baby doll, and come sit on Daddy's lap."

Sienna glanced down and kept her face casually disinterested, careful not to show her disgust at the groping man's hands roaming her ass.

"I don't need a daddy, sugar. Been there, done that. Now, if you want my time, the money's gotta be right," she purred, trying, unsuccessfully, to pluck his meaty hands away from her ass.

"Oh, I got the dollars, baby, you better believe that. Now come on over here and sit that fine ass down on my lap. Be a good girl and give Daddy a dance."

He grabbed her, circling her wrist with one beefy hand. Caught off-balance on her stilettos, Sienna landed, hard, in his lap.

"I didn't think I'd ever get this chance. To think I almost let my wife nag me into staying home with her instead." He breathed the comment alongside her neck; his hot whisky-and-cigarette breath nearly singeing the fine hairs alongside the nape of her neck, beneath her wig.

She tried hard not to cringe at the way he slurred his words, asking her to sit in his lap—his dick already hard and pointing straight at her—along with his creepy reference that he was her daddy.

God, Damian knew just what to do to humiliate her, Sienna thought. He knew she hated this part of stripping more than anything.

She swallowed and closed her eyes, allowing her body to take over and forcing her mind away from what she was doing. What she had to do.

She was starting to bounce on his lap when she felt a hand cover her hand, calmly removing the drunk's beefy hand from around her wrist.

Startled, she felt her eyes fly open.

"I believe the lady promised this dance to me," a deep baritone voice intoned with little inflection.

Sienna glanced up swiftly. Her gaze slowly traveled up a long, hard body, settling on a stern face she'd come to look for in the crowd over the last week.

Her heartbeat quickened. It was him. The man she hadn't been able to get out of her mind, the one she'd been dancing for—him and him alone—over the last week . . . hoping she'd see him again, yet praying he wouldn't come back.

Ignoring the drunk's protest with a hard look, the man calmly lifted Sienna off his lap, tucked her under his arm, and led her away to a darker, more secluded area of the club.

Quiet, unnerved by not only his presence but his overall masculinity, Sienna allowed him to lead her. He sat down and held out a hand. Hesitantly she placed her hand in his and looked into his deep, light gray eyes. Although she knew he was asking her to dance for him, it seemed as though he wanted something more.

By taking his hand, she was agreeing to give him what he wanted.

"I'm sure one of the other girls would be much better at this than me. It's been a while for me," Sienna whispered, her eyes trained on the sensual full curve of his hard mouth.

Her gaze traveled over his angular face, taking in his deepset gray eyes, framed by short, thick lashes, before traveling down his aquiline nose, sensual, hard full mouth, ending at his squared chin, which held the faintest hint of a cleft.

His thick sable-brown hair was cut close to his finely shaped head, tapering to almost skin past his ears. If not for the slightly longer length on top, he could be a poster boy for the U.S. Marine Corps.

"This isn't something you do often?" he asked, sitting farther back in his seat, settling her on his lap.

"No, I don't. At least not in a while. I dance on the stage, occasionally do the smaller stages, but that's it."

She forced the words out of her mouth, straddling his hard thighs, trying her best to concentrate on dancing for him, and not get caught up in the erotic fantasies she'd had going on about him over the last week.

"What's your name?" he murmured, catching her off-guard with the question.

"Sinful Feathers. Sin."

"No. Your real name."

She began to dance, slowly gyrating her hips, rolling her buttocks along his jeans-covered, hard thighs.

Sienna never gave her real name to anyone at the club. It was such an intimate thing—as crazy as it sounded, considering she regularly shed her clothes for scores of men.

"Mine's Garrett. Garrett McAllister. Friends call me Mac." He gave his name, although she hadn't asked.

Just as she used a spin on her real name to give her emotional distance, she'd never wanted to know the names of the men she danced for. She needed the space, and with this man, she definitely hadn't wanted to know his name. She didn't want to feel as though this were anything more than it was. A dancer providing a service for a client. Nothing more, nothing less.

He waited for her to respond. Instead, she turned her head away from his piercing gaze and continued to move her body in time to the music.

She glanced around the room, feeling as though everyone were staring at them.

No one was giving them any more notice than any of the other dancers performing one-on-one for the male clientele.

"It's just you and me, Sin, it's just the two of us, alone. Forget about everybody else."

"I can't." She choked out the words, turning reluctantly to face him. "I can't just forget they're there, watching." Sienna felt as if everyone were watching her as she straddled his hard thighs, riding him. She carefully avoided his hardening shaft thumping against her belly.

"Yes, you can. It's just you and me."

She didn't know Garrett McAllister at all. Over the last few years she'd worked at the club, she had men who'd come in faithfully, but none of them had ever made a dent in her shield. She had never longed to *know* any of them, as she did with this man. It made no sense. God, it made no sense.

But she wanted to know him. She yearned for him. In ways she never had for any man. Even more so than she had for Damian, when she'd first met him, before she learned of his true nature.

She'd noticed him the first time he'd entered the club. He and the black guy he came in with. They'd sat to her left, never making any catcalls, never coming up to the stage—yet she'd *felt* his stare. Among a roomful of men, she'd been aware of his intense gaze on hers. Each night, she'd thought he'd be waiting for her.

Nervous, afraid that he would be there, she'd left the club as soon as she'd collected her money for the night and had cashed out. Disappointed, despite self avowals to the contrary, she realized he'd never been waiting for her.

Her nipples rasped against the rough material of his blazer, spiking in arousal. Her vagina clenched, coming into scorching contact with the bulge lying beneath his zipper, despite her intent to avoid it. The music playing was a slow, sensual beat. Sienna reveled in the rhythm and closed her eyes.

"Yes," he rasped, easing her body closer to his, touching her, although it was forbidden to do so. "Just like that. There's only you and me." With his words, Sienna gave in to what her body demanded she give him.

No longer was she performing a service, a lap dance. Instead, helpless, she feverishly worked her body against the long, hard length of pipe lying hot and thick between her legs.

Grinding her body against his, she lost touch with her surroundings and, with it, her inhibitions loosened.

"That's good. That's real good," he encouraged. "Don't

think of anyone. It's you and me. And what you're doing to me." He uttered the words in a guttural tone, unashamedly referring to his hardened penis centered between her thighs.

She felt the heat of embarrassment; lust and passion flushed her cheeks, yet she continued to ride him. Everyone in the club had to know of the cream now flowing from her. She felt the ease of it, down past the lace of her thong, traveling her thigh and saturating his lap.

The burdening weight of a hundred pairs of eyes seemed to mock her. She tucked her head against his chest in shame. "No," she whispered.

"You can," he insisted gruffly.

Again, ignoring the club rule of no touching, he placed both hands on her waist and centered her directly on his massive erection. "Now rub that sweet snatch all over this dick, and make me come, baby. Make me come," he demanded.

He then did the unthinkable. He snaked his tongue out and gently swiped at the seam of her lips.

Sienna forgot about who might or might not be looking at them. Daringly, she stuck out her tongue and engaged in a short duel with his, lapping her wet tip against his before retreating it back into her mouth.

With those words, that short kiss, and the hot feel of his shaft knifing against the seam of her vagina, Sienna felt the unmistakable beginnings of an orgasm shake her quivering body.

"Oh God, I can't believe this," she whispered, her voice breaking. "I can't do this. I—"

He pressed one finger against her lips, while the other kept her steady, riding him. "Sssh, it's okay. I'll protect you. Just come for me. Let it go," he whispered, and adjusted her body, positioning them away from any chance onlookers.

The music faded, smoothly blending into the next song; this one slower, the rhythms heavier, more sensual. A soft cry escaped her lips. Sienna closed her eyes, allowing the music to take over.

"No, open your eyes. Look at me," he demanded, and captured her lips, again, in a short, soft kiss.

"Oh God—" she whimpered, yet obeyed his dictate.

Sienna ground against him, tight swirls with her hips, curled her spine and smoothly popped her buttocks up and down in his lap. She didn't know what was affecting her so strongly—the music, the dark, or the man she was riding. Or a combination of all three.

Whatever it was, she was lost in the moment. She completely gave in to the sensations coursing through her body, the feelings this man had helped to create.

She kept her eyes trained on Mac's eyes, her forehead barely touching his. She swallowed her automatic cries of passion while she slid her body along his.

His deep, harsh breath fanned against her forehead, telling her he was as caught up in the feelings they'd generated as she was.

"I—I think I'm going to come. Please let me go. I can't . . . ," she begged when her pussy tightened and the orgasm began to curl in the pit of her stomach.

"Yes, baby, just like that," he whispered. "It's okay, release it. Let go," he encouraged. His husky words, the music, and the feel of him between her legs, so hard and strong, were her undoing.

He grasped her hips, helping her to ride him, and she let out a cry that he swallowed. She arched her back sharply, desperately clutching his broad shoulders.

"What the fuck do you think you're doing?" an angry voice intruded, harshly ending the orgasm rippling through her body.

6

With a painful cry, Sienna felt herself snatched, bodily, from Mac's lap and thrown to the floor. Disoriented, she was barely able to catalog the swift movement from the man who had been inches away from giving her the ultimate pleasure.

She scrambled to her feet, only to encounter Damian's twisted, red, angry face, his hand raised, fist closed, prepared to strike her. She covered her arms over her head, readying herself for the blow.

Instead of feeling a fist connecting painfully with her jaw, she saw Mac towering over Damian. He grabbed Damian's much smaller clenched fist within his and spun him around.

"Don't fucking touch her," Mac barked.

"Get your damn hands off me!"

Posturing, aware of the small audience now paying avid attention to the threesome in the dark corner, Damian wouldn't back down, Sienna knew, despite the fear she saw blazing in his dark brown eyes.

"What the fuck do you think you're doing?"

Dragged abruptly from the hot feel of her body riding him,

Mac quickly jumped to his feet once Sin had been torn from his lap and stood, cowering. He grabbed the smaller man's hand before he could hit Sin.

"Nothing, Damian! I was just giving the man a dance. What the hell are you doing?" she hissed, glancing around at the small group of onlookers, who boldly watched the drama unfold.

"Dancing, my ass, bitch! You were fucking him! This ain't that kind of place. If you wanna whore, you need to take that shit somewhere else."

Had Mac been in the frame of mind to laugh, he would have done so, outright, at the comment. He knew for a fact the Sweet Kitty offered much more than stripping and lap dances, if the price was right.

But at the moment, he had more pressing things to take care of. He tightened his hold on Marks's hand, and watched in satisfaction when Damian nearly buckled to the floor in pain.

He had been completely enthralled by Sin's overwhelming, yet unique, womanly smell; the scent of their combined lust; and the way she danced in his lap, grinding her sweet pussy on his dick, as she uttered the small, helpless cries of pleasure.

He wanted nothing more than to unzip his pants, release himself, grab her by the back of her hair, and slam his body into hers, repeatedly, driving his dick as far into her wet, slick heat as he could, until he reached the back of her womb.

Mac couldn't believe he'd gotten so caught up that he hadn't noticed Marks approaching them.

From the first moment he'd laid eyes on her dancing on the stage, working her agile body on the thick pole, she'd been working him into a sexual frenzy.

All frustrated sexual thoughts were cast aside as he easily crushed Marks's hand within his. He ignored Damian's frantic cries for Mac to release him. Instead, he concentrated solely on Sienna as she stood helpless. A red haze of anger clouded his vision.

"If you so much as lay a goddamn *pinky* finger on her, I'll rip your ass apart." He raised his other fist, the image of smashing the motherfucker's face paramount in his mind.

Sienna leaped from her crouching position and grabbed Mac's thick forearm, moments before it connected with Damian's jaw.

"Stop it, please! Just let him go!"

It took both of her hands to circle his thick bicep, yet her fingers couldn't connect around the corded muscles bunching beneath them.

For long, tense moments she held on, until she felt his muscles loosen. Still, he maintained his grasp on Damian's fist. Sienna glanced at Damian and saw the deep-red flush line his pale skin. She thought if Mac didn't release his hold soon, he'd break Damian's hand.

Mac turned to her, his jaw clenched, an angry glint in his eyes the only testimony to his rage. "Get your stuff. You're coming with me," he said.

"What? She ain't going no—" Damian's words were cut off in a strangled gasp.

He wanted to take her with him! She wanted to leave with him, leave Damian and the Sweet Kitty far behind. God, she wanted to go, so badly. She wanted to run and never look back.

"Ja-Jacob," Damian uttered the one name, he knew, would keep her in check.

She couldn't leave.

Her brother's face flashed before her eyes. Despite the pain in Damian's eyes, the threat of what he could, and would, do to Jacob shone brightly in his eyes. He'd come after her. After Jacob.

With a cry in her heart, she turned to Mac. "I can't."

His unwavering stare held a hint of softness, one at odds with his overall hard exterior. The look in his eyes silently asked her if that was what she wanted. Sienna could only turn away, unable to hold his gaze.

He turned back to Damian, any traces of softness left his eyes, and his face hardened.

"I'm watching your ass."

He finally released his hold on Damian, and Damian leaped from his cowering position, massaging his knuckles. He turned to the small group of gawking onlookers.

"This ain't no damn show. Get the fuck out of here or go back to what your asses came here for!"

He straightened his clothes and reached for Sienna.

Mac grabbed him by the collar of his shirt and hauled him close, Damian's feet dangling inches from the floor.

"Remember what I said, motherfucker. I'm watching you. Touch her again and you're a dead man." With that, he released Damian and strode out of the club.

Sienna watched him leave, her heart thudding loudly in her ears, wanting to cry out for him to come back to her.

She turned to Damian. "Don't you ever, *ever* think your ass can get away with pulling shit like that with me. I *will* leave one day. And there ain't a damn thing you can do about it!" She straightened her shoulders, swallowed her fear, and looked him dead in the eye.

7

God, what in hell was she going to do? How would she ever escape Damian or the club now? How could she, when she knew Damian was capable, and willing, to carry out his ugly threats against her brother?

After Mac left, Damian told her to get on the stage, excusing her from any further lap dances. She didn't question why, but gratefully left the floor and prepared to dance.

Sienna was on pins and needles for the rest of the evening. Between fear of Damian's reprisal and furtive glances over the audience looking for Mac, she missed steps and performed on automatic, not into the dance or the stage as she normally was.

When Damian left the club early, leaving his manager to close, some of the queasy feelings in her gut went away.

The evening passed without a return appearance from Mac. For that, Sienna didn't know if she should be happy or sad.

In the end, she was grateful when the club closed and she cashed out for the night, collecting her money, with no more interactions from either man.

Presently she couldn't think about any of the drama that had transpired earlier. She needed time. Time to plan and to figure out what—*how*—she could get away, and take her brother with her.

Her first priority was to make sure Jacob was safe. Everything else was secondary to Jacob's protection. If that meant she had to figure out another way to get away from Damian, then she would, without jeopardizing Jacob's safety.

She sighed and shoved aside the fear for the moment. She couldn't wait to get home. As soon as she stepped through the door, she planned to snatch the itchy wig off her head, take a long, hot shower, and crawl into bed, assuming the fetal position and going to sleep.

"I'll probably cry myself to sleep thinking of all this mess," she murmured out loud.

As soon as she spoke, she knew she sounded pitiful, but damn if it wasn't true. A good cry, get it all out, and then she could wrap her brain around what she needed to do in order to save both her brother and herself.

The cool air brushed against her skin, and goose bumps peppered her flesh when she stepped out of the club. She gathered the ends of her old faux-fur coat closer, wrapping the ties around her body to ward off the chill.

She bowed her head while the wind whipped the strands of the blond wig around her face. The only sound in the nearly deserted parking lot was the rushed, rhythmic, staccato tap of her stilettos against the cement.

"I waited for you."

Sienna's steps came to a halt when the deep voice carried along the wind, like notes to a familiar song.

"Wha-what are you doing here?" She clutched the ends of her coat closer, staring at the man, nearly camouflaged, leaning casually against the door of a gleaming black SUV. After what had happened, she thought she'd most likely never see him again.

"We have unfinished business."

Her heart stuttered against her breast—fear, nerves, and arousal all warred for dominance. Mac unfurled his long frame from leaning against his car and ambled toward her.

"What are you doing here?" The catch in her voice was discernible to her own ears. He stood tall, so *dominating* over her. She took a small step back and caught herself. Stiffening her back, she straightened her body and plastered what she hoped was an indifferent look on her face.

"That should be fairly obvious." He reached a long finger out and moved strands of hair away from her face.

Sienna shivered, but not from the chill in the air, but, instead, from the electric bolt that shot through her from his casual touch. She averted her face and his finger slid away, softly feathering her cheek.

"Whatever you *thought* was going to happen, isn't." She turned to go. He caught her arm, preventing her from leaving, forcing her to look at him. "Look, I'm tired. I just want to go home. Please let me go." She whispered the words.

"Come home with me."

The quiet demand in his voice brooked no argument. Helpless, she gazed up at him. "I can't—"

"Yes, you can. Just say *yes*," he returned, and the light from the moon cast a sensual luster to his stern, handsome features. "Please," he added.

He pulled her into his arms, holding her briefly. She buried her nose in the vee of his neck and breathed in his spicy masculine scent, wanting, *needing*, this man for this space of time. His hand came out to stroke the top of her head, reassuring in its casualness.

She leaned back in his embrace and studied his face. His chiseled chin, the hard line of his jaw, and the strong, yet sensual, curve of his lips conjured up hot images of the two of them, naked, bodies twined as he made love to her.

No, he wouldn't make love to her. That was too tame, and

he was far too hard of a man to do *anything* tame. He'd devour her. He'd pin her down to the bed and rock into her, relentlessly. She wouldn't be able to do anything but allow him to have his way with her in any way he chose.

Sienna knew she would surrender, welcome his every heated demand. This moment had been building for a week, one that was inevitable, destined to happen from the moment he'd come to the Sweet Kitty.

She made a decision, and she refused to delve into the reasons for it. She chose to only listen to her heart, for once, and nothing else. If only for one night, he would be hers.

"Yes," she finally answered.

He pulled her toward him and covered her mouth with his. His hard mouth slanted over hers in a hot, turgid kiss. As quickly as he began to devour her mouth, he released her.

Her eyes locked with his. His face was starkly highlighted against the light gleaming from the moon and the harsh lights in the parking lot. The look on his face was frightening in its intensity. Sienna felt like running fast and far away from the hot promise in his light gray eyes.

He must have read her intent. He gathered her beneath the shelter of his arms and, with her in tow, briskly walked back toward his SUV.

"I'll drive. We can pick up your car later."

8

"Thank you," Sienna murmured when Mac removed her coat and, along with his leather jacket, hung both inside the closet near the front door.

Sienna walked farther into the living area and placed her bag on the oversized white sofa. "Your home is beautiful."

"Thanks. But it's temporary digs for me," he replied, and leaned against the door frame, observing her.

His intent stare unnerved her and she caught herself fidgeting, playing with the strands of hair on her wig, before stopping herself. "Temporary?"

"Yes. I don't live in this area. Just here on business." He peeled himself from the wall and walked toward her.

"What type of business?"

"I'm a private investigator. My partner, Kyle, and I were here on a case. We were put up in these accommodations from our client. But he's out. For the weekend."

The clarification didn't go over her head. He wanted her to know that they'd be alone for the weekend.

"Can I get you something? Food? Drink?" he murmured,

the heat from his body reaching out to cocoon her in its warm embrace.

She licked suddenly dry lips. "Something to drink—non-alcoholic—would be nice."

"Why don't you sit down." He waved a hand, indicating for her to choose somewhere to sit amongst the comfortable-looking chairs and sofas scattered throughout the large room. "I think I have something in the fridge. I'll be right back."

She glanced around the tastefully furnished, if sterile, room. She wasn't surprised that it wasn't his home. It didn't fit his personality. Sienna imagined the place Mac called home would be much less put-together, yet just as appealing. It would be ruggedly attractive, much like he was.

Various prints were mounted and framed, carefully arranged around the room. Glass knickknacks were set on the built-in shelves and lined the mantle of the whitewashed brick fireplace.

Instead of sitting down, Sienna roamed the room and ran careful fingers over the art on the walls.

"All I have is apple juice and milk. Hope the juice is okay." Mac interrupted her perusal of the beautiful print she was admiring.

"That's fine." She accepted the juice he held out for her. Despite the flutters in her stomach, she sat down next to him on one of the small love seats and placed her drink on the table in front of them.

Sienna reached for her drink. His large hand covered hers and brought it to his mouth. He opened her palm and placed a hot kiss directly in the center.

"You don't have to be nervous. I'm going to take care of you, Sin."

Mac pulled her closer and slanted his lips over hers, completely covering her mouth. After what had transpired between the two of them during her lap dance, he'd been as horny as his seventeen-year-old randy nephew.

Despite what happened in the club in front of that asshole, Damian Marks, Mac knew it had been more than a dance, more than a grind, for her as well.

He'd felt her slight body tremble, quivering, as she danced in his lap, grinding her body against his cock, and had witnessed the complete ecstasy in her eyes as the orgasm burned through her.

He'd been seconds away from coming as well—to hell with whoever was looking. For once, he'd been as caught up in a woman, a moment, as the woman he'd been pleasuring. Even if it had been in public, in full view of anyone who happened to glance their way.

Damn.

He didn't know if he'd ever been that turned on. Not since he'd been a grown man, at any rate. Had it not been for his concern for her, his desire to shield her from gawkers, he wouldn't have given a damn who saw what he was doing to her in the club. What she had been doing to him.

And now he planned on finishing what they started.

He pushed her down on the sofa and covered her body with his, not giving up the connection of her lush, beautiful lips with his.

He tunneled his fingers through her hair, pulled her head tighter, closer. "Why are you still wearing this?" he asked, pulling on the wig.

"I can take it off." She sounded hesitant, almost shy. With a brief nod, he asked her to remove the wig.

She pulled out several pins and removed the wig. She wore her dark hair short. The thick curls softly framing her face made her look younger than she did in the heavy makeup and fake hair she wore while dancing.

"God, this is the wrong time to ask this, but how old are you?" He held his breath. Shit! If she wasn't legal, no matter how much he wanted to make love to her, there was no way in hell he'd have sex with a minor.

Her startled laughter rang out. "No fears. I'm definitely over the age of consent. I can show you ID if you need it." Despite his raging hard-on, Mac felt like laughing at her quip.

"No, I'll take your word for it," he said, and pulled her full, bottom rim between his teeth and sucked it, pulled on it, bit it, licked it, and shoved his tongue into the moist cavern of her mouth.

"Damn, your mouth is sweet." He broke away from her. He'd wanted to take it slow with her, as slow as he could. But he couldn't. He needed to feel her, naked and writhing, beneath him.

Mac watched her closely as he unbuttoned her blouse and unclipped the front closure of her bra. He stifled a groan when her small, creamy brown breasts, slightly lighter in complexion than her face, tumbled free, and her dark cherry budded nipples stood erect and proud, begging for his touch.

He cupped one of the perfect mounds in one hand and stroked a hard, calloused thumb over the protruding nipple, fascinated by the way it stretched and elongated the more he manipulated it.

"Hmmm," she groaned, and his gaze flew to her face.

"You like that?" he asked gruffly, and she nodded, eyes closed.

"Yes," she answered, her breath coming out in soft puffs of air.

"You'll like what I'm going to do next, more. Lift your hips."

She lifted her small hips and Mac slid her jeans, along with her panties, down her legs in one smooth motion, exposing her.

He tossed the clothes on the floor without looking, keeping his eyes locked on her bared body. One of her legs dangled off the side of the sofa, the other was perched on one of the cushions, leaving her open to him.

He'd seen her dancing, nearly naked, for a week, yet it hadn't prepared him for what she'd look like nude.

Although small, her breasts seemed large in comparison to her waist, but her hips and thighs flared out, toned and smooth.

Instead of being shaved smooth, as he suspected she would be, she had a small thatch of hair covering her pussy. It was centered, in a perfect line, down the middle of her mound. Short enough that he could see her tiny clit poking out.

Mac's index finger feathered over her tuft, seeing if the curls were as soft as they appeared, before separating the lips of her vagina. It turned him on that the skin of her inner lips was a darker brown than the skin on her body.

He dipped his fingers inside and screwed his fingers inside her drenched slit. He withdrew them, soaked with her juices, and licked her cream away.

His own breath was becoming as labored as hers when his gaze traveled to her face and he saw the stamp of arousal there. His nostrils flared as the heady smell of her arousal wafted up to his nose, engulfing him in its heady embrace.

He wondered how many men she'd done this with. How many men had she danced for and allowed to take her home, allowed to stroke and lick her?

How many men had tasted a bit of sin?

"What—what's wrong?" she asked.

He felt her immediate unease and schooled his features away from the anger he felt tightening his face. The hesitancy, the aloneness he'd detected in her from the moment he'd first seen her on stage, was starkly at odds with the side of her personality that allowed her to strip her clothes and dance for a bevy of strangers on a nightly basis.

Mac was uneasy with the duality in her nature. He also felt uncomfortable with his anger.

The urge to find the score of nameless men she'd shed her clothes for, exposed her beautiful body to, and knock their teeth down their collective throats raised a red haze of anger, clouding his vision and his mind.

He clenched his teeth and forcibly shoved the need out of his head and concentrated on the woman in front of him.

"Nothing's wrong. You're beautiful."

"Thank you," she returned huskily. He knew he hadn't said enough to reassure her. She needed reassurance that only he could provide.

He wasn't an eloquent man. He didn't know how to communicate to her, the need he had, the newness of it, the connection he'd had with her from the moment he'd seen her on stage—something he didn't understand.

"You can trust me."

She needed the flowery words, but he didn't know how to express the intensity of his attraction to her.

Damn, he hoped she trusted he would take care of her, if only for this night. She didn't need to fear him.

Her pink tongue swiped the generous swell of her lower lip. His heart clenched when she gave a hesitant smile. "Yes," she said, and cleared her throat. "I trust you."

He groaned, leaned down, pressed himself against her, and captured her lips within his. Minutes passed as he sucked and caressed her lips, until both of their breaths were ragged.

Reluctantly he released her mouth and trailed lingering kisses down her throat; his dick hard, pressing instantly against her bared core. He laved her neck, swirling his tongue in the hollow of her throat.

One hand found and cupped the soft swell of one breast, tugging at the erect nipple. The other hand trailed down her body, searching for and finding the minute thatch of curls guarding the entry at the apex of her thighs.

He tunneled his hands past the furred vee, separated the lips of her vagina, and alternately stroked down each side. She was hot and creamy, her sweet dew sticky, covering his fingers, and Mac groaned, imagining the feel of it saturating his cock.

He slipped one finger inside her tight, moist opening and

massaged her plump clit, rubbing the hard, blood-filled tip until she whimpered, crying out from the pleasure he gave her.

He inserted another finger and rubbed her clit with his thumb as he pumped his fingers in and out of her body.

Sienna tossed her head against the soft cushions on the sofa and arched her body sharply into his. "That feels good, so damn good."

He stifled his own groans when her silken walls clamped down on his fingers. While one hand continued to minister to her pussy, the other molded her breast.

He nibbled kisses on her lips, licking the full lower rim, nipping it, before recapturing her mouth in a hot kiss. Her luscious lips were soft and wet. Perfect. Just like the rest of her.

Mac gently pried open her mouth, inserted his tongue, and groaned into her mouth, searching for her tongue.

He released her mouth and rained kisses down her throat, between her ample breasts, before journeying over to capture one tight, erect bud, pulling the long nipple into his mouth and nursing from her.

He reluctantly released his hold on her breast and pulled his fingers out of her clenching walls, ignoring her cry of protest. Easing his body down the sofa, he dropped to his knees on the floor and arranged her body, placing both of her legs over his shoulders, and leaned into her pussy.

Mac inhaled deep, taking in her heady scent. He placed two fingers alongside the lips of her vagina and separated them. He licked the side of her thigh, laving a trail to the core of her, and stroked her from the back of her opening to the tip of her hood, and pulled the hidden treasure inside his mouth.

"Oooh!" she screamed, her body jerking, her thighs clenching against his head, keeping him right where she wanted him to be.

9

When his rough tongue lapped against her thighs, and his sweet, hot kisses traveled to her vagina, Sienna nearly came.

Sienna half-raised her body from the soft cushions of the sofa, her legs clamping against his face.

The sight of his dark head between her thighs, his hot breath scorching the skin of her inner thighs, was enough to send liquid from her. Embarrassed, she tried to close her legs.

"No, let me finish eating you," he said, and opened his mouth wide. Using his entire tongue, he lapped at her core.

The words and incredible feel of his tongue against her pussy forced her cream to rush from her body. Sienna relaxed her legs and opened herself to his mouth, his lips, his demanding tongue.

With slow licks and soft bites, he ministered to her, swirling his tongue alongside the soft tissue of her inner core, ignoring her whimpers and cries. Sienna was dizzy with the onslaught of erotic sensations.

"Oh God . . . that feels so good," she moaned.

"Do you want me to stop?" He murmured the words against her quivering pussy.

"No! Please don't stop!" Sienna cried out when he blew a hot breath against her inner lips, her body slumping back against the cushions when he curled his tongue around her clit.

He used his talented fingers and kept her lips separated. He suckled on her and she bucked against him, accepting his oral loving, her hands clutching the corners of the seat cushions on either side of her, grabbing one and holding it against her mouth to muffle her cries of pleasure.

In sensual agony, she accepted the wicked glides of his tongue, teeth, and lips, in and around her pussy.

He carefully worked one, two, until he had four of his thick fingers embedded deep inside her drenched channel. He curled them inside her body, rotating them in smooth, circular movements, and Sienna screamed as she released.

Before lifting her in his arms, he withdrew his fingers and kissed her sensitive flesh. Her release was so prolonged, drained her so completely, that afterward she was too weak to do anything but lay back in his arms when he strode out of the room with her nestled in his arms.

She barely cataloged in her mind the journey down a long hallway toward a closed room. He kicked open the door to the bedroom, carried her inside, pulled back the thick comforter, and placed her on satin sheets.

Sienna watched in blissful contentment as he shucked his clothes and walked over to a bureau and opened the top drawer. Her heart raced when he withdrew several foil packets and tossed them on the side table near the bed.

She moaned when he crawled onto the bed, naked, shoved her legs up, and held on to her knees. His beautiful, hard body brushed against her sensitive skin.

The clarity of his intent shone brightly in his light-colored eyes.

Save the light from the hallway, and the illumination of the moon, the room was bathed in a sensual glow of semidarkness.

Yet, Sienna could clearly make out the hard length of his thick, curved penis resting against the muscled planes of his softly furred stomach.

As he ripped one of the condoms open with his teeth, she swallowed the melon-ball size of lust and desire. Before he could roll the prophylactic on, she reached down and trailed her fingers over his tight erection. The contrast of hard cock and soft skin was as enticing as it was beautiful.

She caressed him, stem to root, and grasped the soft sac covering his testicles, the weight heavy and warm to her touch. She feathered her fingers up his length and smoothed her fingers over the bulbous, pre–cum-tipped head.

His gaze was hot, intent, focused on her as she played with him. With a small smile, she opened her mouth and licked her fingers, the taste of his cum both sweet and salty.

"No," he bit out harshly. "If you keep that up, this won't last long."

"Turnabout is fair play," Sienna murmured, her eyes trained on his beautiful cock.

She never gave a man head, never wanted that closeness when a woman willingly took a man's shaft in her mouth, deep, and made love to it.

Yet, with this man, she longed for that closeness, even if it was temporary.

She closed her eyes and swallowed the excess of fluid in her mouth.

The thought of her going down on him, taking every glorious inch of him deep inside her mouth, of him bathing the back of her throat with his cum, was a tantalizing fantasy in her mind.

One she wanted to come true. She opened her eyes and smiled at him.

"Later, maybe. Now I want to feel that pretty pussy wrapped around my dick," he replied in a coarse voice. He must have read the purpose in her eyes and she stifled a need to laugh.

All humor evaporated when he rolled the condom onto his shaft, shoved her legs farther apart, spread her wide, and pushed into her.

"Ummm . . . wait—wait," she panted as he began to fill her.

He paused at her portal.

Sienna felt her walls clamp down, firm, against his invasion. She'd made love before—it wasn't as if she were a virgin, and hadn't been one for longer than she wanted to remember. He'd also sufficiently prepared her downstairs, but he was a lot bigger than his hand. And she didn't know if she'd ever had a man the size of Mac inside her.

"We'll take it slow." His breathing was harsh, yet he stopped, pulling out a little, the round knob of his dick resting at her entry.

"God, you're big."

Mac gave a rough laugh and waited.

One thick finger came out to play with her clit. She felt the gush of liquid saturate his finger as he flicked and toyed with her.

He turned his head and brushed a kiss along the inner skin of her thigh. The simple caress was her undoing. She cried out and her legs relaxed, opening more to him.

"No, close them."

He forced her legs closed, bunching them against each other. The action stimulated her clit. Her thighs brushed against the sides of her mound, forcing the lips of her vagina to rub against her inner folds, intensifying the pressure.

He leaned away from her and slowly pushed his length inside, filling every square inch of space within her clenching walls. Sienna cried out in protest. He was so thick and hard, she felt stuffed.

And he wasn't all the way in, yet.

He pushed on, unwavering, until she felt as though the tip of his dick brushed against the back of her womb, he was embedded so deeply.

He slowly began to screw his hips and Sienna released a mangled groan of pain and pleasure. He captured her cry within his lips, shoving his tongue deep inside her mouth.

Slow, hot, drugging kisses mimicked the way he dragged his dick back and forth inside her. He'd positioned her legs tight together and forced her clit into direct contact with his groin. In the position he held her, the root of his cock ground against her clit until Sienna felt the tight, coiling sensation spiral in her womb, and welcomed the release she knew was forthcoming.

Each advance and retreat of his flexing hips drove his dick deeper inside her wet heat. With each downward stroke, she felt the fine, wiry hairs surrounding his groin rasp against her wet folds, her clit, intensifying the sensation.

Sienna mewled and whimpered against his mouth as the pressure built.

"Not yet, sweet girl, not yet." Mac released her lips and breathed the words against the side of her mouth and stilled his movements.

Sienna was dragged back from the edge of release when he stopped moving.

"What—what you are doing?" she yelled at him, frustrated and ready to climb the pinnacle just out of reach.

Mac pulled out until the knob of his cock hovered at the lips of her pulsing vaginal lips. He inserted two fingers inside her drenched walls, scooping out her thick cream. Sienna's breathing hitched, her heart beat loudly, and she waited.

She felt his hands spread her cheeks wide and circle his lubed fingers over the small, tight ring of her buttocks. Before she had time to react with more than a loud gasp, he'd slipped two thick fingers inside, and Sienna released a sharp hiss at the painful intrusion, the pressure hot, inside her ass.

He leaned down, his body draping hers, and covered her lips, giving her a soul-wrenching, deep, toe-curling kiss, stifling her cry within his mouth. He moved his other hand to cup her warm mound, one lone finger coming out to pluck at her engorged, pulsating clitoris. He slipped two thick fingers deep into her opening and her walls clamped down to capture them, her sphincter clenching, tightly gripping his fingers. Taking deep breaths, Sienna squirmed around the dual penetration.

"It's okay, baby, just relax. I need you nice and creamy." His voice was raspy.

In careful strokes, he manipulated her, his fingers dragging in and out, in hot glides and smooth caresses. Her juices saturated his fingers inside her pussy while easing the restriction inside her ass until the pain passed into pleasure, and she began to move, freely, bucking against him. The warmth invaded her limbs in a slow, insidious heat, snaking through her body, crawling up her limbs. Nearly incoherent with the pleasure, Sienna convulsed, giving in to the pleasure.

Moaning, crying out, she welcomed the fiery orgasm. As she came, he encouraged her, his voice low and husky. "Yes, just like that, Sin. . . . Now let go."

Sienna needed no further coaxing. The orgasm raced through her, devastating and complete.

She'd just recovered, her body still quaking in the aftermath, when she felt the blunt end of his penis nudge her passion-swollen lips and slide deep inside her channel.

Grasping her hips, Mac rode her, jostling her body as he rotated his muscular hips, knifing into her cunt. With a shout, he threw his head back, the muscles in his neck straining, his arms shaking, and sweat pouring down his face.

"Yes! God, yes!" he shouted as he ground against her, digging his fingers into her hips. His straining arms bracketed her body, and his heaving chest touched the tips of her nipples as he drove into her, one last thrust before he came. Covering her lips with his, he swallowed her cries when an unexpected second orgasm hit her as well.

He pulled away from her, allowing his body to rest against hers, his heart beating a wild rhythm against her breasts.

He slowly moved away from his position on top of her and lay behind her, throwing one muscular leg over her hips, his softened penis nestled in her crease as he spooned her body close.

For long moments, they lay in that position, silent, his hard chest blanketing her back.

Once Sienna's heart had calmed and her breathing became more normal, she laid her hands over his, crossed over her waist. She wanted to say something, *anything*, but couldn't rouse any form of intelligent speech in the aftermath of his wild lovemaking.

The satisfaction and contentment she felt had rendered her body boneless, her mind mush. All she wanted to do was sleep.

"How many men have you gone home with, offered your body to, after you've danced for them, Sin?" His light hold on her waist tightened as he asked the question.

She was moments away from drifting off into a sated slumber; his words slammed her back to full awareness. Damn.

10

Sienna's back stiffened against Mac's chest with his abrupt question.

Yeah, he had no damn right to ask her the question he had, but that hadn't stopped the words from flying out of his mouth.

Mac held her close, his breathing calming. The fine tremors she'd elicited from him when he'd first stroked into her were easing, finally, with his release.

"You have no right to ask me that," she said, her voice barely above a whisper. "You have no control over me. My body is my own, to share with whom I please."

She was right; he had no right. But the thought of her allowing another man to rock into her hot, sweet pussy was an image he wanted scrubbed from his mind.

When she tried to move from him, he pulled her tight, his hold strong. He refused to allow her to run away from him.

"Answer me," he demanded, ignoring the truth of her words, intent on getting her to answer his question.

The silence stretched out, until he thought she would refuse to answer. When she did reply, he had to strain to hear her words.

"No, I don't," she answered, her voice clipped. When she offered no further words of explanation, he turned her body around, impatient, forcing her to look at him.

"Why me?" He framed her soft face with his hands and stared down at her intently.

She worried her bottom lip, scraping the lush rim with her small white teeth. She stared up at him, uncertainty in her dark eyes.

"I don't know. Right place, right time . . . right man," she answered flippantly, but Mac saw past the words and the careful, neutral expression. He was trained to read feelings no matter how well someone tried to hide them.

Instead of challenging her, he let the question go. He leaned down and captured her soft lips with his, lingering, pulling her bottom rim into his mouth, before slowly releasing it.

She raised her hands to cover his, cupping the sides of her face.

"Does any of that matter?"

Mac opened his mouth to speak, ready to give her a swift rebuttal, but he clamped his mouth, just as suddenly.

He didn't want to get wrapped up with this woman. Yes, he wanted her, had wanted her from the first time he'd seen her on stage. And after the lap dance she'd performed, there had been no way he'd be able to leave her alone until he'd slaked his lust for her.

And that's all it was. Pure lust.

He captured her lips with his, kissed her until both of them were breathless, before releasing her.

"No, it doesn't. Only the here and now." His gaze traveled down her small nose and lingered on her sensual full lips. Lips stained red from his kisses.

Mac cupped the back of her head and led her to his chest,

lying back against the plump pillows near the headboard of the bed. After a hesitant moment, she laid her head on his chest, her soft curls tickling his nose when he rubbed his chin back and forth over the top of her head.

"You should wear your own hair when you dance. It's beautiful." He fingered a lock of hair between his fingers. It was thick and smooth in texture. "Why don't you?"

"I wear it short, and most of the customers like long hair, adds to the fantasy." She laughed, a short, humorless-sounding laugh.

"Doesn't add to *my* fantasy. You're beautiful. Would still be beautiful even if you were slick bald."

Sienna's answering laugh was more genuine this time. "Thank you." Her fingers toyed with the hair on his chest as she continued speaking. "Also, it adds to the anonymity. All they see on stage is a body. When I wear the wig, it helps to disguise me even more," she disclosed.

Mac was quiet. Over the last week, he'd seen that she didn't dance for anyone but herself.

"How long have you danced?" He lifted her body, until she was laying on top of him, her head resting comfortably beneath his chin.

"Jac . . . I had been living in a real dump, couldn't afford anything decent after I moved to DC. I struggled for a few years, working odd jobs here and there, along with working as a waitress to make ends meet."

Mac caught the slip. She was about to utter the same name Damian said earlier in the evening. The name Marks choked out, which had made cold fear appear in her eyes.

"I've been dancing at the Sweet Kitty for four years," she finished.

"How old were you when you ran away?" He brushed a strand of hair away from her forehead. She leaned away from his chest and peered into his eyes, intently, in the dark.

"Who said anything about me running away?"

"Didn't you run away?" he asked, leaving it up to her to share or not.

A fraction of silence before she answered, "Eighteen. I was eighteen when I left."

Mac stroked his hands over her hair as she spoke, silent, listening intently.

"I left home as soon as I turned eighteen, hadn't even graduated from high school. But it was time. So, on my eighteenth birthday, I left."

"Did your family ever look for you?"

"I don't have much family to speak of. Lived in foster homes most of my life," she told him. The admission didn't surprise him. "Didn't see any use in hanging around a place I wasn't wanted. As far as anyone looking for me? No."

"Wouldn't your foster parents notify your caseworker?"

"Why would they? They still got their check from the state for me until I turned eighteen. Once the checks ended, they didn't give a damn one way or another. I'm sure they got another kid to fill my bed." She laughed without humor.

"I'm sorry to hear that," he murmured.

"It's life. I learned at an early age life wasn't fair. You work the cards you're dealt, don't rely on anyone but yourself, and don't get caught up, don't get hurt that way."

Mac ran one hand down her back, caressing her soft, satiny skin.

He'd always thought he was a hard son of a bitch, detached. He'd helped raise his kid sister, did his stint in the army, got banged up, and tended to play his emotional cards close. Or so he was always told. He wasn't the warm and fuzzy type. He now wondered who was the most closed off emotionally—he or the beautiful woman who lay on top of him.

11

Sienna wanted to tell him everything. Wanted to unburden herself to a complete stranger. Wanted to release the anger and pain of growing up the way she had. Of the stupid choices she'd made along the way.

Choices she had to make, in order to protect her brother and survive.

"Why did you come to the Kitty?" she asked.

He moved their bodies so they were lying facing each other.

"Why does any man come to a strip club?"

"Well, yes, I know that. I meant, I hadn't seen you around before last week. I notice all the regulars. At first, I thought you were one of Damian's associates."

"Damian, as in the asshole you work for?" he asked gruffly. "No, I wouldn't call myself a 'friend' of your employer." His voice sounded grim.

It was her turn to wait for him to expound on his answer. For the first time in years, Sienna wanted to get to know a man beyond the superficial.

"My partner and I are here on business. He came to the club

a few times with me. You may have seen him. He's the big, bald black guy who sat with me at the table a few times," he finally answered.

Sienna recalled seeing the handsome black man sitting next to him during several of his nightly visits to the club.

"You said you were an investigator? What types of cases do you take on? Do you help—" Sienna stopped herself before she could ask him if he could help her out of her situation.

Allowing a man to help her out when she was in need was one of the reasons she was currently stuck in a situation she didn't have a clue in hell how to get out of.

Damn, what the hell was she thinking?

She would figure it all out, by herself. Rely on no one but herself, and she'd avoid getting hurt.

"Help what?"

Sienna said nothing. No, it was best to stop all thoughts that she'd found her knight in shining armor. She'd given up believing in fairy tales a long time ago.

She decided to stop herself from wanting something she'd never get and enjoy the moment for what it was. To forget who and what she was, and glory in the feel of him, of catering to her sexual needs instead.

Nothing more, nothing less.

To want anything more—to dream that he could help her, be her prince storming the castle and bringing down the dragon— was a setup for heartache.

"Did you enjoy the way I loved you?" Mac abruptly changed topics.

He wanted to press the issue, wanted her to trust him enough to unload her burden, burdens he knew she carried like deadweight.

But he'd wait.

He had every confidence he'd gain her trust before the

weekend was over. He planned on keeping her, beneath him, for the next forty-eight hours, until he made sure that happened.

He brought her close and kissed her, grinning in satisfaction against the warm hollow behind her ear when he felt the small goose bumps rise against his mouth.

"Ummm, yes," she whispered.

"Do you want more?" He gently tugged her head in order to see her face.

The light of the moon cast a shadow on her face, one side darkly shadowed, the other illuminated, giving her the look of a harlequin.

It was like seeing two sides of the same woman, mirroring the two sides of her personality: the open, hedonistic woman who stripped and danced in a seedy club, and the thoughtful one who was shy, unsure of herself, yet held a quiet dignity.

Sin was an enigma.

She held secrets and he found himself more intrigued by her, the longer he was with her. Before the night was over, he was determined to ferret out her closely held secrets.

"Yes," she answered, her eyes trained on his.

He captured one of her perfect nipples in his mouth, tugging on it, laving it with his tongue before releasing it to swallow her sweet moan of delight.

Mac blindly reached behind him and retrieved a second condom from the nightstand table.

Releasing her lips, but keeping his eyes trained on hers, he ripped the foil with his teeth and sheathed himself.

He pulled her into a straddling position over his body and lowered her down onto his throbbing dick. He carefully pushed past the swollen lips of her labia until he was fully embedded inside her tight, slick walls.

"Good, because I'm not done with you yet." Mac grasped her hips, steadying her for the ride.

After she adjusted her body around the tight fit of him deep inside, he allowed her to set the pace.

In the moonlit room, he stared up at her, watching the play of emotions on her face, her moans of passion, the way she closed her eyes, lips partially opened, lost in the feel of their bodies joined.

His balls grew heavy, tingling.

Damn. He could come just from looking at her ride him. His jaw tightened as he mentally tried to gain control.

Her slick walls clamped down on him, her cream saturated his shaft as she moved.

She bounced and rolled her ass, gyrating along his dick, making him lose his mind.

"God, you feel good! So damn tight. So juicy." His hands grasped her hips tightly.

"You feel just as good. Hard and thick." She was panting. "I can barely move."

"You're doing a damn good job." He laughed roughly.

A sensual smile graced her full lips while she rode him. Her moves were at first careful, painfully slow.

Light strokes of slick heat massaged his shaft. Her inner walls gripped him, milking him.

Like a thousand feathers caressing his dick.

Sweat broke out on Mac's forehead.

He sat up, grabbed her round, firm buttocks, and ground their bodies together, smashing his pelvis against hers, stroking into her heat in hard-driving thrusts.

She cried out, wrapped her arms around his neck, and rotated her hips, fucking him as desperately as he fucked her. Mac felt the tingling sensation of his cum swelling his balls.

His climax was close, building to a crescendo, one he couldn't hold back for much longer. He didn't want to come without her, though.

He inserted his hand between their bodies, found the hard

nub of her clit, and used her own sweet juices to spread over the blood-filled nub.

He lightly pinched her plump clit, massaged her steadily, and covered her mouth with his. He kissed her as he rocked into her, back and forth like a seesaw, while plunging his tongue deep into her mouth, stroking her all the way to the back of her throat.

She snatched her mouth away from his, flung her head back, and screamed. Her body jerked in hard spasms as she came, and Mac was finally able to surrender to the pleasure her body had given his.

Violent pleasure washed over him, completely destroying him—leaving him open, vulnerable, for a small space in time. Even as he released deep inside her, he felt both renewed and annihilated by their physical bond.

Once he'd completed his orgasm, he fell back on the bed, taking her with him.

Her groan was a mixture between a satisfied sigh and soft laugh. "That was amazing."

Her head lolled off his chest, landing on a pillow beside his head, her soft breasts cushioning his chest.

She reached over and pressed a kiss directly to the center of his chest, above his heart.

"Thank you," she whispered, placing her hand where she'd kissed him.

Mac's gaze fell on her face. She looked relaxed. Young and innocent.

Her passion-reddened full lips were softly parted, light breaths of air whispering against the top of his arms. Her eyes were closed, the thick lashes fanning her cheeks. So innocent.

Mac stared up at the ceiling, gathered her close, and allowed the moment to overtake him. Closing his eyes, he went to sleep.

12

"Come on, Sin, you know this is what you want. It was good before. It can be good again."

"Please . . . just go away. I told you to leave me alone!"

"You want it—"

"I don't want it or you, Damian!" Sienna yelled. "Don't you understand? That was a long time ago. Get away from me! I work for you at the club. I'm not your personal whore." She wrenched herself away from him and ran toward the door. She had gotten only a few feet away when she heard her skirt rip.

"One more time, for old times' sake. Soon you'll belong to him. But until then, I think I should get one last sample of the goods, don't you?" He roughly turned her around and pinned her against the door.

"What are you talking about?"

He ignored her, kept a punishing hold on her upper body with one hand, the other he used to unzip his slacks and shove them far enough down to release his cock.

Sienna screamed, kicking and punching him, desperately trying to get away when he she felt the end of his penis brush against her naked thighs.

"Before we do that, why don't you show me what you can do with those sinful lips of yours. I've been dying to feel them wrapped around my dick. You never would do that for me, before. This may be my last chance."

He laughed cruelly and grasped her by the shoulders, trying to shove her down to her knees. She struggled and fought, her nails scoring down his face.

"Let me go. Damn it! I swear to God, I'm leaving this place, Damian!" Sienna pushed him away, using all of her strength. Damian stumbled back, wiping the trickle of blood running down his face.

He moved as though to grab her.

"I mean it. I'll leave," she threatened, her chest heaving with her exertions.

He opened his mouth to speak, when his phone rang. "Don't move." He kept his eyes on hers as he picked up the phone.

Seconds later, his body snapped to attention, his hand whitened around the knuckles as his grip tightened on the phone. He placed his hand over the mouthpiece and hissed, "Get back to work."

Whoever was on the other end of the phone had put the fear of God into Damian. Enough so that his attempt to screw her was no longer paramount in his mind.

She silently thanked the anonymous person and ran out of the office.

Sienna struggled even as she knew she was in the thrall of a dream. She struggled against sleep, fighting to wake up, to get out of the clutches of her dream. With a wrenching cry, she sat up in bed, sweat pouring down her face, heat flaming her skin.

She inhaled deeply and released the pent-up air, her body slumping back against the headboard.

Damn. Although she'd banished the memory of Damian's attempt to force her to have sex with him again, weeks ago, it was there in her mind.

No doubt she'd dreamt it because of all the drama she'd gone through last night.

As she took another fortifying breath of air, she caught the delicious scent of food and looked around.

Across the room, the blinds were closed, yet the morning stream of sun, filtering past both blinds and the heavy curtains, spilled into the room.

The heavy aroma of frying bacon assaulted her nose, and her stomach grumbled, reminding her that it had been nearly a day since she'd last eaten. She raised her body from the bed, twisted her spine, and released a groan. She flipped her legs over the side of the bed and gingerly sat up, the soreness between her thighs from last night's excess making her wince.

It had been the early hours of the morning when finally, completely sated and unable to move, she'd fallen asleep in front of Mac, his hard body spooning against hers tightly.

"Oh God." She took a deep breath.

Erotic images of their bodies tangled, hot and sweaty, of Mac working her body *all night long,* were vivid in her mind, erasing the lingering memory of last night's nightmare.

Damn, I need to leave all that alone. It was one night. And one night only. Sienna shied away from the memory of his fine body draped over hers as he made love to her in ways she'd never experienced.

She also forced away the memory of his intense, unwavering gaze as their eyes locked while he stroked into her with single-minded determination. . . .

Standing, she searched in vain for her clothes, and unable to find anything, she picked up Mac's discarded T-shirt and pulled it over her body, the ends fanning her thighs.

She walked over to the large mirror mounted to the wall above the large chest and scrutinized herself.

Her hair was a hot mess, all over her head, seriously giving new meaning to "bed head," she thought in disgust.

Picking up the small wire brush set on the chest, she pulled it through her hair, straightening some of her curls, only making it look more like the proverbial rat's nest.

"I'd better stop while I'm ahead," she murmured, grimacing at her reflection, her natural curls springing back within seconds.

After fingering her hair one final time, Sienna turned away from the mirror and followed the smells down the stairs toward the kitchen.

She came to a stop inside the doorway, an unknowing smile on her face. Mac stood in front of the oven, wearing nothing but a pair of jeans, partially open, with a spatula in his hand, turning food in the large cast-iron skillet.

Her gaze trailed over him from the top of his spiked hair, disheveled from sleep, down over his exposed, muscular chest, and down to his large bare feet.

She cleared her throat. "Smells delicious. Is there room at the table for me?"

Her voice startled him. Mac jumped back as the sizzling butter in the pan popped. He avoided the splatter on his bare chest, just in time. After turning off the burner and sliding the omelet onto a plate, he turned around to face her.

"Of course, have a seat," he said, his eyes greedily drinking in the sight of her, starting at her bare feet, with their brightly painted pink toes, and traveling up her body. His gaze paused at the dark thatch of hair shadowed behind his shirt, up to her pointy nipples stabbing at the thin fabric of his T-shirt.

"I'm sorry, I couldn't find my clothes—"

"No, that's fine. You look better in it than I do," he said with pure male appreciation. "Have a seat. I'll have this ready in no time." With a smile, she walked over to the bar stool and hopped onto the seat, careful to keep the ends of the T-shirt tucked under her bottom.

Mac turned away so she wouldn't see his grin after seeing the faint blush across her bronze skin when she caught him eyeing her plump, naked cheeks before she'd pulled down the shirt.

She continued to amaze him with her moments of schoolgirl shyness.

"I didn't want to wake you. You looked so peaceful sleeping. Decided I'd better get the hell out of there, before my chivalry took a flying leap, and I picked up where we left off last night."

Mac turned back around to walk toward her, plate in hand, and caught the blush increase, staining her cheeks a healthy rosy color. He placed the food and silverware in front of her.

"Smells great! I'm starved."

"What do you want to drink? Got OJ and milk," he said after opening the refrigerator door and pulling out the choices. "I have coffee brewing as well." He nodded his head toward the percolating coffeepot.

"I'll take the juice. When the coffee's ready, I'd like a cup of that as well. I'm not quite human before my morning cup. Although, even coffee won't help the way I look this morning." She ran a hand over her short, curly hair.

"I don't think it would matter what time of day it was, you'd still be beautiful."

Sienna made no comment. Instead, picking up her fork and piercing a bit of the omelet, she took a healthy bite and closed her eyes.

"Ummm, this is good!" she said, and snapped her eyes open when his rusty-sounding laugh rang out.

"You say that like you're surprised. I cooked in the army and for my kid sister growing up."

"I wasn't expecting it to be so good," she admitted sheepishly.

His finger captured a bit of cheese, caught in the corner of her lip. When he put his finger to his mouth, licking off the cheese, Sienna refrained from groaning out loud.

This man was lethal, she thought.

"In basic training, in the army, I did plenty of KP duties."

"KP?"

"Kitchen patrol," he laughed.

"Oh." Sienna smiled in return. "You should do that more."

"KP?"

"No, laugh. I like your laugh."

"Thank you."

They ate in companionable silence before he spoke again. "I raised my sister. I got plenty of experience cooking for her."

Sienna paused, midchew. "What happened to your parents?" she asked cautiously, swallowing the last bit of egg and taking a sip of the orange juice.

When he stood, and motioned for her plate, she nodded her head for him to take it. He took both their plates and placed them in the sink, along with the assortment of dishes he'd used to prepare the meal.

The muscles in his bared back flexed and bunched when he reached for the soap and began to wash the dishes. The smooth play of his corded muscles reminded her how it felt to be the recipient of all that power.

All that concentrated power.

Sienna shuddered.

"My mother passed, soon after I left for the army."

"And your father?" she asked after a moment of silence.

"My dad?" He laughed. This time, his laugh held no humor, was instead almost painful to hear. "Hell, even when my mom was alive, he wasn't there much. Papa was a rolling stone, as the old song goes. When Mom died, he stuck around for a while, and then he took off."

"I'm sorry to hear that."

He turned to face her, swiping his hands on a small dish towel near the sink. "I wasn't. Most of the time, when he was around, he was drunk or wasted. He did us a favor when he left." Mac went to the coffeepot and poured them both a mug of the steaming brew and set her cup beside her.

"Thank you," she murmured after taking a sip. "If you were in the army, who took care of your sister?" Despite her intention of enjoying him for the moment only, Sienna found herself wanting to know everything about him.

"Our aunt—my mother's sister. As soon as I was stationed in a stable duty station, I sent for Chrissy. By that time, she'd gotten pregnant, and had no one, besides me. My aunt came along with her, and her son, to help. I was deployed a lot. She was young. She needed someone with her when I was away."

Sienna's heart clenched at the level of his commitment to his sister, his dedication. She felt tears threatening to fall and turned away.

"Hey, what's wrong?" he asked, turning her back around to face him, one calloused finger beneath her chin.

"Nothing," she said, her voice hoarse, clogged with tears she refused to allow to fall. She understood what it was like, trying to care for a sibling. She'd spent her entire life caring for her brother.

For a while, she thought he was going to question her further as he stared intently into her eyes. When he dropped his hand, she released a pent-up breath. Whether it was from relief that he'd let it go, or disappointment that he didn't demand she answer, she chose to ignore.

"How did you go from the military to private investigation?"

"I was Special Forces. After nine/eleven, my battle buddy and I—my partner, Kyle Hanley—were sent to Afghanistan. It was a mess, chaos everywhere, a real hot spot. We got caught in an ambush. I took a direct hit, shot in the leg. The close range shattered my kneecap."

"God, that's awful." Nausea swelled. She had to swallow down the taste of bile in her mouth.

Sienna studied his face. Little or no expression showed, yet the pain of his experience was reflected in his eyes.

She remembered the terror, chaos, and fallout in the States after the attack, and could only imagine what Mac faced.

"Yeah, it wasn't pretty, that's for damn sure. I was medevaced out and sent to Walter Reed," he said, mentioning the large army medical facility in DC. "I got a medal for my efforts, medically discharged from the army, and wondered what the hell to do with my life. I'd planned to make a career with the military. The army was all I knew. But time wasn't a luxury for me. I had to take care of my sister, as well as her son."

His dedication to his sister was obvious again. Sienna knew if she stayed around him for much longer, she would be in jeopardy of losing her heart to him. She shoved the uncomfortable thought away.

"So I took a couple of courses in law investigation at the local community college, was pretty damn handy with a weapon, and after I recruited my battle buddy to go into business with me, I received my license. The rest, as they say, is history."

"But you didn't want to live in DC," she said.

"No, actually, I own a small house in Hampton, Virginia. After I was discharged from the service, I returned. Once she got on her feet, a few years back, my sister and her son had moved out. But my aunt stayed on and took care of everything while I was away."

"I didn't even wait around to get my high-school diploma, two months shy," Sienna said, wanting to share more of her own history with him.

"Your home life was that bad?" he murmured.

"Yeah. Even though I hadn't graduated from high school, it was time to go. I was just biding my time."

"How long before you hooked up with Marks? Before you started stripping?"

Restless, not wanting to see any censure in his eyes, Sienna jumped up and carried her cup to the sink. She rinsed it, taking much more time than needed to rinse the mug out, before placing it in the strainer by the sink.

She didn't hear him approach her. Startled, she jumped when his warm hands settled on her shoulders, turning her around to face him.

"Look, I'm not condemning you. You did what you thought you had to, to survive."

"I had choices. At the time, that one seemed the best. I was stupid."

Mac started to speak, then abruptly clamped his mouth shut. Instead, he gathered her in his arms, tilted her head back, and lowered his head.

His warm breath fanned her cheeks. He planted small, heated kisses over her face, across her closed eyes, down the bridge of her nose, until he reached her lips.

She shivered when he kissed her, pressed biting caresses down her neck, burrowing his hands in her hair. He tilted her face up and captured her lips, devouring her with his kisses, enveloping her in his warmth.

Her hands quickly circled his broad shoulders, completely giving in to his toe-curling kiss. His tongue swiped at the seam of her lips, demanding entry.

He tugged at her lower lip, sucking it into the warm cavern of his mouth, before releasing it.

Sienna moaned at the expert way he handled her. No man had ever made love to her, much less kissed her, the way Mac did. He gave attention to her mouth in the same exquisite way he loved her body—with hot, detailed, mind-blowing precision.

When he pulled away from her, she whimpered in protest.

13

Mac rested his face on top of her head for a fraction of a moment before easing her away.

She sucked her swollen full lower lip into her mouth; hesitancy and uncertainty reflected in her eyes. He bit back a groan.

Damn! If he kept kissing her, he wouldn't stop. He'd take her right there on the kitchen island, and not stop until he'd gotten his fill of her, rutting in her until they were drained, sore, and satisfied.

"Sin, would you consider staying with me? For the weekend."

He saw the flare of hesitancy in her eyes. "You could go to work at nights. Just spend the weekend with me. Please," he added when she said nothing.

He waited for what felt like an eternity before she spoke.

"Okay. I'll stay with you," she finally said, and Mac released a breath he hadn't realized he was holding.

"Good," he said brusquely, clearing his throat. "There are toiletries upstairs in the bathroom. In the cabinet mounted on the wall, you'll find a spare toothbrush, as well as a robe that should fit you, on the inside hook."

Mac knew she thought he brought women to his temporary

digs, regularly, because of the amenities he kept in the bathroom. He started to reassure her that due to the nature of his job, he often needed to keep these on hand in case one of his clients needed them.

But he resisted the urge. He'd never explained himself to anyone before. No matter how much he wanted her, how different he felt with her, he wasn't going to start now.

"Thank you," she said quietly, staring into his face.

With a final, contemplative look at him, she pulled completely out of his arms and left the kitchen.

She gathered her hastily discarded clothes from last night, strewn across the sofa. With one final glance over her shoulder at him, she headed back upstairs.

Standing in front of the large vanity beside the glassed-in shower, Sienna loosely tied the ends of the borrowed robe. She peeled the packaging from the toothbrush and squeezed a dollop of paste on the bristles and started brushing her teeth.

As she brushed, her gaze fell to her breasts, peeking through the gaped vee of the robe. Memories of the way Mac had handled her last night, until the early-morning hours, filtered through her mind. Her spiked nipples became unbearably sensitive against the soft, silk robe.

She washed away the last bit of toothpaste from her mouth and, with hesitant fingers, pulled the robe farther apart, her small breasts spilling free, fully exposed.

She'd turned on the shower, allowing the steam to fill the room, and now her skin was dewy from the humidity. Her breath hitched. Closing her eyes, her fingers feathered over the rosy, tight buds, imagining it was Mac's thick fingers pulling at her.

The sensation caused a chain reaction.

Moisture eased from her vagina, down her thighs. Lost in her thoughts, longings, and lust for Mac, her other hand found her moist heat, and her fingers delved between the swollen folds of her vagina.

"I hope it's my hands you're imagining on your body. My hands between your thighs."

Her eyes flew open and she stared into the fogged mirror. The object of her desire stood framed in the doorway, nostrils flared, eyes half-closed, gloriously naked, watching her touch herself.

14

As Mac walked into the room, he kept his eyes glued to the mirror and her startled gaze.

"I—I didn't hear you walk in," she stuttered, quickly removing her hands from her body, closing the robe and belting it tightly.

He stopped, standing behind her, close. So close, she could feel the heat from his naked chest against the thin robe. He kept his gaze on hers and lowered his head, his lips grazing the side of her neck.

"Hmmm," Sienna moaned in appreciation, rolling her neck to the side.

She closed her eyes when she felt his tongue snake out and leisurely lap a caress against her skin. The moisture increased between her thighs. After last night, she didn't think she'd be able to bear any more of his heated kisses.

She was wrong.

His hard body blanketed hers, his erection thick and insistent, lying against the curve of her back.

As he kissed her, he reached around her body, inserting his

big hand inside her robe, and palmed one of her breasts. The other hand pushed aside the robe and trailed to the triangle at the top of her thighs, brushing back and forth over her springy curls.

Her eyes flew open when one lone finger eased inside.

In the mirror, she watched their twin reflections.

She, with her eyes glazed-looking; he, watching her, his hot gaze fanning her body.

A cry escaped from her lips when he opened her wide, two fingers separating her vaginal lips, another smoothly pushing deep inside. She arched her back, her buttocks popping against his groin when he withdrew from her and pinched her clit—not hard enough to hurt, but enough to make her *feel* the stinging caress.

He released his hold and turned her toward his body, swallowing her whimpering cries.

His tongue shoved into hers, swirling inside her mouth, suckling her top rim. She felt the kiss deep inside her body.

Turning fully into his embrace, Sienna leaned up, on tiptoes, and wrapped her arms around his shoulders, bringing him closer.

With a harsh groan, he pulled away from her, lifted her into his arms, and walked the small distance to the shower stall. Once inside the steamy shower, Mac placed her in front, her back to his chest, and withdrew a sponge and liquid gel from the caddy.

"Let me wash you."

Sienna nodded her head. She leaned back against him when he ran the soapy sponge over her breasts, down her stomach, leaving a sudsy trail the warm water quickly washed away.

He paid careful attention to her body, cleansing her even as he heated her with his touch.

She widened her stance when he nudged her thighs apart, and she moaned when she felt the sponge glide between her folds, lathering the soap along the seam of her pussy.

He pulled her head back with one hand and covered her cries with his mouth, his other hand continuing to manipulate her, the soap running down her thighs.

Suddenly he flipped her around and pulled her closer. He raised her legs and wrapped them around his waist, the long, hot length of his shaft nestled between them. She ground against him, impatient to feel him inside her body, anywhere, just as long as he entered her.

Sienna was frantic, crazed, with the need to house him inside her. She held her breath, her heartbeat speeding up when he lifted her higher. He grasped his cock and rubbed the rounded tip over her anus. In breathless anticipation, her heartbeat kicked up a notch as he feathered it back and forth. She wondered if he'd take her there, in virgin territory, a place none had ever entered.

He seemed to hesitate before he adjusted her legs, moved his cock away, and slowly pushed into her pussy, past her tender tissue, until he was balls deep inside her.

"Oooh, yes. Oh yes," Sienna cried, despite the tender almost painful feel of his hard dick shafting her. Her forehead rested against his water-slicked chest. "Just like that, please," she begged, biting her lower lip, screwing her hips around his dick, her buttocks pressed tight against the wall of the shower.

He raised her hips higher, angling her clit so that it hit the top of his groin as he began to grind into her.

He set a smooth rhythm, slipping in and out of her drenched heat as his fingers bit into her hips, thrusting and grinding, rotating the twin globes of her ass cheeks, screwing his hips clockwise as he plunged inside her.

Her head dropped to her chest, her breathing labored, while he fucked her in short, tight thrusts.

"We can't finish this way," she panted. "I'm not on any protection. I—" She screamed when he slipped a hand between their close bodies, stroking the seam between her pussy and ass, before easing a finger inside her anus.

He slammed her body against the shower wall, and she helplessly rolled her buttocks against his finger. Tears slipped down her cheeks in ecstasy as she accepted his thrusting strokes in both ends.

The hard length of his dick competed with the unyielding shower wall, the friction exquisite, until the pressure built to unbearable proportions and spilled over.

The orgasm ripped through her body. Her body jerked when the spasms hit, hard. Replete, she slumped forward against his chest. Had he not had such a tight hold on her, her body would have crumpled, falling down against the marbled tile wall of the shower with the power of her release.

Mac ground his teeth and bit back his own release. He held off until he was assured she'd completed hers. Once her cries died down to a mewling whimper, he pulled out of her clenching, warm sheath. Grabbing the base of his cock—and with two, three jerks, yelling—he emptied his seed. His thick cum jetted over her belly as he held her hips steady with one hand.

Once his own racing heart calmed, he eased her legs from around his waist. Grabbing a sponge, Mac washed away his semen from her breasts and followed the sticky trail to her stomach with shaky hands. He turned off the showerhead, still holding her quivering body close to his.

He opened the shower door and stepped out, grabbing a towel before he turned back to her. Without bothering to dry himself, he ran the towel over her and lifted her into his arms, carrying her out of the bathroom and into the bedroom.

In his arms, she lay quiet, her eyes closed, lashes fanning the swell of her high cheekbones, and Mac felt his heart clench at the picture she presented of trusting, sated innocence.

Laying her down on the bed, he swiped his body with the towel before gathering her, laying her on top of his body. Within minutes, they were both fast asleep. His last waking thought, an uncomfortable one.

He didn't know if he could let her go, once the weekend was over.

15

"*Stop playing games! Acting like you're some kind of virgin innocent. I've seen the way you flounce around here, purposely switching that ass in front of me. You want to be fucked. Don't worry, I'll give you what you want. But first, I'll eat this sweet cunt, make you feel real good before I stuff my dick in your mouth and let you suck me. Stop fighting and let me in. Let me in, damn it!*" Although his voice was low, it held a distinct nasal quality.

Sienna felt her thighs being parted, and struggled against hands that held her down, not allowing her to move.

"No," she moaned, tossing her head back and forth. "I don't want this! I never asked for this! Please let me go!" Sienna begged, crying out when she felt a warm, wet tongue lap between the seam of her vagina.

In horror, she felt the stirrings of arousal, despite the humiliation of what he was doing to her. She grew moist, her limbs grew shaky, and cream eased down her legs as she spread for him, welcoming him, inviting him to take what he wanted from her.

He separated her vaginal lips, and with aching slowness, he

ran his tongue over her clit, sucking and pulling the hard nub with his mouth, before releasing it.

"You like that, admit it, Sin. Admit that you want what I'm giving you." Sienna felt the tears run freely down her face as she ground her pussy against him, moaning and whimpering.

He laughed a rough, satisfied laugh and opened her lips wider with two fingers. He shoved his tongue deep inside her, spooning out her moisture. He lifted her buttocks high in the air so that her ass was positioned directly in his face. Using her cream he'd gathered from her pussy, he laved the small puckered hole. Sienna screamed.

"Hmmm, so good, so damn good."

He licked her ass, giving it as much attention as he'd given her pussy, rimming her, until she felt as though she were coming apart. He inserted a thick finger inside her vagina at the same time that he shoved his tongue deep into her ass; she bucked against him, crying out in both shame and ecstasy as the orgasm swept through her.

"Please—"

"Tell me you want it! Tell me! Now! You want me, and only me. . . . Say it!" he demanded, his voice was different, deeper, less nasal.

Sienna was suddenly consumed with wanton need, aching for him to finish what he started.

Horrified at her reaction, Sienna renewed her struggles.

"No! I don't want this! I don't want you! I don't, I don't, I don't, I . . ." Her litany became a piercing wail, a cry of pain, arousal, and shame when he continued to stroke into her until, giving in, she came. Her release was harsh.

She felt the tears stain her cheeks as she accepted his final caresses.

"Sin! Baby, wake up!" The hands that once held her down now came to rest on her shoulders, shaking her strongly, forcing her eyes to slam open.

"Wha-what?" she stammered, confused, caught between the dream/nightmare and consciousness, her skin tight and itchy, hypersensitive and aching.

"You were having a nightmare. Damn, I'm sorry. I shouldn't have done that to you. I thought you would wake up and enjoy it. . . . Goddamn, baby, I'm so sorry." Mac looked down into her eyes, his own filled with apology. He gathered her into the warm shelter of his arms, without another word.

Grabbing at his shoulders, clutching him, she helplessly returned his hug and allowed the pent-up emotions from her dream free rein.

She cried hard and long—deep, aching tears flowed. Cried for what happened in the dream, cried because her life was a mess, and mostly cried from self-loathing.

She was no better than what she'd been told she was, from the time she was little more than an adolescent.

She was nothing more than a whore.

Mac ran his hands over her hair, down the length of her back, clutching her body to his, and waited for her to calm down. He felt like shit. Complete and utter shit.

When he'd woken, she'd been sound asleep, resting peacefully next to him, her beautiful face bathed in the bright sunlight that had broken. She looked so beautiful, lying close to him, that despite their early-morning intense session in the shower, he'd grown hard in moments.

Easing his body down hers, he'd parted her legs. His dick grew hard as he simply looked at the soft nest of curls guarding her sweet entry.

Crouching between her thighs, he'd run his fingertips over the soft curls and laid a soft kiss at her center. When she'd stirred, moving her thighs to the side, he took advantage of her, spreading her legs wide. He covered her mound with his mouth.

She'd begun to moan, murmuring in her sleep as he'd started to lick her. Soon he'd felt her excitement grow; even in sleep she was receptive to him. Within seconds, her dew covered his mouth as he greedily feasted on her.

He'd then lifted her sweet bottom high in the air; her small, puckered hole beckoned him to taste it, to swirl his tongue around its perfect circumference.

Mac had given in to the temptation and played both ends of her, laving her hole while plunging his fingers deep inside her warm well.

She'd cried out in pleasure, begging him to keep loving her. Mac had gotten caught up in the pleasure of pleasuring her—so much so, he'd become demanding. Thoughts of her letting another do this to her ripped through his mind, the image burning his retinas.

In anger, he'd demanded she acknowledge he was the only one she'd allow to make love to her.

He wanted to be the one, the only one, to bring her to shattering release.

She'd cried out, demanding that he stop, but he'd been unable. He'd held her thighs, forcing them to stay widespread, until she'd completed her orgasm.

He'd come to his senses when he raised his body, only to see tears falling down her cheeks, eyes closed, chest heaving.

He'd realized that she was asleep, and having a horrible nightmare.

She eased out of his embrace, turning her face away.

"No, don't turn away. Please."

She turned back to face him. Uncertainty and some other unrecognizable emotion shone brightly in his eyes.

"I didn't know. I thought you were awake. Had I known—"

"It's okay. Forget about it."

"What happened in the dream? Were you being hurt?" he asked, uncertain. He saw the shaking tremors that continued to rack her body, although she'd moved away.

"It was nothing. Just a dream." She forced a grimace of a smile to stretch across her mouth.

"I thought you were enjoying it, Sin. I thought you were awake. You seemed to be—" He stopped, not sure what to say.

"I know."

"You can talk to me—"

"Really, just forget about it. Please," she pleaded, her face tense, the determined smile still in place.

"Fine," he agreed.

She turned to lie down, facing away from him, and Mac eased his body behind hers.

He pulled her close, expecting her to rebuff him. She didn't. Instead, she snuggled her body back even closer, her hands coming to rest on top of his, placed around her waist.

Mac took a deep breath and exhaled. The puzzle of who Sin was, heavy on his mind.

Sienna listened as his breaths eventually evened out, signaling that he'd fallen asleep.

He was right. She had taken pleasure in what he had been doing to her. So much so, that even in her dreams, he'd made her come.

The thing that filled her with the most shame was that she didn't know to whom she'd been responding: Mac or the man in her dreams—the faceless man who represented the many who'd used her, mentally and physically.

16

"Honey, I need to go downstairs and do some paperwork, make a few calls. I brought your purse upstairs, in case you needed anything."

Sienna was awakened from a deep sleep when Mac's deep, scratchy voice murmured near her ear. She stretched her back and yawned, raising her body from the comfortable mattress.

"No, don't get up. You rest. I'll be back up, soon." He kissed her forehead and she smiled sleepily, mumbled an incoherent assent, and lay back against the soft down pillows covering the bed. The bed dipped when he left and she hugged her pillow tightly, closing her eyes.

She'd only had her eyes closed for a minute; then she heard an insistent beep. She tried to ignore it and keep sleeping, but she realized it was her cell phone.

Struggling against the hold of sleep, she forced herself to consciousness. Untangling her body from the satin sheets, she leaned over to the side of the bed where Mac had placed her purse.

Fumbling with its snap, she finally reached her phone and

flipped it open. She saw the small text-message icon and pressed the envelope to retrieve the message. Squinting her eyes, she read it.

Small goose bumps peppered her arms after she read the single sentence: *Have you checked on Jacob today?*

Nerveless fingers dropped the phone. Sienna jumped from the bed and frantically pulled on her clothes.

"I need you to stay away for the next day."

Mac held the phone propped against his shoulder and ear. He leafed through a string of documents, until he located the one he wanted. He straddled the armchair in the room he used as an office in his temporary lodgings.

"Stay away from the strip club?" Mac heard his voice echo back, and knew his partner had him on speaker.

"The town house," Mac answered as he read over the report he had faxed. In disgust, he tossed it to the side when the information wasn't what he needed.

He stood and walked over to the refrigerator. He scrounged inside, taking out cold cuts and salad fixings, wanting to have something for Sin to eat when she woke.

"You paying to put me up elsewhere?"

"What's wrong with your current digs? Trouble in paradise?" Mac heard two distinct feminine voices in the background, Tawny and Tanya, the two women who'd followed him to DC, calling out for Kyle to get off the phone and come back and play. Kyle spoke directly into the phone, taking him off speaker.

"I'm cool. What's up with you? Any reason why I can't come back to the town house?"

"I've got company."

"Oh yeah? Who? That stripper from the club?"

"Her name is—" Mac stopped, embarrassed that he didn't know Sin's real name.

"Damn, man, I was just bullshitting. You've really got the stripper—wait, you don't know her name! I don't want to hear any more shit from you about me and my lovers. At least, I get their names before we fuck!"

"Screw you—oh hell, don't take that to heart. I don't swing that way, dude." With a satisfied grunt, Mac located the mayonnaise in the far corner, in the back of the refrigerator. He unscrewed the lid, sniffed the contents, making sure it wasn't rank.

"Hell, even if you did, I prefer my threesomes to involve a couple of sets of nice, big, soft tits and curvy asses, not dicks, balls, and rough skin."

"I haven't had any complaints about my dick, balls, or skin, last time I checked."

"Let's just say, you're as safe from my charms as I am from yours. Too bad for you, you'll never get to sample my sweet chocolate delight." Kyle laughed and Mac felt the side of his lips curl up in a half grin.

"I'll take my chocolate with cream, minus the cum. Sin's chocolate is more than sweet enough."

"Hmmm. Like that, is it?"

"That and more. A hell of a lot more." In satisfaction, Mac recalled their morning lovemaking session, a session that had left them both exhausted, but well sated.

He'd woken, a second time that morning, and unlike the first time, he'd carefully woken her up, not wanting a repeat of the last time. Slowly, languidly, he'd made love to her, catering to her every need, stroking her entire body, from her beautiful face to her toes, and back. He'd paid careful attention to her erogenous zones, like the bend of her knee. When he licked, caressed, and lightly nibbled that area, she squirmed in delight and sighed in satisfaction at the same time.

He'd not asked her again about the dream, but he hadn't forgotten it. One of the reasons he'd gotten up had been to call his partner and have him run a check on Sin.

"Did you come up with anything more on Marks?"

"Other than he's running some kind of side game with Medeiros?"

"Yeah, could your snitch get any more information?"

Kyle had several informants he utilized whenever he needed information Mac couldn't get. Kyle had a way about him, a charm, which Mac didn't possess, nor had a clue in hell how to utilize even if he did, that got them the information they needed.

He'd somehow found a small "in" within Medeiros's close inner circle and had ferreted small but useful information. Mac was hoping he'd be able to find out the link between Marks and Medeiros.

"Still working on that one. Give me more time. I'll get it," he said. Although Kyle's tone was light, Mac knew that Kyle wouldn't stop until he'd struck gold.

"Good enough. Oh, I also need you to see what you can come up with on her."

"The strip . . . Sin?" Kyle asked. Mac silently applauded his friend on catching himself before he referred to her as the "stripper" again.

"Yeah, anything you can pull up."

"Why can't you? You have your laptop with you, don't you?"

"Can't," Mac said around a mouthful of food, chewing and swallowing down the bite of sandwich before continuing. "Don't know how much time I have before she gets up. I need to run a check on Marks."

"We've done that. I doubt there's anything new since the last time we looked. You searching for something in particular? A connection beyond employee and employer?"

Mac scowled and put his sandwich down on the plate, considering his partner's question. He didn't want to believe there *was* a connection beyond business between Sin and Marks. He didn't want to think the way they'd made love hadn't been different, special.

She *couldn't* be in a relationship with the fucking club owner. She couldn't. He stalked out of the kitchen, heading toward his computer in the den, when he heard the bedroom door open and close.

"Just see what you come up with, I need to go."

"Wait—how the hell am I supposed to find anything on her, when you don't even know her real name?"

"You're an investigator, investigate!" At the sound of the curse on the other end of the phone line, Mac grunted in satisfaction.

He turned toward the stairs, his smile grew wider when Sin descended. As he walked toward her, his smile slowly dropped when she drew nearer. He noticed the pinched set to her features.

"Babe, everything okay? What's wro—"

"Take me to the club," she interrupted, walking past him. He dropped his hand to his side and followed her.

"What do you mean? You're staying for the weekend."

"No, I'm not. Please take me back now." She stood at the front door, arms crossed over her chest, her face set. She'd turned her face to the side, not looking at him.

"What happened? Why do you want to leave?"

"Look, it was cool, last night. But I need to go. I made plans I forgot about."

"It was *cool*?" Mac's eyes narrowed, anger rose sharp, immediately, in response.

"I enjoyed it—"

"So glad I could provide *pleasure* for *you*."

Mac now stood directly in front of her, less than a foot away. He saw the dark flush run over her cheeks. He reached out and grabbed one of her shoulders, turning her around to face him, forcing her to look into his eyes.

"Plans? What plans? Your plans are with me."

"No! I said I have to go now. Please, just take me back to the club so I can get my car." She shrugged his hand off her shoulder and cried out when he grasped her by the chin, forcing her to look at him.

"What the hell kind of game are you playing with me, lady? One minute, you're hot, burning for me. Now you have plans you forgot about? Who? Who do you have plans with?"

"Damn it, that's none of your business! I don't owe you any explanations. You don't own me. It was just sex—"

"It was a hell of a lot more than just sex! Or do you need a reminder of how much more it was . . . than just sex?" He yanked her close, rasping the last words against her neck.

Sienna struggled against Mac, trying to shove him away from her.

He didn't budge.

Instead, he buried his face in her neck, rubbing his face against hers. He pulled away enough to grasp her by the head, angling her face and slamming his mouth over hers.

Sienna forced her moans of pleasure to stay clamped behind her clenched teeth. He gentled his kiss, licking at the seam of her lips, stroking her, his touch begging her to open for him. With a helpless little moan, she obeyed his silent demand, wrapping her arms around him, as he crushed her body to his.

The message on her cell phone flashed in her mind, and her eyes snapped open.

Dear God, what was wrong with her?

Her brother could be hurt, and here she was, like a cat in heat, rubbing her body against a man she'd just met, forgetting all about her fear of what could be happening to Jacob.

She pulled her mouth away from his and shoved, with every ounce of strength she possessed, at his hard, unyielding chest.

She caught him off-guard and he stumbled, giving her enough room to maneuver out of his arms.

"I said, I need to go!" She ran the back of her hand over her swollen mouth, heart racing in her chest, as she watched him coldly assess her.

"Fine. You want to go? Go! I'm not begging you to stay. I'll take you back to the club," he said, his gray eyes darkening. The tic in the corner of his mouth was the only giveaway to how angry he was.

They stared at one another for long moments, both of their breaths coming in harsh gasps, before he spun away from her. He strode over to the round table in the corner of the room, picked up the keys, and, with a grim look, motioned for her to follow.

She followed him out the door, and felt like crying in protest.

But she had no choice.

She had to get away, out of his presence while she could. Her brother's life could depend on it. And as much as she wanted to stay with Mac, as much as it hurt like hell that she couldn't—if only for one more day—her brother came first.

He always had, and he always would.

Mac turned to face her.

"So I was only a good fuck for you, huh?" he asked, his face set, unreadable.

"No. I—" Sienna stopped, looking away from the angry glower on his face.

"Well, I hope you enjoyed the screw. Next time I'm in the club, we can just go upstairs, use one of the rooms. At least, you'll be on the clock. May as well get paid for what you do so well."

The minute the words left his mouth, Sienna hauled back and slapped his face as hard as she could.

When she went to slap him again, Mac grabbed her hand.

They stared at each other for long, tense moments. Sienna held back the tears stinging the backs of her eyes with grim determination as he held her hand in a punishing grip.

His face softened, and his hold on her eased. He allowed her to withdraw her arm. She let it drop to her sides, not wanting to give him the satisfaction of seeing her rub the circulation back into her wrist from his simple hold.

"Let's go." He didn't have to say any more. The disgust, the anger, was all there in his eyes for her to see.

She swallowed bitter tears and followed him out the door.

17

As soon as Mac drove up to the near empty lot of the Sweet Kitty lounge, he unlocked the passenger side on his console.

"Mac, I—"

"Just go." He stared ahead, refusing to look at her. He simply wanted her to get out so he could get the hell out of there.

"Please."

"Please what?" He turned to face her and waited for her to tell him to turn around. To take her away from the lounge.

She remained silent. The tension was thick, palpable, as he waited for her to say something, anything, that would give him a reason to ask her to go back home with him.

He gritted his teeth and forced himself not to reach out to her; with a sorrowful, yet resigned, look in her dark eyes, she turned away from him and lifted the door handle. He forced himself not to beg her to stay when she stepped out of his SUV, and closed the door, not looking back at him.

He forced himself not to demand she tell him what the hell happened. One minute, she was willing to stay with him; the next, she was demanding he take her back here, pretending—

and he damn well knew she was pretending—as though she felt nothing. As though their night, morning, and damn near most of the afternoon of lovemaking hadn't meant more to her than a good lay.

When she got out of the car and, without a look over her shoulder, walked toward her car . . . he forced himself not to spin out of the parking lot like some rejected, love-struck high-school fool. He was a grown man, not some immature young punk who'd gotten dumped.

He put the SUV in reverse, yanked down on the gearshift, floored the accelerator, and peeled out of the lot.

Fuck maturity.

Sienna resisted the urge to rub her hands over her arms in response to the chilled look in Mac's stainless-steel–colored eyes. She'd made herself turn away, knowing that she was seconds away from begging him to take her back to his town house and help her forget all her problems. Wanting, *needing*, his love-making to help her forget.

She sighed when he roared out of the parking lot and seconds later raced down the street, nothing left but the dust the wheels of his car had kicked up in its wake.

Swallowing, she turned to face the deserted Sweet Kitty. She searched the lot, turning toward Damian Marks's reserved parking spot, near the entry. Her gut clenched in fear, bile rising in her throat. His car was there.

She knew Damian was behind the cryptic message left on her cell phone. The minute she'd received the text message, she'd called the home where her brother lived. She'd asked, her nerves stretched taut in fear, if he was okay, if he'd been harmed.

The on-duty nurse had assured her he was okay, but he had suffered a small accident. They'd been going to call her soon. Sienna's heart sank at the news, and she'd begged to speak to Melanie, his personal caregiver. The nurse had tried to reassure her that Jacob was fine, but Sienna couldn't relax until she'd heard from the woman who cared for her brother daily.

When Melanie had finally gotten on the phone, Sienna didn't know whether to cry or laugh in nervous relief when Melanie had assured her that Jacob was fine.

"Sienna, he's fine! You know I would have called you right away if he had been involved in anything serious!"

"I know, Mel, it's just that I got this strange message—"

"A message about Jacob? I didn't send a message. No one from here had. I did plan on calling you later, to tell you that he'd fallen, but that was minor. He wasn't hurt at all!"

"He fell? How? What happened?"

The pause on the other end of the phone was just long enough that Sienna knew she wasn't mistaken. Something was going on.

"No, it *wasn't* major, Sienna. Please believe me when I say that." Melanie sighed and Sienna waited, with bated breath, god-awful dread pooling in her stomach. "It was a bit strange, how it happened. Jacob was playing the piano, as he normally does for the residents. He plays so beautifully," Melanie said, and Sienna smiled, despite the fear weighing down on her chest. Jacob was autistic. Although he rarely spoke, he loved playing the piano and was extremely gifted.

At the request of the residents and staff, he would play during their weekly Friday-night party. Sienna hated that she rarely got to hear him play on Fridays, as she was at the Sweet Kitty working. She made up for it by coming on Sundays. Jacob would play for hours for her as she curled up in one of the lounge chairs in the rec room.

"After he finished playing," Melanie continued, "one of our new residents got up and went over to him and hugged him. When we tried to stop him, the resident wouldn't let go, no matter how much Jacob screamed. It took two of us to get the resident off Jacob."

"Oh God," Sienna murmured.

Jacob couldn't stand for anyone to touch him. Besides herself and Melanie, no one was able to come close to him or he'd start screaming, and it would take a very long time for him to calm down. And for someone to actually hug him, Sienna could only imagine how her brother had protested.

"In the struggle, Jacob fell, bumped his head on the piano. It only dazed him a bit, no real physical damage," she quickly assured Sienna.

"No physical, what about—"

"He's fine, Sienna. Trust me. Actually, I was surprised at how well he recuperated. I think maybe the bump on the head helped him calm down sooner. I think his attention was on the pain to the noggin and he forgot about his indignation over being touched!"

"Thank God!" Sienna laughed in relief. "I'll be in tomorrow, as usual, to check on him. I'll call him later today, Melanie."

She got off the phone, partially relieved. She trusted Melanie, and if she said her brother was okay, he was.

But the text message was another question. Without a shadow of a doubt, she knew that Damian had something to do with sending the message to her, and that's what scared her most.

She'd never told Damian the name of the expensive home where her brother lived. The bills were sent directly to her, and Damian had given her the money, initially, to have the care set up.

Once she'd begun making good money at the club, minus the sizable reductions to pay off her debt to Damian, she'd been able to take care of the payments herself.

So the question was how did Damian know where her brother lived, and who did he have working at the home that kept him abreast of her brother's activities?

Why did he have someone watching her brother?

She took a deep breath and quickened her steps, hastily walking inside the club.

She'd taken only a few steps inside when she was met by the man she had come to not only fear, but to deeply loathe.

"Well, well, well. Look what the cat dragged in," he jeered, lighting a cigar, the light from the match illuminating his pale-colored skin.

Sienna straightened her back and faced him, no fear showing in her eyes. "I'm tired of playing games with you. What the hell do you want from me, Damian?"

18

Twenty-two months later

Sienna turned from the blackboard and faced her small gathering of students, clapping her hands together. She glanced at the white utilitarian clock on the wall, noting it was five minutes until the class, as well as school, ended. She hid a smile. "Okay, guys, we have *just* enough time to do one final review!"

The collective groans from her eighth-grade social studies class predictably greeted her and she laughed out loud. "Okay, okay, just kidding. I think you all are ready for the T.A.S.K.," she said, referring to the annual academic assessment test. "No more review, I promise! Class is dismissed. Go have fun and get started on your weekend."

When her announcement was met with loud cheers and chairs scraping against the floor in a mad rush to gather backpacks and leave, she held up a hand. "Now, if any of you *really* want more practice, I'll be here this weekend to go over any material you'd like to review, as well as this week."

"Man, Ms. Featherstone, don't you guys have a life?" one of her students, Daniel, groused, and Sienna laughed.

"We do . . . and it usually centers around the students! We want to make sure you all receive the best instruction you can. We want our students to shine!"

"Well, these babies will be shining on the beach this weekend," Daniel chirped in a crackling, preadolescent voice.

Sienna bit the inside of her cheek to prevent the laugh from escaping when the teen shoved back the sleeve on his uniform polo shirt, exposing his thin arm. There was a barely discernible muscle housed beneath his pale, blue-veined skin.

"We're going to the Poconos. I need to start getting this hard body honed for the girls for spring break."

"Oh yeah, we're all foaming at the mouth to see all that *hard* body revealed." Christina, one of the girls, giggled. Daniel's pale cheeks blushed crimson red.

"Okay, be nice!" Sienna automatically cautioned before turning back to her desk and gathering her things. "Have a great weekend, everyone," she said over her shoulder, "and make sure you've handed in your reports, please!" The students who hadn't handed in their book reports tossed them on her desk, with a hearty chorus of return good-byes, before they stampeded out of the classroom.

With a chuckle, Sienna stacked the reports neatly in a corner on her desk.

Turning around, she saw that Daniel was slower in gathering his things, still hovering around his desk.

When the last student filed out, and he was still loading his backpack, she gave him her full attention.

"I thought you'd be the first one out the door, Daniel. I think you turned in your assignment at the beginning of class, right?" she questioned, thumbing through the papers.

"Yes, Ms. Featherstone, I did."

"Oh, okay, good." She smiled, adjusted her small, square-framed glasses, and perched on the desk, careful that the hem of her skirt didn't rise above her knees. "Was there something else you wanted to talk about?"

"Umm, well, kinda. I did. I mean, I—I do," he stammered, his face flushing even more.

Sienna waited patiently for him to continue.

"Ms. Featherstone, I know I'm not doing so good."

"You're doing a lot better since you started working after school with the student tutor. The improvement in your work shows."

"Thanks. I guess I'm just worried about the exam and all. The essay part of it. I know they kinda give an idea of how well we're doing, and determine where we'll be placed for high-school courses. I was hoping to do well enough to try my hand at some of the advanced courses they offer in creative writing. I like to write poetry. Doubt that I'm good enough with my grammar, though. But I wanted to try," he mumbled, kicking the toe on his high-tops against the linoleum floor.

"You're doing great, Daniel. And you are definitely smart enough to try one of the advanced courses. You are a wonderful writer. I've enjoyed the poems you've written and shared with me. You have a wonderful imagination. Grammar can be learned, that's not a problem. Imagination and talent are things that can't be taught, and you have an abundance of that." Although he slid his glance away from hers, Sienna could see that he was flattered with her compliment.

"And if you want to try your hand at one of the advanced courses offered next year, I'll recommend you. And make sure you tell Ms. Dotson, your home room teacher, okay?" She tilted her head to the side, to try and see his face. "The tests are not the only indicator of how well a student is doing, Daniel. You're a smart young man. You have great determination and your writing style is beautiful," she reassured him, reaching a hand out to pat him on his thin shoulders.

When he blushed again, and nervously glanced around the empty room, as though checking to see if one of his classmates had witnessed the exchange, Sienna withdrew her hand.

Although this was her second semester teaching, it was still something she had to get used to, the way many of her students, particularly the male students, reacted to her touch.

She'd used her sexuality so casually in the past, had used her body as a weapon in order to survive. Now she often had to remind herself that the population of men she worked with on a daily basis were not only much younger, but also much less experienced with being around women.

"My uncle says that he'll pay for private tutoring," he blurted, shifting from foot to foot. "He wants me to do better. He's been gone for a while, but he's back now, and he and I had a talk. Could you tutor me? I talk about you all the time to my uncle." He laughed and blushed.

Sienna smiled. "I'm sure I can arrange something. If I can't tutor you, I'll find a good tutor for you, Daniel. We have plenty of university students who offer that type of service. Among your mother, your uncle, and me, we'll work something out."

"Uncle Mac helps me and my mom out a lot. I've told him a lot about you since he got back last week. He's a private detective. He's gone a lot on cases. He wants to know if you could tutor me? I mean, do you do that sort of thing for your students?"

When he said his uncle's name, along with his job, a strange feeling swept over Sienna.

Sienna felt dizzy and gripped the corner of her desk tightly, her fingers curling, biting, into the scarred wood until her knuckles ached.

She shook her head in denial.

There was no way his uncle Mac was the same man she'd met nearly two years ago, the same man she'd made love to and left after one of the most incredible nights of her life. A night that had marked her, one she'd never forgotten, not one moment, for nearly two years.

"Do you and your mother live with your uncle?" she asked with feigned nonchalance, her breath hitched in her throat, waiting for his reply. She remembered everything Mac had told her about his nephew and sister.

"No, not anymore we don't. Used to when I was a kid, though. I'm the man of the house now," he said, puffing out his chest. Despite the strange sense of impending doom, she inwardly smiled at the way he poked out his thin chest.

"What's your uncle's full name?" She racked her brain, trying to remember the name on Daniel's personal information on his school card. She shut her eyes briefly.

Before he could answer, the door to the classroom opened.

Sienna's eyes flew open.

She stared across the room at the one man she didn't think she'd ever meet again; yet in her subconsciousness, she'd known all along that she would. That she'd picked this small town near Hampton, Virginia, because she remembered he said it was where he and his sister lived.

She was forced to acknowledge that she had chosen to move her and her brother from DC to Langston, Virginia, with the hopes of seeing him again, no matter how she denied it to herself.

Garrett McAllister.

19

It was her.

Sin.

Mac strolled across the room, his gut tied in knots.

As he approached her, she nervously bit at the full rim of her bottom lip, her cheeks flaming with color.

Her startled gaze behind her glasses roamed over his face. He saw that her breaths increased, her chest rose and fell, her breasts pushing against the silk blouse she wore.

His own gaze lit on the buttons of her blouse straining with every deep breath she took, the pink lace-scalloped edge of her bra visible.

For two years, her face, her body, still burned a hot memory in his mind.

In two years, he hadn't forgotten how good she'd felt lying beneath him. The way she moved, wrapped her body around his as they'd made love, calling out his name as he catered to her body.

In two years, he hadn't forgotten the feel of her hands feathering over his body as he rocked into her hot, wet sheath.

In two years, he hadn't forgotten her casual dismissal of him as a onetime momentary diversion.

No.

Mac hadn't forgotten one thing about her. He felt his jaw tighten in anger.

He forcibly unclenched his teeth and relaxed his tightening facial muscles.

He stretched his lips into a semblance of a normal smile and casually ruffled the top of his nephew's hair, his gaze still locked with hers.

"Uncle Mac, I'm not a kid!" Daniel protested, but he didn't try and remove his uncle's arm from where it settled across his shoulders.

"Sorry about that, Daniel." Moodily Mac watched her hop down from the desk and take two steps back.

"Aren't you going to introduce me to your teacher, Dan?" he asked, his eyes never leaving hers, hungrily taking her in, from head to toe.

There were small changes in her appearance. She now wore her hair much longer than before. It lay like a thick, heavy curtain down her back in a riot of curls.

She was wearing a prim short-sleeved silk blouse and a demure midknee-length black skirt, where Mac caught a glimpse, when she hopped down from the desk, of her well-formed knees.

He gritted his teeth in anger when his body reacted, fierce and immediate, to being in her presence.

"Uncle Mac, this is my teacher Ms. Featherstone. Ms. Featherstone, this is my uncle Mac," his nephew introduced them proudly. His introduction brought them out of their absorption of each other.

Mac offered his hand for her to shake. Reluctance clearly on her face, she placed her small hand in his, her tongue coming out to snake at the lush rim of her bottom lip.

"It's nice to meet you, Mr. McAllister. Daniel has told me a lot about you," she said, quickly trying to extract her hand from his.

Mac held on.

"Hey, how did you know his last name, Ms. Featherstone?" Mac hid his grin, wondering how she would answer the question.

She broke eye contact with Mac. "I've read all my students' files. I believe your uncle is listed as a contact in case of emergency?"

Although angry with her, Mac gave her cool points for the handy response. Lame, but handy.

When she tried again to remove her fingers from his, he reluctantly released his hold.

"Uncle Mac, Ms. Featherstone has agreed to tutor me!"

"Oh, wait. I haven't agreed to that yet, Daniel. Perhaps your uncle would like to choose another tutor. I can refer you to some excellent tutors who would be able to give you—"

"I'm sure you'd be perfect for the job, Ms. Featherstone," Mac interrupted. "Unless there's another reason to prevent you from tutoring Daniel . . ." He allowed the sentence to dangle. When she threw eyeball darts at him, his mood was strangely improved. She quickly schooled her features into a tight grin.

"No, there is no other reason. Although I wouldn't accept money for tutoring Daniel. That wouldn't be ethical."

"I understand that. I'm sure your ethics are very important to you, Ms. Featherstone. I wouldn't want to compromise your . . . *integrity*," he murmured.

With a tight smile, she turned away from him and spoke to Daniel. "We can arrange a time later to arrange for some extra tutoring, Daniel."

"Thanks, Ms. Featherstone!" Daniel looked from her to Mac, a puzzled look on his young face. He may not know exactly what was going on, but he was astute enough to pick up on the strong undercurrents running back and forth between them.

"You two don't know each other . . . do you?"

"Yes."

"No!" Sienna said simultaneously, and Daniel's face became even more confused.

"Which is it?" His eyes darted back and forth between them. Mac took pity on Sienna and answered, "Ms. Featherstone reminds me of someone I knew once, that's all, son." He turned to give Sienna a hard glance. "But, obviously, I was mistaken. Right, Ms. Featherstone?"

There was an awkward pause. Sienna's eyes widened and she cleared her throat. "I believe you were, Mr. McAllister." She, too, gave Daniel her attention. "Your mother should have my home phone number, Daniel. Have her call me, and we can set up a time," she said, smiling at Daniel.

She turned to Mac and he noted the facsimile of a smile on her face was much more strained; the fine lines bracketing her mouth, more pronounced.

"I didn't catch your first name, Ms. Featherstone."

The look she cast his way, from beneath the dark fringe of lashes, clearly said it was because she hadn't *thrown* it.

"It's Sienna," Daniel volunteered, and blushed wildly. Mac made a mental note to add a few bucks to his nephew's weekly allowance.

"It was nice meeting you, Mr. McAllister." She stuck out her hand and he grasped it. Unable to resist, he ran a caressing thumb over her knuckles. He saw the goose bumps run along her arm from the contact; he felt satisfied at the telling reaction.

"I've got to get ready for a late-night session. I look forward to hearing from your mother, Daniel." The dismissal was friendly, but direct. She wanted Mac to leave.

Fine. He'd go. For now.

But as soon as he got his nephew safely home, a few blocks

away from the school, he'd high tail it back to the damn school before she had a chance to escape him—something he had no intention of allowing her to do.

Mac turned to his nephew. "Okay, buddy, let's go. Your mom is waiting for you."

He turned and gave Sienna a final look. "I'll be back," he promised. A thrill of anticipation coursed through him when her eyes widened and a look of pure fear, mingled with desire, lurked in her deep brown eyes.

As soon as the door closed behind the pair, Sienna rushed to gather papers on her desk and stuffed them, sans protective covers, inside her briefcase with shaky hands.

Dear God, there was no *way* she wanted to be here when Mac returned. And return he would, no doubt about it.

The wicked, almost predatory look on his handsome face promised her he would. It also promised there would be no talk of her tutoring his nephew.

Hell no.

The look in his light gray eyes, along with the heated glances she'd received from him, promised he had an altogether different type of *tutoring* in mind.

She glanced at the clock. The impromptu conference with Daniel, along with Mac, had cost her time. It was well after four o'clock. It was Friday, so the school would be empty or near empty, especially since spring break was around the corner.

She'd told Principal Skinner she'd be available after school to go over a proposed change in the curriculum for next year, and she knew she needed to be there. She enjoyed teaching, and was damned if she'd allow another man to have her running scared. She'd go by his office before he could make it to her room and make her excuses. . . .

"Ms. Featherstone?" the cackle from the intercom on her desk startled her, and she dropped her briefcase.

"Damn it," she mumbled under her breath. She caught herself from falling just in time.

"Yes, sir?" she called out, hoping the principal hadn't heard her cursing.

"I'm going to have to reschedule our meeting for next week, if that's okay with you?"

"That's fine, sir. I think I'll leave now as well," she answered in relief.

Sienna looked at the clock, anxious to get away before Mac could return. After more idle talk, the principal finally said good-bye and Sienna quickly picked up her things, pulled her lightweight sweater from her chair, and prepared to leave.

With her nerves on edge, Sienna dropped the sweater and bent down to retrieve it. She missed her door quietly opening. The click of the lock registered and she whipped her head around, doom settling in her gut.

"So this is where you've been hiding out. You've been a bad girl, Sin. . . . It's taken me a long time to find you."

Sienna gasped in surprise and horror when she saw the man lounging casually against the door. The jeering look of arrogance on his thin face, one she'd hoped she never would have to encounter again.

Damian Marks.

20

Mac turned into the private cul-de-sac and drove into his sister's driveway.

He'd made the ten-minute drive in less than five minutes, and thanked good fortune he hadn't gotten busted by a cop.

Daniel had thrown him curious glances during the short trip. But, thankfully, he hadn't asked his uncle any probing questions—the kind most kids his age seemed to enjoy—along the drive.

He parked the car, without cutting the engine.

"Aren't you going to come in? Mom's making pizza," Daniel quizzed, one hand on the door handle, the other hooked on his backpack.

"No, son, not tonight. I have something I need to take care of."

"Going back to talk to Ms. Featherstone?"

Mac looked in surprise at his nephew. Obviously, he'd passed some of his intuition, or overall nosiness, to his nephew.

"Maybe," he conceded, and ran his hands over Daniel's head, knowing it would irritate him. He laughed when Daniel ducked away. "How 'bout I take a rain check on dinner? Tell your mom for me, okay?"

"Sure, Uncle Mac," Daniel agreed, and opened the car door to leave. Before he closed the door, he leaned in, his face serious. "Uncle Mac?"

"Yeah, son?"

"Uh, Ms. Featherstone is real nice. I like her a lot." His young face had a look of maturity stamped on it; Mac got a glimpse of a much older, grown-up Daniel and felt his heart clench.

"Yes, I can tell."

"Well, I think she's kind of had a rough life."

"What makes you say that, Dan?"

"I don't know. She never really talks about her personal life or anything. Some of the kids ask her questions all the time. Stuff about her family, what she did before she taught, stuff like that."

"And?" Mac prompted.

"Well, once, Sean, one of the kids in class, was talking about his sister. I guess she has something . . . wrong . . . with her."

Daniel looked away and bit his lip, his face scrunched.

"Sean got piss . . . mad when one of the other guys made fun of his sister. He got in a fight and got suspended from school."

Knowing that Daniel had something more to say, Mac waited for him to continue.

"Well, the next day, Sean was back at school. He told me that Ms. Featherstone got him out of trouble. She went to the principal for him."

"What did she say?"

"She said that no one should get in trouble for defending their family. If family couldn't rely on family to take care of them, who could they rely on?"

With that, Dan eased his face out of the open window. "I'll see you later, Uncle Mac. I'll tell Mom what you said about dinner." With a cheerful wave good-bye, his nephew pulled his backpack farther up his thin shoulders and galloped toward the house.

As Mac watched his nephew walk inside, his thoughts focused on the enigma of Sienna Featherstone.

"Ms. Featherstone, you and I have a lot to talk about. And this time, you're going to open up. I'm not letting you go, again," Mac said aloud.

"What are you doing here? How did you—"

"Find you?" Damian laughed and strolled toward her.

Sienna glanced nervously around.

Damn. She was alone. The school was nearly deserted and he'd locked the door.

Unless someone came by her room, specifically looking for her, no one would know she was still there.

Then she remembered the intercom. Maybe she could catch Principal Skinner before he left.

She spun around, ran back to her desk, and pressed the intercom button. Before she could open her mouth to speak, it was covered with Damian's hand, while his body covered hers from the back.

"I wouldn't do that if I were you. You and me got unfinished business, bitch," he snarled, low, in her ear.

Sienna spun around and shoved him away, wiping her mouth with the back of her hand.

"What business do we have?" She cried out when he snatched her by the shoulders and yanked her back toward him, her body slamming into his so hard, her teeth jarred.

"You still owe me." He ran his hand up and down the side of her cheek, and Sienna flinched in revulsion. "And I'm here to collect."

Although Sienna couldn't believe he found her, she wasn't surprised. When she'd escaped Damian and the Sweet Kitty, she knew she hadn't seen the last of him.

"What final debt?"

"The one for your brother."

"I don't owe you a damn thing, Damian, you know that! You took almost everything I earned when I worked for you!" She slowly backed away from him.

"No, you *do* owe me. Until I say the debt is paid, ain't shit paid! Unless you want something *unfortunate* to happen to Jacob, I suggest you play nice."

When he mentioned her brother, chills danced along her body. She turned to face him, her shoulders slumped. "What do you want?"

His thin lips stretched wide in a parody of a smile. He walked toward her, propped his body against her desk, and crossed his long legs, near his ankles.

"Simple. I got a new gig I need you to work."

Sienna stopped her pacing and turned to face him. "What gig? Stripping? I'm not doing that! Listen, I have a new life here. I have a respectable profession. No one knows—"

"And they don't have to know your dirty little secret. As long as you do this last gig, no worries. It's not stripping in a club. And it won't be here. I need you to come to Virginia Beach, a *respectable* distance from this quaint little community."

"And do what?" she asked warily.

"I've got a group of investors that need to be entertained."

"What type of entertaining?"

"The kind you do best, baby. Nothing hard about that. Just come with your costume, and you and the others will simply entertain while we conduct business. You'll like it! We have a big, beautiful yacht anchored off the marina. All you have to do is a bit of dancing, look pretty, and earn a few greenbacks in the process!" He spoke as though he were offering her a wonderful island getaway vacation.

"What kind of business? I'm not getting involved in anything illegal!"

* * *

Back when she worked for Damian, she knew he had dealings with "businessmen" dirtier than he. She'd once accidentally walked in his office when he'd been in the middle of a meeting with one.

Sienna had backed up when the men had turned to her—Damian's face irritated, the other man's a mask of fury before he quickly closed down his expression.

"What the hell do you want? I'm in the middle of something. You don't just come in here any damn time you want!" Damian had yelled at her.

Sienna had been too surprised at the way he'd spoken to her to say anything. She'd mumbled an apology as she stumbled out the door, quickly closing the door behind her.

She'd turned away from the door and stopped. Unable to resist, she'd looked up and down the hall to see if anyone was looking. Then she'd leaned her face close to the door to try and hear what they were talking about. She was curious as to who the sophisticated-looking, well-dressed man was. She wanted to know what he was doing talking to someone like Damian.

". . . yes, she's perfect. Absolutely perfect. Not that I'd expect a simpleton like you to see that." The unknown man spoke so softly Sienna had to strain to hear him better.

"Yeah, she's got a perfect ass, *sí, amigo?* I can't wait to sample a piece of that." The next thing she heard was a loud gasp. She heard the choked-off exclamation through the door.

"Wha—what did I do? Let go of my neck!" Damian squeaked out.

"You will keep your hands off her. You'll do well to remember that . . . *friend.*" There was a long silence before she heard anything more. Nervous, afraid to stay and listen to any more, yet unable to leave, Sienna stayed rooted to her eavesdropping spot in front of the door.

"Give her this. I want to see her wearing it the next time she dances," the unknown man spoke again.

A moment later, she heard Damian exclaim, "No problem. Damn, you didn't have to choke me! If you want me to do something, all you gotta do is ask. You know that," he cried.

Sienna would have stayed to listen to more, but she heard voices and scurried away from the door, swiftly walking away, just as two dancers passed her in the hallway.

After that episode, she'd learned the man's name. Carlos Medeiros. The few times he came to the club, he would stay for her set, sitting at a secluded table, alone, his dark eyes never leaving hers as she danced. When she came back out to the floor, he was nowhere to be seen. After a few times, she dismissed it, but it always left her unsettled the way she'd only see him during the times she danced.

During one of his infrequent visits to the Sweet Kitty, he'd been sitting at a VIP table with several businessmen.

All the men looked out of place in the club. They weren't the normal nine-to-fivers who frequented the Sweet Kitty. They wore their hard sophistication as elegantly as they wore the expensive clothes on their bodies. Although they watched the dancers, there was an air of detachment surrounding them. She'd avoided their cold-eyed stares. Particularly Carlos's.

Sienna shivered, remembering the hard, cold, calculating look in his eyes as he watched her dance.

"Now dance for me." Damian's demand wrenched her out of her memories.

He leaned back on the desk, crossed his arms over his chest, and grinned a nasty smile.

"Wha-what do you mean, dance for you? I've agreed to do the damn party—what more do you want?" Sienna cried out, completely humiliated, nerves stretched taut.

"I need to see if you still got it. It's been a while, baby girl. You've been out of the biz for a while." He got up and strolled around her room, touching the art on the wall, the bulletin board she had with each student's picture pinned up with a thumbtack.

"I wonder what your precious students would think if they knew their teacher used to strip, and get men off, for a living?" he asked, turning to face her, an evil look on his face. "Or how would their parents feel if they knew? Hmmm?"

"I already told you that I'd do it! Please, Damian—"

He walked closer, until he was inches from her. The smell of his cheap cologne cloying, making her nauseous. He lifted a strand of her hair. "I like the new look. Softer, more womanly." When she flinched, his face hardened.

"Although I'd bet the fathers wouldn't be as judgmental. I bet a few of them have already had fantasies surrounding hot little Ms. Featherstone."

"I'll do whatever you want. Just don't—"

"Don't what? Spoil your new 'gig'?" He laughed. "No fears, baby girl, just show me what you got."

Sienna bit back the tears of humiliation and schooled her features. She closed her eyes, inhaled deep breaths, and slowly began to gyrate her body. Listening to the music in her head, tuning out Damian's mocking face, she began to dance.

21

Mac parked his Jeep and vaulted out of the driver's seat, locking the door with his remote.

Glancing around the near-empty parking lot, he hoped he caught Sienna before she left the school. He had no idea what car she currently drove. If memory served correctly, she last drove an old Corolla, and he saw no sign of a Corolla in the parking lot. The only cars he saw were an old, beat-up–looking maintenance truck, a small compact, and a gleaming black Mercedes-Benz. Maybe the Ford was hers. He didn't think she'd be driving a Benz.

Hell, if teaching paid enough for her to afford a luxury car like that, he was in the wrong line of work.

He walked to the door, and wasn't surprised when he found it was locked.

"Fuck!" He tried the revolving door, with no luck.

He banged on the glass door for several minutes before giving up. He must have missed her. Damn it!

Turning to go, he caught sight of a uniformed man ambling toward the door. He motioned for the man to come, and waited impatiently for him to finally open the door.

"What can I do for you, young man? You banging so hard

on the door, you'll wake the dead! Nobody here, school is closed for the weekend," the old man said around a mouthful of what looked like chewing tobacco.

"Are any of the teachers still around?"

"Didn't you hear what I said? You deafer than me, or what? Told you, nobody's around. Gone for the weekend." The old man started to close the door in Mac's face after that pronouncement. Mac grabbed the door edge before he could.

"There's a couple of cars in the lot. I thought my son's teacher may still be here. We were supposed to meet for a conference." He uttered the lie completely straight-faced.

"Which one?"

"Ms. Featherstone."

"Who's your kid?" the janitor asked, swirling the tobacco from one side of his gaunt cheek to the other, his eyes suspicious-looking.

"Daniel Rhodes."

"Hmmm. What's your name, again?"

"Garrett McAllister," he answered, impatiently wanting to get past the inquisition to see if Sienna was still in the building.

"Hmmm. Thought he lived with his mama. Never heard your name mentioned as the father. Different last names?"

"He's biologically my nephew. I take care of him and his mom. Could I please come in?" Mac answered shortly.

After a long perusal, where the old man's eyes roamed over him, head to toe, he finally opened the door, allowing Mac to enter.

"Haven't seen Ms. Featherstone leave yet. Usually, she's the last to leave for the night. Know where her classroom is?"

"Yes, but thanks," Mac answered.

He walked through the empty halls, making his way toward her classroom, hoping he'd caught her before she left. He had no desire over the next few hours to hunt down where she lived. Something he knew he'd do if he had to.

He rounded the corner that led to her room and sprinted the

last few yards. He stopped in front of her door, hand on the knob, and peered inside the stained glass window.

Mac stopped short of opening the door, a red haze of anger clouding his vision.

Wearing nothing but the pink bra he'd glimpsed beneath her blouse, and the demure straight black skirt, she was on her knees, rolling her hot little body.

The man she was on her knees in front of, taking off her clothes for, was Damian Marks.

"Yes, just like that, baby. Show daddy what you got," Damian taunted.

Sienna continued to ignore him, pretending she danced for herself and no one else. Just as she'd done before.

She rolled her upper body, snaked her hands down her chest, alongside her breasts, before cupping them. She completely lost herself to the sensuality of the dance.

"Open your eyes and look at me."

Reality crashed in on her, and she opened her eyes as he commanded.

"Now come up real slow," he demanded. She began to rise, only to have him stop her.

"No, not like that." He laughed loudly. "Turn that sweet ass around and let me see it from the back."

Sienna clenched her teeth and kept her face blank. She refused to give him the satisfaction of seeing her angry, letting him know how much she hated him and what he was forcing her to do.

She spun around on her knees, grabbed her ankles, and rotated her body upward, allowing her ass to jut back as her fingers slid up her ankles, past her knees. She lifted the hem of her skirt, exposing her thong-covered buttocks to his leering eyes.

"Yeah, just like that. You can take the whore out of the club, but you can't take the club out of the whore!" He laughed at his own lewd comment.

She raised her head, ready to turn to face him, and her glance fell to the door. Her heart leaped.

Very clearly she could see the outline shadow of someone behind the translucent glass.

She clutched her hands in front of her near-nude body, desperately trying to cover herself. Dear God, who had witnessed what she'd been doing? she wondered, frantic. She spun around to face Damian.

"Get out, damn it!"

"What?"

"You heard me. Get the hell out of here! I promised to come. I'll be there! Now just get out!"

His jaw clenched, a small tic flickered. He stared at her for so long, she thought he'd ignore her. When he shoved her away, she breathed a sigh of relief. She watched nervously as he reached inside his double-breasted jacket and withdrew a slip of paper and threw it on her desk.

"Just be there. These are the directions and my cell phone number."

When he walked away, her body sagged with relief. She needed him gone, now.

At the door, he looked over his shoulder and paused, his eyes hard. "Don't be late. Remember, I know where you live. Don't make me have to come and get your ass. And I know where Jacob lives. Remember *that*." He turned the lock and flung open the door, slamming it behind him.

When the door closed behind him, Sienna waited five full minutes before she swiftly gathered her things and left the classroom.

She glanced around to see if the person she'd glimpsed outside the door was around. When the empty hallways echoed only her footsteps, she prayed to God it had been her imagination, and no one had witnessed her stripping in her classroom.

Dear God, would she ever escape her past? She swallowed bitter tears and rushed out of the school.

22

"Same dance, different city."

Sin—*Sienna*, Mac mentally corrected himself—jumped when he spoke. He spoke as though he were picking up a pleasant conversation between two friends, and not ex-lovers.

He'd been waiting for over an hour for her to come home. Images of her dancing for Marks, her hot little hands touching the other man's body, screwed with his head.

After witnessing her *dance*, Mac had driven around for a short time, enraged, trying like hell to cool down.

He didn't trust himself to go back to the school, to confront her. And if Marks's ass was still there, there was no telling what the hell he would do to the man. To say he wanted to rip him apart was putting it too mildly. He *had* to calm down.

And now he knew her address and phone number.

He'd stopped at a gas station, picked up a phone book, and searched for her listing. She had an unusual last name, not common. He wasn't surprised when there was only one listed, and when it had the initial *S*, with no full first name, he knew it was a good chance it was hers.

He'd impatiently punched in the number and waited.

Her voice mail picked up, and when he heard her soft voice directing the caller to leave a message, his lips stretched in a grin of satisfaction.

He'd disconnected, taken note of her address from the phone book, and had driven the small distance to her house.

When no lights shone in the small town house, no evidence of her being home, Mac made his move.

Easily picking the lock, he'd entered. Once inside, edgy, he'd stalked through her home, familiarizing himself with the layout before returning to her small den in the front of the house, near both the front door and the small entry to the garage.

He wanted to catch her when she *finally* came home, no matter which entry she chose.

"Wha-what are you doing here? Who the hell are you? H-how did you get in my home?" she stuttered, her large eyes wide and frightened as she stumbled back from his advancing body.

He kept to the shadows of her den, knowing that his face was half-shadowed, wanting—needing—her to fear him.

"I wonder if the school board knows they have a whore for a teacher?"

"I don't know who you are, but you'd better get the hell out of here before I call—"

"You're not calling anyone, and neither are you going anywhere."

Mac swiftly caught her before she could turn the knob on the door, his hands lying on top of hers heavily. As he came out of the shadows, his face fully exposed, she was able to see who he was.

Mac saw the look of relieved recognition, followed quickly by some unknown emotion close to longing, flare in her eyes.

"Mac!" She turned frightened eyes up, to stare intently into his face.

"Sorry to disappoint you, Sin. Expecting someone else, maybe?"

They weren't touching; yet her heat seared him, called out to him. His dick was hard as a rock, pushing against his zipper. His body needed hers, longed to feel her soft curves moving along his body, needed to feel her wrapped around him.

But no way in hell was he going to touch her.

He might hurt her if he did, in his present state.

Angrily he crowded her, shoved her body tight against the door, her face away from his. Her back was flush against the hard wall of his chest. He buried his face against the soft curve of her neck.

"Oh God, Mac," she moaned when he grasped her hair and moved it aside for his lips and teeth to scrape the long line of her neck. "I didn't know it was you at first. You scared me. . . ." Her admission that she'd recognized him eased the anger beating at him. He shoved his relief to the side.

"Why did you lie to me, and why are you still hooked up with that motherfucking, Damian Marks?" he asked harshly. He stopped himself from asking why she left him two years ago.

His hands came up to cup her shoulders, easing up to stroke alongside her throat. His hold tightened, squeezing her fragile neck, lightly. A warning.

"I don't know what you're talking about, and neither do I owe you any explanations!"

He moved in closer. One hand remained around her neck, the other grabbed the ends of her hair, pulling her head back so he could see her face.

"Let me go, goddamn it!" Her throat constricted against his hand. When she tried to move away, she winced when his hold tightened.

"I'm surprised you remembered me. You whore for so many, why remember me?" He whispered the harsh words against the side of her temple and felt her tremble.

When she refused to answer, he spun her around to face him, slamming her body against the door. "Look at me, damn it! And stop the damn pretenses!"

"What are you talking about? What pretenses? Let go of my hair," she cried out. Continuing to avoid his eyes, she further angered him.

"I will, when you admit who you are and stop fucking playing games," he spit out grimly, *forcing* her to look him in the eyes.

Long, tense minutes followed, both of their breathing harsh, staring at one another, neither willing to relent.

In disgust, he released his hold on her and she jumped away, easing away from the door, warily assessing him as she massaged her scalp.

His eyes angrily roamed over hers when she wrenched away. "Come to me, Sin."

"No." Sienna's breath was coming out in gasps as she slowly backed away, never taking her eyes away from his.

He narrowed his eyes to slits, his nostrils flaring when her heady, unique scent assaulted his senses. Mac forcibly stopped himself from pouncing on her like a caged beast.

As she slowly walked backward, he stayed still, not moving an inch, allowing her to retreat. But when she turned, her intent to run away from him obvious, the beast demanded release.

That was her first mistake. Turning her back on him.

She'd made it to the entry to her garage, hand on the door-knob, turning it, when he clamped one hand down, hard, on top of her shoulders, spinning her around to face him.

She slapped his face, hard, and jerked herself away, her face filled with fear.

That was her second mistake.

Not the slap, but the fear shining brightly in her deep brown eyes. As though she needed to be afraid of him.

"Wrong answer, *Sin*!" This time, when he grabbed her, his hold was steely. He gave her no time to react. He flipped her around to face him, forced her head back, and slammed his mouth over hers, crushing her body to his.

His hands roamed her body, refamiliarizing himself with her sweet curves, the slope of her hips, down her small, softly muscled ass, and back up her body. He shoved his hand inside the vee of her blouse. Buttons popped, flying everywhere, as he inserted his hand and cupped a warm mound.

Hands, which first were pushing him away, now clutched, before delving under the ends of his shirt.

Impatiently he pulled the shirt over his head, leaving his chest bared. She ran her small, capable hands over his chest, and Mac clenched his teeth together to prevent himself from ripping off her clothes.

With his hold on her hair firm, he gathered the long strands tighter around his fist, pulling his mouth away from hers, his breathing harsh and loud in the dark room.

He kept his eyes on hers and tore her blouse, ripping the silk to shreds, carelessly throwing it to the floor to land near his.

He closed his mind to the fear reflected in her eyes and attacked her skirt, shoving the material up her long legs, bunching it around her waist. His hands ran up her thighs before he found what he wanted.

"No, Mac, please . . . not like this."

"Be quiet."

He inserted a finger inside the lace edge of her panties, pushed past the lips of her vagina, and inserted a finger. Her cream soaked him and he groaned harshly, before he eased his honey-coated finger out of her creaming slit.

He brought his finger to his mouth and licked her essence away. His dick hardened to painful proportions.

Pushing her down, he forced her to her knees, in front of him, his hand at the opening to his slacks.

His gut clenched at the picture she presented, her small, perfect breasts cresting the top of her delicate-looking bra as her chest heaved, her eyes on his. One hand went to the front of his pants and unzipped.

Her eyes widened when he shoved his pants down far enough to allow his cock to spring forth, hard and ready.

She closed her eyes when he slapped it, lightly, against her soft cheeks. Her small tongue snaked out to run along the full rim of her bottom lip.

Mac grasped the base of his shaft in one hand and rubbed it slowly, back and forth, against her lips, his pre-cum liquid dampening her mouth, silently demanding her to open for him.

She stubbornly kept her lips clamped shut.

"Open, goddamn it!"

"No!"

"Yes." Mac lightly grasped the back of her head, forcing her head back, readying her for him. "Tell me you want this," he demanded. She stared at him, her eyes angry, defiant . . . yearning.

"Go to hell, Mac."

For long, tense moments, they stared at one another, both of their breathing harsh in the quiet, dark room.

"Tell me you want it. That you want me. *Tell me, Sin.*"

When her mouth opened, Mac shut his eyes briefly and exhaled the pent-up breath he didn't know he'd been holding. He began feeding her his cock, easing the round knob inside, inch by inch, his shaft gliding between her lips.

"Yes, take it, take *me*," he rasped, easing as much of his penis into her warm, wet mouth as he could, until he felt the end bump the back of her throat.

Her throat worked convulsively, her eyes shuttering closed. Her hands came up, a slight tremor in them, as she held his marauding cock steady.

"Open your eyes. Let me see you."

He needed to see her beautiful eyes, needed to see that she knew whose cock she was bathing with her tongue. He flexed his hips, moving his shaft in and out of her warm receptor, clenching his jaw in pleasure when her teeth grazed him.

She opened her eyes and stared into his. The look in her orbs forced his heart to thud harder against his chest.

Her eyes held a wealth of emotion—sadness, anxiety, lust, and acceptance.

Tears, unshed, shimmered before one spilled down past her long, thick lashes, down her smooth brown cheek.

23

What the hell was wrong with her? Sienna thought desperately.

She didn't want this, didn't know this angry Mac, and had no idea what she'd done to incite him so. She had every right to not seek him out, to deny knowing him. Why in the hell couldn't he have just left well enough alone?

Now he had her on her knees, his dick in her mouth.

Instead of biting it, doing him and it serious damage, she shamefully gloried in having him embedded in her mouth.

She gloried in the feel of his thick shaft cradled in her warm mouth, loved the feel of *him*. Just like the whore he called her. Loving him in ways she'd never willingly done to any man.

She licked him, her tongue sliding under and around his thick shaft, nursing from him like a babe on a bottle.

She dragged his penis from her mouth. As she gazed down at the thick stalk with its blushed round head, she felt her sex clench in remembrance of what it felt like stroking inside her.

Sienna glanced up at him, grasped the root of his shaft, and with her eyes trained on his, she licked the head. It bobbed against her tongue. She leaned closer and engulfed him farther into her mouth.

She sucked him hungrily, her tongue playing over the soft skin wrapping the hard length of cock in her mouth. Her suckling became more urgent, harder, pulling at him. Her cheeks hollowed with every tug and draw. When he groaned, his legs trembling, she knew he wasn't as unaffected as he pretended to be.

She glanced up and saw his eyes shutter closed, his thick lashes hiding his expression. Sienna felt a surge of feminine power swell within her.

She widened her legs in her kneeling position in front of him and firmly grasped the back of his hard, thickly muscled thighs, her nails biting into his skin.

"What are you doing to me?" He groaned.

She pulled her mouth away from him. His hands came out to grasp her by the back of her head and pull her back into close contact with his throbbing cock. She licked the tightly drawn sac of his balls and blew air across them. His groan was loud and harsher than before at the contact.

"Isn't this what you wanted, Mac? Me on my knees, sucking you off?" Before he could respond, she swallowed his dick, whole. Her breast slapped against his thighs as she drew him in, closer.

In earnest, she laved and suckled him, her hands cupping the sac of his tightly drawn testicles. The warmth from his hot cum nestled inside scorched her hand.

He held on to her head, his big body shaking her, thrusting his hips, forcing more of his length inside.

Sienna reveled in the power reversal, his shuddering, his body hers to pleasure. She slid forward, taking him deeper, deep-throating him, bobbing her head along his shaft.

"No, not like this!" His voice came out a strangled gasp of pleasure, cracking.

He tried to push her away, but Sienna held on, *refusing* to allow him to end what *he* had started. She moved her hands upward, held on to his muscled butt cheeks, and continued to work his cock.

"Goddamn it, Sienna!" he growled, his hands gripping her hair tight as he pumped into her mouth. Once, twice, a final thrust, and he released.

Throwing his head back, he yelled as he came ferociously.

His hot cum scorched her mouth, splashed down her throat, spilling out of the corners of her lips as she milked him.

Unrelenting, she refused to release him until she'd drained him.

Spent, Mac opened his eyes and glanced down at Sienna on her knees. Her eyes were passion-glazed, with his semen easing down her chin.

He finally pulled away from her, forcing her lips to let go of his dick. When she moved as though to stand, he stopped her.

"I'm not done with you. I need to feel that sweet snatch grip my cock."

Sienna's lids were half-closed and drowsy-looking. Her full reddened lips were partially open. The sight of his cum on her smooth, soft cheeks, trickling down her neck, kept his erection hard and throbbing.

There was a look of such wanton need stamped on her beautiful face he knew he'd have a hell of a time not coming, again, the minute he stroked into her.

Mac hoped like hell he wouldn't embarrass himself and could make it past a few strokes before he exploded inside her.

He lowered his body, pushed her down onto the carpet, his fingers trailing down her face, gathering the sticky evidence of his arousal. He smeared it down her body.

The hot visual of his white cum on her creamy brown skin made his balls tingle; his dick hardened, painfully.

He flipped her so that her belly lay flush on the carpet, her round ass an invitation he couldn't resist.

Leaning down, he moved the thin scrap of her panties to the side and stroked his tongue over one perfectly shaped brown globe.

He held on to her waist, pulled her body higher, separated her cheeks, and stroked his tongue between the crease of her pussy and ass. Before she could do more than cry out sharply, he withdrew. He kept her raised high in the air; the position thrust out her heart-shaped ass, the swollen glistening lips of her pussy pronounced.

At the angle he had her, he could see white cream that surrounded her delicate lips, evidence that sucking him had excited her.

Reaching a hand between them, he eased her skirt off her body, along with her panties, down the length of her legs. He lifted her so her knees came off the floor and threw her clothes next to the small pile collected near their bodies.

Repositioning her, Mac felt her tremble beneath his hands as one lone finger stroked between her seam, slicing between the lips of her vagina. He blindly reached for a condom from his wallet as he moved in closer behind her, spreading her wider. He settled his body between the backs of her open thighs.

Grasping the base of his shaft, he quickly sheathed his erection and targeted her seeping entry, nestled between her sweet folds.

"Oh God . . . ," she groaned, her body bowing down, her back arching against his chest, as he rubbed his dick over her vagina.

"You're so damn juicy, so creamy. Just waiting to be fucked."

He inserted one finger between her slick lips, massaging his fingers over and around her pulsing clit. She keened when he pushed two fingers deep inside her cunt, rotating, before withdrawing them. He lifted his fingers to his lips and tasted her.

"Just as good as I remembered." Mac drew in a deep, steadying breath, trying to rein in his need to drive deep into her, push into her as far as his dick could reach.

And ride her hard.

He wanted a nice, long fuck.

Needed to jam her body and drench himself in her essence. He'd been obsessed with thoughts of her, dreaming of her, unable to get her out of his mind, for nearly two years.

After leaving DC and returning home, he'd bedded as many willing bodies as he could, unsuccessfully trying to drive the image of her welcoming body, beautiful face, sweet snatch, out of his mind.

After a year of fucking as many women as he could, he'd realized it was a damn moot point.

Every time he'd surged into a willing woman, a warm body, the only face he'd seen had been Sienna's, the only body he wanted it to be had been hers.

After that, he'd given up. He'd been celibate, knowing that no one could take her place.

Several months ago, he'd decided to go after her, to return to the Sweet Kitty and see if he could find her. He'd taken too long.

When he'd returned to DC, not only was she gone, but the Sweet Kitty had changed owners. Marks had sold the place and no one knew where he'd gone. The few dancers who remained hadn't known what happened to Sin, either.

He would have continued his search, but a new case had come in and he'd had to focus his attention on it, instead. After returning home, and making sure his sister and nephew were okay, his plan had been to return to his investigation.

Then he'd walked into his nephew's classroom and there she was.

And his world had turned upside down.

He ran possessive eyes over her slight form in front of him.

In the dim light shadowing the room, her small honey-colored breasts and tight cherry nipples hung low, begging for his touch.

He ran his eyes down her body, her smooth back, her perfect ass. He'd replayed this scene over in his mind countless times—the things he wanted to do with her body, the ways he'd planned to make her, his.

He pushed into her drenched pussy in one hard thrust until he was embedded, balls deep.

"Damn, you're wet," he said with a groan. "Slippery, but so tight!"

The pulsating walls of her pussy clenched down on his dick so hard, Mac pulled out, despite her mewling protest. He then clamped his fingers down over the end of his cock, with one hand on the base, to stop his cum from jetting forth.

"Aren't you going to make love to me? What do you want from me, Mac?" She turned her head to glance at him over her shoulder. Her breathing was labored, red lips lush and enticing.

His nostrils flared with the scent of sex, heady and palpable in the room.

"I want to fuck you senseless."

24

His strokes were hard and strong, jostling her body with the force of his thrusts. Sienna whimpered and moaned, forced to lower her upper body, her elbows and forearms flush on the carpeted floor as she accepted his glorious fucking.

As he plunged and retreated inside her drenched sex, his balls insistently tapping against her backside, she reared her ass back, grinding on his cock, twisting her body to better accommodate his thick girth. She mewled and cried with every corkscrew drive of his hips.

When one of his big hands strongly smacked one of her ass cheeks, she yelped.

He withdrew from her, easing himself out, and Sienna cried out, "No, please—"

He reached a hand down and she felt him replace his shaft with one of his fingers. He pushed into her vagina far enough to swirl a thick finger inside her creaming core, withdrawing some of her juices, before plunging his cock deep inside her once more.

He covered her back with his chest, his breath ragged and hot against the back of her neck. He inserted his finger into her mouth.

Sienna knew what to do.

"Ummm," she moaned, and clamped her lips around his finger, suckling as he continued to move inside her. He kept his hand in her mouth and slammed his body in and out of hers, in an orchestrated dance.

Some of his thrusts were short, tight, the others long, nearly easing himself out completely, his round knob resting at the mouth of her sex, before he'd ram back into her.

The strokes were so deep, so powerful, they edged on painful. Sienna accepted each one, though, grinding herself on his shaft, welcoming the power and the pain/pleasure of his depth.

Soon she felt the beginnings of an orgasm unfurl within her belly. Rolling her hips to capture every inch of his pounding cock, her breasts brushed against the carpet, her nipples overly sensitive, and she cried out.

When he removed his finger from her mouth and captured her clit between two fingers, swirling the blood-filled tip, her orgasm broke.

"Yes, God, yes, just like that. Please, just like that, please, *please* don't stop—" Her keens reached a crescendo, and when she felt another stinging slap to her ass, she screamed loudly, the pleasure intensifying to nearly unbearable proportions.

"This is mine! Damn you for fucking that asshole Marks! Never again, do you hear me?"

"I didn't! I was only—"

He slapped her ass again, harder, in rhythm with his jabbing cock and toying fingers on her clit, over and over, sending her cresting the top, her orgasm shattering her body into a million pieces.

The power of her release shook her small body. Shaking and trembling, she was limp, unable to move as he rocked into her. Her pussy fastened down, milking him as ferociously as he was rocking into her.

"Yes, goddamn! Yes!" He roared and held on tight, his fingers digging into her hips.

He gave one final thrust before he shouted as his fingers gripped her hips even tighter, and he, too, released.

When it was over, when he'd completed his orgasm and withdrew from her, his big body was draped on top of hers.

As he lay on top of her back, pressing her into the carpet, the sweat from their combined bodies quickly cooled in the air-conditioned room.

Sienna shivered from both the cool air and in reaction to the man who'd delivered on his promise—to fuck her senseless.

25

"You okay?" Mac asked, easing away.

He had to force his body away from the temptation of hers, afraid he'd hurt her during his rough lovemaking.

"I'm fine. Why?" she asked, her voice quiet yet strained-sounding to his ears.

Mac glanced worriedly over at her as he yanked the condom off, tossing it in the small trash can.

He pulled his slacks back up the length of his legs and shrugged his shirt up over his head.

In his haste to get inside her, he had only shoved his slacks far enough to release his dick and get at her. Now, dressed, his pants fastened, he offered his hand to her.

He saw the hesitancy in her expression before she placed hers inside of his, allowing him to help her stand.

"I shouldn't have been so rough with you," he muttered.

She didn't respond, simply gathered her torn clothes, and attempted to put them on.

"Here, let me help."

"No. I'm fine," she replied in a soft yet clipped tone. She turned her body away from him to put on her clothes.

Mac's hand dropped at his side.

He ran both hands through his hair in frustration, spiking it over his head. He felt like shit as he glumly watched her pull her torn blouse on, her averted face flushing when she pulled the ragged ends together, fisting the fabric, to keep it closed, because he'd ripped the buttons off in his haste to get at her.

"God, I'm so sor—"

"Look, you don't owe me any apologies," she interrupted, cutting her eyes toward him before turning away. "I'm sure it was pretty obvious how much I wanted it, toward the end there. Actually, from the beginning. You turn me on, even when you're calling me a whore." She laughed, without humor. "You know the way out. Same way you came in."

She brushed past him, walking down the hallway and out of sight.

He waited, undecided.

Turning, he walked toward her front door. He paused, with the door open, torn.

After the way he'd just made love to her, he knew she probably wanted him to get the hell out of her house, and out of her life.

A grim determination settled over him.

There was no way in hell he was going to do that.

She had gotten under his skin two years ago, and no matter how she denied it, no matter what she said to him, or herself, he knew he'd gotten under hers as well.

No woman reacted the way she had, creamed all over a man's dick, moaned and cried out as he fucked her, the way she did—if she didn't have *some* type of feelings.

Even if the feelings were all about the sex.

He'd build on that.

Mac's mouth set, determined; he closed the door and set out after her, striding down the hallway, searching for her.

He came to a stop in the entryway to her darkened living-room area. He saw her as she was walking into the kitchen after turning on a small light. Her steps were slow, careful, as though she held the weight of the world on her small shoulders.

After Sienna turned on the light, she made her way to the oven.

Closing her eyes, she braced her hands on the counter and inhaled a deep, shaky breath before opening them again.

Glancing down at her blouse, with the ripped buttons, she felt a renewed sense of shame.

She'd allowed him to take her like an animal.

No, scratch that.

She'd *gloried* in him taking her like an animal.

The image of his hard back draping hers as he'd rocked into her had her squeezing her thighs together—an exquisite memory of having housed him deep inside her body.

Sienna shook her head, trying her damndest to chase the image out of her mind.

She opened the door to one of the cabinets. Standing on tiptoes, she blindly tapped around the upper shelf, searching for her Baggie of specially blended tea to help her relax.

She wanted nothing more than to crawl into bed, curl her body around her favorite pillow, in the fetal position, and go to sleep.

"Ouch!" she cried when she lost her balance and stumbled, hopping on one foot. She would have fallen, had not a strong pair of hands caught her around the waist, steadying her. His touch caused a current of electricity to pass from her to him, and she yelped.

Spinning around in Mac's loose embrace, her heart thudding loudly, Sienna glanced up at him, startled.

She'd assumed he'd left when she heard her front door open and close.

She licked dry lips and swallowed, their gazes locked. She coughed and tried to ease out of his embrace.

When he tightened his arms around her waist, instead of releasing her, she waited patiently.

She wasn't going there with him again. No more angry, hairpulling, dominating sex for her. She was still reeling from the last one.

"Thank you," she murmured when he released her.

"What were you trying to reach? I'll get it for you."

"Thought I'd have some tea. There's a small plastic bag of my favorite blend on the upper shelf. Don't know why I had it so far back on the shelf, as short as I am," she said with a self-deprecating shrug.

His gaze, hungry, roamed over her body, making her aware of her state of dress. Or undress.

She clutched the ends of her blouse together.

"You're perfect," he murmured in a low voice; then he turned away and searched for the tea. He found the bag and dropped it in her hand. "Would you mind making me some of that?"

"You drink tea?"

"Yes. Why?"

She shrugged and maneuvered away from him, easing around his big body, careful not to actually touch him.

"I don't know. You don't seem like the tea-drinking type, I guess." She shrugged.

Sienna walked over to the sink and removed two clean mugs from the strainer and filled them with water before placing them in the microwave to heat.

"There's a lot you don't know about me, Sienna. Tea drinking is just one. I also like long walks in the rain, bubble baths, and watching old romantic movie classics late at night."

She jerked her startled gaze to his. A small dimple appeared in his cheek. "Long walks in the rain, huh?" She bit back an automatic answering smile.

"You didn't mention the bubble baths." He leaned against the counter, his gaze unwavering, steady on her.

"Well, I don't find that one too hard to believe."

"That's one thing we haven't done together . . . yet. One of the few things," he said in his deep, sensual voice.

"There's a lot we haven't 'done' together, Mac. We don't really know each other."

"Whose fault is that?"

She turned away from him, busying herself at the sink, wiping away the small splattering of water on the counter. She turned to face him.

"Look, what happened between us was a long time ago. A chance encounter."

"You've made that clear." That small tic appeared in the corner of his mouth—the quirk she'd come to know meant he was angry.

"I don't know why you're so mad at me. It was almost two years ago." The microwave dinged and she removed the steaming water, sinking small tea bags inside each cup.

"I never forgot you, Sienna."

"Do you want sweetener?" The mundane question seemed to throw him. He shook his head. "No."

She handed him his mug and then opened a small jar and scooped out a healthy spoon of sugar and emptied it into her mug.

Mac took a drink of the tea, watching her over the rim of the mug, before he set it down. "Did you forget me?" he asked quietly.

Sienna sighed and walked to the other side of the counter. She placed her drink in front of her and settled into one of the high-backed bar stools before she faced him again.

"It was a long time ago, Mac. I was a different person—"

"I didn't ask you that. Did you forget me?" he interrupted her. His voice remained low, but she heard the anger, the hurt, in the casual query.

How did she explain to him that her past, although she wasn't ashamed of it, wasn't something she wanted to revisit, even in her memories?

Yet . . . she'd moved to the same small town where a man from her past lived.

When she'd made her plans to leave DC, sent out her résumé to various schools on the East Coast, Mac had been at the forefront of her thoughts, no matter how she denied it.

No. She'd never forgotten him, either.

She remembered everything about him. Every word he'd shared about himself, his life, his family, she'd cataloged and stored in her mind.

Before moving, she'd found a perfect community for her brother to live near her in the small town. Not only was it affordable on her teacher's salary, but the staff was wonderful, provided excellent care, and seemed to genuinely care about the residents.

She'd found an affordable house to buy and moved into it, feeling at home for the first time in her life.

And in the back of her mind, she'd been waiting for the day she'd meet up again with Garrett McAllister.

The wait hadn't been long. She'd been as relieved as she was nervous, on pins and needles waiting.

How did she explain something to him that she herself didn't understand?

"I've never forgotten you, either, Mac." Once the words were out, she searched his face, looking for clues that he would use her feelings against her.

His eyes sparked before he closed down his expression.

"Take me to your bed?" he asked, his hand out, waiting for her acceptance.

He wanted her willing, she knew that. He wanted her to admit that she wanted him, as much as he wanted her. She needed to invite him to her bed.

By doing so, she would be inviting him into her life.

Sienna worried her bottom lip with her teeth.

Her eyes roamed over his face, cataloging each feature, committing to memory what was already there.

His face was nearly expressionless, but his eyes told a different story.

In his eyes, she read fear. Fear that she'd reject him, as he thought she once had.

He stood there, hand outstretched, waiting for her to reject him again.

She placed her hand in his and allowed him to pull her to him.

Quietly she led him through the small house, up the short flight of stairs, which led to her bedroom.

26

Mac quickly shucked his clothes, withdrew a prophylactic, sheathed his erection. He laid her down on the mattress and settled his body over hers.

Placing small kisses over her face, he lifted her by the knees, spreading her legs to accommodate his invasion, planting her feet on the mattress.

Sienna gloried in the feel of his hard cock as it stretched her wide, impaling her. He pushed deeper inside her, that final inch of dick pressed tight, nearly to her womb. His breath coming out in harsh gasps, he stayed that way, not moving.

"You don't have to hide anything from me, Sienna. *Trust me.*"

With her hands tightly held within his, he rotated his hips, screwing them clockwise, his thrusts short yet deep.

The look in his eyes was intense as he gazed into hers, his expression as intense as his lovemaking.

Moans and sighs of gratification were the only sounds in the dark room. To Sienna the lovemaking was as simple as it was beautiful.

He made sweet love to her, as he did the first time. Gentle, passionate, eyes locked together, as they held each other's gaze. Mac grasped her hands within his, interlocking their fingers. Slowly he began a heated pull and drag . . . pushing deeply into her, cramming her body full. The hot feeling of being stretched by him was made more erotic with the intense way he stared deep into her eyes.

Their release came quickly. Mutually they reached orgasm, this one much more subdued than their earlier coming together.

When their breaths calmed and the sweat cooled from their bodies, Mac pulled her deeper against him, spooning his body tightly behind hers. No words were shared; their calming breaths were the only sounds in the dark room.

"You don't have to hide anything from me, Sienna. Trust me." He repeated the same words he'd uttered to her before he'd made love to her.

She pressed her back closer to his chest, her head pillowed on his outstretched arms.

"You know that, don't you?"

"Yes. I do."

He waited for her to continue speaking, stroking his hand over her arm, down the length of her body, the indentation of her waist, over her hips and back to her waist.

His hand crept to the front of her body and he feathered his hands over the springy curls covering her mound, the heat from her pussy warm in his hand as he cupped her.

One finger plied between her folds, gently stroking her crease.

"Are you going to tell me why you're still with Marks? What's his hold on you?"

Her heart raced again, at his words, so unexpected. God, she wanted to ignore his question, wanted to avoid it.

The main thing on her mind was basking in the glow of how good her body felt, how it still hummed . . . how content she was, how *right* it felt to be lying in front of him after he'd loved her.

But she knew it was beyond time to open up to him.

"My mother died when my brother, Jacob, and I were kids. She died of an overdose," she began, and stopped.

She took a deep breath and swallowed.

He gathered her closer, nestling her head under his chin, his strokes on her body gentle, strangely soothing.

She cleared her throat. "Anyway, mom was rarely around, was always out in the streets trying to score the next 'high.' I rarely remember her being sober. So I took care of my brother."

"You took care of your brother? Is he younger than you?"

"No. I'm two years younger than he is. But my brother isn't . . . normal," she said quietly.

"Can I ask what's wrong with him?"

"He was born fine. A healthy little boy." She gulped down the constriction in her throat. "Perfectly fine, just a little hyper. What little boy isn't? Anyway, Mama went out once and left us alone with one of her boyfriends, Keith. Keith was into sex with Mama and drugs, too. Not so much into babysitting." Mac felt her shrug one elegant shoulder.

But he felt her body tense. He pulled her closer, almost afraid to hear what happened next.

"He wanted to calm my brother down, he said. Make him sit down."

"What did he do?"

She blew out a breath of air, shuddering. "He gave Jacob something. . . . I don't know what. It really messed my brother up. He was so young, too young for his body to accept whatever it was, at the dosage he gave. I couldn't calm him down, he was too strong, the adrenaline rush made him too strong for me. I was only six years old, but I couldn't—" She broke off, a strangled cry on her lips.

"I'm sorry, baby." Mac turned her around to face him, buried her face in his chest, her cries muffled.

"Keith just laughed, wouldn't help me get Jacob under control. Eventually Jacob calmed down. He crashed. He fell out in a heap on the floor and I stayed with him, put his head in my lap, and waited for him to wake up." She cried in earnest now, and Mac felt sympathy for that small child she once was, trying to care for her brother. Sympathy, and anger at the son of a bitch who gave a small child an overdose of drugs, and did not give a shit what happened.

"I thought he was asleep. I lay next to him, and something woke me up. I woke up and didn't see his chest rising. He'd stopped breathing." Her thin frame now shook with tears, her body trembling. She lifted tear-drenched eyes toward him.

"A neighbor helped me. Called an ambulance."

Mac tightened his hold, kissing her tears away before covering her lips with his, at a loss as to what to say. He slowly withdrew from her. "Sssh, baby, it's okay. We don't have to talk about it." He felt helpless, at a loss.

"They got him to breathe again. But . . . he wasn't the same. He had a tracheotomy, to help him breathe. Had to wear a tube for so long, months, that when it was taken out, his voice was barely above a squeak. His mind—"

"Dear God, I'm sorry, Sienna." The words felt about as useful as a limp rag, the rage bubbling within him just as useless. Wasn't a damn thing he could do to help heal that long-ago hurt to her brother, or to Sienna.

"My brother was placed in a home. My mom died shortly afterward, and I was placed in foster care."

She stopped talking and he held her tightly. The sobs racking her body eased, her breathing evened out, and Mac thought she'd fallen asleep until she spoke up again.

"The place he was in . . . was bad." She laughed, without humor. "That's putting it mild. At least, they allowed me to visit him. The homes I stayed in were bad, but not nearly as horrific as the place my brother was in. I had to deal with abuse, harassment, at an early age, but nothing like what my brother went through."

"What harassment?"

She feathered her soft hands over his chest in an absent-minded way, as though not aware of what she was doing.

"I was molested. A few times." The words came out in a rush. Her reluctance to disclose, obvious. "I stayed around long enough to make sure I could get my brother out, could take care of him."

She blew off her own pain and humiliation as though it were nothing. The anger he felt toward the injustice on her brother didn't come anywhere near the exploding anger he felt at what happened to her.

"I'd just turned eighteen. Convinced the social worker to give me custody of my brother. Wasn't really too hard. The system is screwed, too many kids nobody wants anyway. Two less made no difference. I took him out of the home and we ran. Left Chicago far behind."

"Is that when you moved to DC?"

"Yes. I chose DC because my mother grew up there, and she had family living in the area."

"Did you contact them when you came?" He was afraid to hear the answer. From the sound of her life, he didn't expect her mother's family received her with open arms.

"I tried. I knew their names, general area they lived. None of them wanted anything to do with us." She sighed. "So I went to work. I hadn't graduated high school and took whatever job I could. Got a job waitressing, but the pay wasn't enough. My brother needed care. Care I couldn't provide for him."

"That's when you started dancing?" he guessed.

"Yes. Damian came into the diner one night. Gave me his card and said if I ever wanted to make real money, give him a call. So I called a few nights later."

"Did you know what he did? What kind of business he was in?"

"Yes, I knew. I also knew I couldn't afford the care Jacob needed, and he was more important than the shame of taking my clothes off for strangers. After a while . . . it grew easier.

"The first time I danced, took off my clothes, the embarrassment . . . God, it was humiliating." Her voice broke. She cleared her throat and continued. "The utter humiliation was too much. The catcalls from the men, their leering stares, groping hands. I almost quit then—even though I'd made more money in tips the few hours I worked there than I did if I worked two weeks at the diner."

"What made you stay?"

"After the first night, I told Damian I couldn't do it again." She licked dry lips. "He took me into his office. Told me he'd take me off the floor, I could work the stage, avoid contact with the men. He was so kind, so understanding, I thought. I opened up and told him about my brother, our situation."

Mac grunted.

The son of a bitch knew exactly what he was doing. Assholes like him ran games on women for a living, took advantage of the young—with no qualms at all. She was a beautiful woman, unusually so. Marks saw her potential. The potential she had for making him more money.

"Not only did he take me off the floor, he lent me money. Enough money to put Jacob in a better home. A nice one, with his own nurse. God! I was so stupid! I should have realized that he wasn't doing a damn thing out of the goodness of his heart."

"You weren't stupid, baby. You were young, worried about your brother." He soothed her, his hands running over her back.

"He said I could work off the debt. Put me up in a nice place, took care of my brother's expenses, and all I had to do was dance for him at the Sweet Kitty . . . as well as special parties. . . ." Her last words trailed off.

Mac didn't need to hear the rest.

He knew what else she had to do for the money. He knew all about Marks and his "special parties." Before they'd left DC, he and Kyle had found out about the parties Marks threw for special clients. He didn't know that she'd been a part of that.

"I only did a few of them. Didn't do the hard-core ones. I danced, stripped, but that's it. But I knew it was only a matter of time before Damian wanted me to do the special parties. I'd heard from one of the dancers what went on."

Relief rushed through Mac. He, too, knew what happened— the same thing that happened in the upstairs bedroom suites at the Kitty.

"I had a plan, and dancing didn't figure into it. The hours at the lounge allowed me to go to school. I got my GED, then took courses at the junior college. When I finished that program in less than a year, I transferred to Howard University and finished my bachelor's in education."

The pride in her voice stirred deep emotion within Mac. He roughly cleared his voice. He knew she was special, different. Had known it the first time he laid eyes on her.

"Why did you tell me to go? Why didn't you leave? I would have . . ." He didn't finish the sentence. He would have done any damn thing for her, he'd been so hooked. The anger he felt when she dismissed him still lingered.

"I couldn't!" she cried out. "Damian threatened me. Called and left a text message about Jacob the morning I woke up after we'd made love. I was scared. I couldn't let anything happen to my brother."

With her disclosure, Mac felt a rush of relief, and then dawning understanding.

"He's threatening you again, isn't he?"

She pulled away and looked up at him, her eyes glistening with unshed tears, fear shining brightly in her dark eyes.

"Yes. I left him, thought he'd never find me. He did. Now he says I owe him. If I don't dance, entertain, he's going to hurt my brother. I can't let that happen, Mac. I can't," she whispered, and buried her face against the column of his throat.

He felt her warm, wet tears stain his skin.

He laid her flat on her back and climbed over her.

He took her face between the palms of his hands and feathered kisses over her slightly open lips.

He smoothed away a few wisps of hair from her forehead. One finger trailed down the short bridge of her nose, dipped in the small indentation above her full lips, before caressing the seam between them, urging her to open for him.

When she obeyed his silent edict, he dipped a finger inside the lower lush rim, and swirled inside the moist, warm cavern. He withdrew his fingers and trailed them down her chin, circling his hands around her throat.

He leaned down to kiss her again. This time, he drew her bottom lip between his teeth, gently biting down, before suckling the small injury, pulling her lip farther into his mouth.

He took his time kissing her, sucking and pulling on her lips—long, drugging kisses—until she began to whimper and moan. He traced his fingers over the long column of her smooth brown throat, delicately moving the pads of his fingers over her strongly beating pulse.

He placed a kiss in the center of her throat, licking the hollow as her body squirmed.

He licked a hot path between the valley of her breasts and palmed one of her small mounds in his hand, bringing it to his mouth, and licked the cherry nub of her nipple before he allowed it to pop out of his mouth.

"Do you like that, baby?" he asked, his voice low.

Sienna nodded her head. With a feral grin, enjoying her sighs of delight, he fastened on her, filling his mouth with one of her breasts.

His other hand cupped her mound, his finger delving between her swollen, slick folds, searching for the heart of her femininity. He flickered her clit, smoothing her dew over the engorged tip, plucking and tugging gently, continuing to nurse from her plump, turgid nipple.

27

After her disclosure, Mac had soothingly run his hands over her back, encouraging her to tell him everything. She'd gone on to detail what Marks wanted from her, and the yacht he'd secured to "entertain" a group of investors.

"He told me that I only had to do it one more time for my *debt* to be paid."

Fat fucking chance, Mac thought, but said nothing.

Now that Marks had found her, there was no way in hell he would let her go.

Mac tried to convince her to give him the information Marks had given her—his location, cell phone, everything.

"I don't know, Mac—"

"You told me that you trusted me."

"I do," she quickly reassured him. "I just don't want you involved in this mess. That's the reason for my hesitancy."

The satisfaction he felt from her obvious trust in him made him want to go all caveman and claim his woman.

And hell yes, he'd claimed her.

"Don't worry about me, baby. I can take care of myself. More important, I'll take care of you. I promise you."

"Hmmm. That feels so good, Mac." Her body jerked in response to his kisses.

"You like when I play with this pretty pussy, don't you?" He had released his suction hold on her breasts. "When I suck these perfect little breasts?" He stroked his fingers over her soaked vaginal lips, between her slit, and back over her clit.

"Yes." She choked out the word, her body rising.

She grabbed the back of his head and pulled him back down to her breasts, holding him tight as he alternated laving one and the other, giving equal, hot attention to each one.

As he delved and toyed with her pussy, finger fucking her, her cream ran down the length of his hand, the moisture easing the glide of his fingers.

She was so damn responsive to his every touch, so hot and sexy. His dick was engorged, pressed tight against her stomach. His breathing grew harsh and ragged as he tore his mouth from her.

"God, it's not enough! I need more."

Despite her whimper of denial and distress, he withdrew his hand from where it was buried between her thighs.

When he lifted one of her feet from the bed and she felt his warm tongue bathe the top of her foot, shivers raced over her body.

Sienna arched her back sharply when he pulled her big toe into his wet mouth and fastened down on it, suckling it as he had her breasts, in long, dragging pulls.

The shot of pleasure reverberated through her body, straight to the heart of her pussy, her inner walls clenching and releasing with each tug of his mouth on her toe.

He released her toe and grazed the underside of her foot with his teeth, nipping her, before his talented tongue swirled around her ankle, up the calf of her leg, delivering scorching kisses along the way and ending at the bend of her knee.

Sienna's entire body was on fire from his touch—his sweet, hot touch. No man had ever fucked her, catered to her, *loved her* . . . the way Mac had. Ever.

His tongue, slick and wet, licked the inner flesh of her thigh, the rough stubble of his five o'clock shadow scratchy, teasing, causing a string of delicious quivers to travel the length of her body.

She wriggled her body, and a cross between a moan and soft laugh escaped when his hair tickled her thighs.

The alternating long, methodical sweeps of his tongue and stabbing flicks against her clitoris transformed the garbled laugh to a scream of pleasure.

Sienna leaned up on elbows and peered down at him as he ate her. The top of his thick, dark-haired head was the only visible thing she saw. But dear God, the feeling of him stroking her, his tongue stabbing in and out of her pussy, was unreal.

Her body tensed.

The incredible feeling, nearly painful it felt so good, was overwhelming. She would lay there and let him eat her out, love and lave on her forever, if she could. As good as it felt, as much as it had her screaming in pleasure with each lap against her, her body demanded something more.

She had to feel his cock deep inside her. She needed to house all of him within her body, claiming him as hers.

Mac closed his eyes and slid his face over her mound, glorying in her scent. Her curly, wiry hairs tickled his skin. He nosed between her slit, running over it and around the lips of her pussy, between her folds, and inhaled.

"Even your pussy smells good, damn!" The scent of her cunt was a heady mixture of sex, lust, and her natural womanly smell. An addictive, intoxicating aroma.

He spread her thighs wide and centered himself between them, to better angle his mouth. To better angle himself so he could get at her sweet snatch.

He ground his entire face into her pussy and ground his body into the sheets as he devoured her. He hoped like hell he wasn't scaring her as he rutted his face against her cunt, but he couldn't stop himself—even if he wanted. Her pussy was so juicy, so good and sweet. Her smell was heady, overwhelming.

He felt like a starving man at a buffet, the need to devour her was surreal.

He felt like a damn animal.

He grunted, thinking he was even growling like a damn animal, but he loved pleasuring her, making her moan and writhe as he catered to her. His thrusts into the bed became stronger as he ate her.

His heart thudded heavily against his chest as she held on to his head, keeping him centered where she wanted him, where *he* wanted to be. He grabbed each side of her thighs, forced her impossibly wider, and fucked her with his mouth, pumping his body hard into the sheets.

She yelled and screamed out her pleasure, her body shaking wildly, her arms flailing around her body. He felt the moment the orgasm violently rocked into her.

At that same time, in one final thrust of his tongue deep into her core, he ground his body into the mattress, his cum jetting from his body in nearly painful spurts as he spent himself on the sheets.

28

"We need Runninghorse."

Mac leaned back against the kitchen chair and rubbed his temple, massaging away the headache that had been hovering for the last few hours.

"Yeah, you're probably right. Just a matter of him being available," Mac answered, and shoved the chair back and stood, rotating his back as he stretched.

"I already checked. I called him on the way over. He's back from his last mission. Taking some time off, he said."

Mac grunted out a laugh. Trust that Kyle had already done a recon on the situation.

"Question is, will he be willing to help?" Kyle asked.

Mac didn't answer, knowing the answer already. Mac hadn't ever called in the favor Runninghorse owed him. Once during their time in Afghanistan, he and Runninghorse had gotten caught in rebel crossfire. Runninghorse had taken a bullet in his leg, that, although not fatal, had disabled him. Had Mac not thrown him over his shoulder and run like hell toward their HumVee military vehicle, the rebels would have finished him off.

He'd woken a couple of hours ago, Sienna's body snuggled against his. He'd eased his body away from hers and sat on the edge of the bed.

She'd murmured in her sleep, and he'd leaned down and placed a gentle kiss on her forehead, telling her to go back to sleep.

With a sleepy murmur of consent, she'd relaxed her body, one small hand lying beneath her cheek, and fallen back into slumber.

Standing over her for several minutes, he let his possessive eyes travel over her face and body. In sleep, her face was relaxed, free from the lines of worry he'd noticed bracketing her mouth. She looked innocent, trusting, as she lay curled around the pillow he'd used.

He'd left the bedroom, quietly closing the door behind him, and made his way to her kitchen. He'd soon called Kyle, briefing him on the situation and sharing the directions to Sienna's home.

Now he and Kyle had set up laptops and mugs of coffee on her kitchen table, creating a makeshift office space.

He glanced over at the time flickering on her oven clock. Although it was near midnight, Mac didn't see them going to bed anytime soon.

"Is he in country or did he vamp?" Mac asked.

Whenever he ended a mission, Runninghorse had a tendency to leave the country, or simply go ghost, going wherever, no one knew. Neither did they have a way to contact him when he'd disappear.

But, without fail, when it was time, he'd contact you if you needed him. The man had an eerie ability to *know* when he was needed.

Like Kyle, Mac and Runninghorse went back to his days in the U.S. Army. He and Runninghorse both enlisted with the recruiter in Hampton, although they hadn't known one another prior to the day they signed up. Both had arrived at the Fort Dix Military Entrance Processing Station (MEPS), Special Forces division.

Whereas he and Kyle had been battle buddies, Runninghorse had been a loner. He'd been assigned a buddy when he first entered the army, as all had been in the Special Forces unit they'd been assigned to.

After that soldier had been killed during a simple recon mission, one that had turned bloody and violent, Runninghorse went solo, rejecting each new "buddy" sent his way. In the end, the battalion commander had instructed the unit commander not to assign him any more partners.

Which seemed to be exactly what Runninghorse wanted.

He'd stayed on with the unit, even after Mac and Kyle left. Recently he had retired and entered into service with the FBI as an agent in a specialty unit that dealt primarily with closed-in case files, crimes that had gone unsolved for years.

But Mac knew there was more to Runninghorse's job description, as well as his specialty unit, than what was public information.

"Did he say how soon he could arrive?"

"No. But knowing Runninghorse, I wouldn't be surprised if he came tonight." Kyle laughed at the same time that the doorbell rang, and both men stared at each other, stupefied.

"What the hell? No fucking way! Not even Runninghorse can travel that damn fast! Did he say where he was when you spoke?" Mac asked as both men swiftly walked to the door.

"Nope. I don't even know where he calls home these days. Somewhere on the East Coast, I thought," Kyle said, shrugging his shoulders.

Mac's hand automatically went around his waist, his hand resting on his weapon, before he opened the door. He'd felt naked without his gun, and rarely was without it.

He hadn't taken it to the school, didn't want to get frisked and asked a bunch of questions. He'd been so violent after seeing Sienna dancing for Marks, it was a good thing he hadn't had it. He might have gone out searching for the man.

Mac had asked Kyle to pick up his weapon at his home before he'd come over. He had no intention of leaving Sienna's side, with the new threat she faced. And with the company that hood kept, he was damn sure not going without his piece.

He cautiously opened the door, prepared to see either Runninghorse's solemn face or Marks's, and was thrown when a pimply-faced kid, with a huge pizza in his arms, stood on Sienna's doorstep, chewing gum.

"Somebody order an extra large pepperoni with extra cheese?"

Mac turned to Kyle. "You order pizza?"

With a sheepish grin and shrug, Kyle withdrew his wallet from his pants. "Guess I forgot," he mumbled.

He paid the kid, tipping him generously before taking the box from his hands.

"And since when did you start eating pizza?" Mac grabbed the box from Kyle and walked to the kitchen, throwing the box on the counter, before going to the glassed hutch in the corner of the room and removing two plates.

"Since when did you start using china for pizza?" Kyle asked with one brow raised. Mac looked at the delicate floral plate in his hand. He wouldn't have noticed anything strange about it, had Kyle not pointed it out.

"A plate's a plate. . . . Who gives a shit if it has flowers on it?"

"Sienna will. Trust me. Women care about shit like that. This is her 'good china.' The kind of dinnerware reserved for holidays, dinner parties, and important people," Kyle said, taking the plates from Mac's hand and returning them to the glass shelf. He walked over to her overhead cabinets and searched until he found what he was looking for.

He grunted in satisfaction and placed two plates, obviously less expensive, printed with a floral design, on the counter.

"Whatever. A plate's a plate, just like I said."

"This is why I get all the ladies, and you don't." Kyle laughed.

"Like I said . . . whatever."

After digging into the pizza, they returned to work. Kyle, on the laptop, was doggedly searching for articles online, police reports, anything that mentioned Damian Marks.

Garrett was searching online, going to the chat groups he would frequent when he was on an assignment, using various aliases, posing as another creep on the make, looking to score.

"I'm not picking up anything. Sent a bunch of messages out. Nothing," Mac said, rolling his neck to ease the knot of tension.

"Maybe you're using the wrong lure. Go in as a woman."

"Yeah, did that. No bites yet," he said, his eyes scanning the message board, his fingers typing out a message.

Garrett stood and stretched.

Peering at his laptop screen, his partner leaned over his shoulder and let out a choked laugh. "*Vivilicious?*"

Mac felt heat wash his face, the tips of his ears burning. "Yeah. Once had a girlfriend named Vivian. That was, uh, my nickname for her. She used to want me to call her that while, uh . . ."

"Oh, hell no! You calling out sex names during the heat of the moment? That's too damn funny!" Kyle laughed, and Mac shoved him away and returned his attention to cyberspace and typed in another message.

Vivilicious: Looking 4 ways to make $ dancing. Free-lance gigs are my fav. Anyone got info?

No bites. But he knew he'd get inundated with responses soon. Whenever he posed as "Vivilicious," he usually did. His online persona, "Viv," was a good-time girl. No questions asked. She wanted good times and fast cash. At least, that was the persona he'd carefully cultivated since adding her to his lineup.

She'd come through on more than one occasion for him, getting him inside info he couldn't have gotten elsewhere.

"Damn, man, I'm beat. Let's pick this up tomorrow," Kyle said, and Mac glanced up from the monitor.

"Yeah, I guess. May as well. I didn't come up with anything worth a damn thing," he said in disgust, pushing back from the table. "Did you?"

Kyle stood and arched his back, yawning. "Naw. Nothing. Maybe when Runninghorse gets here, he can get us intel we can't get." He picked up the plates and went to the small kitchen sink and rinsed them, before placing them in the wire dish rack.

"You're the cleanest straight dude I've ever met," Mac commented, rising from the table.

"My mama didn't raise a slob." Kyle laughed, wiping his hands on the dishrag draped over the faucet. "Besides, man, when you grow up with five women, you learn a few things."

"You know, I don't think Sienna should go." Mac's thoughts were tuned in to Sienna, and not on the reason for his partner's anal habits.

"To the yacht?"

"Yeah. I want to keep her out of it. If there's any way we can. I think we can get this guy without her being involved."

Kyle looked thoughtful, before answering, "How're we going to do that?"

Mac ran a hand over his hair, his normal MO when frustrated or thinking.

"Don't know. But with Runninghorse's help, we get the surveillance up that we need, Sienna can stay home. She won't have to see this asshole or worry about him popping up in her life ever again," he finished grimly.

"Might work," Kyle agreed.

"Yeah, it can. We need Runninghorse, though, for it to work. To get the info we need to nab Marks's ass, find out what he's up to."

"We have a week to get the ball rolling, right?"

"Yeah, the *party* is going down next Saturday."

"You coming into the office tomorrow?" Kyle asked.

"No. I think I'm going to set up an office here. Until this shit is over, I don't want Sienna alone."

"What does Sienna have to say about that?"

"She doesn't have any say in it. I'm not leaving her alone until this shit is over."

"Oh, it's like that, huh?" Kyle laughed knowingly.

"Don't know what you're talking about. I'm staying just to protect her, nothing personal about it."

"Nothing personal, huh? Okay, keep on telling yourself that and maybe you'll convince somebody. Did you ask her what she thought?"

"No, he didn't."

Both men turned. Sienna stood in the door, arms wrapped around her body, wearing Mac's discarded T-shirt.

Although the shirt ended near her knees, Mac jumped up and walked over to her, standing in front of her to hide her from Kyle's amused, interested gaze.

"Baby, what are you doing up? You should be asleep." He reached a hand out and ran it alongside her cheek.

"Yeah, nothing personal."

Mac ignored his partner's taunt.

"I'm fine, Mac. What do you mean you're staying here? We never talked about that." She stared up at him, her big eyes questioning.

"It's late . . . or early. Whichever way you want to look at it, I'd better go. Looks like you two need to discuss a few things." Kyle stood directly behind Mac as he spoke. "I'll see you tomorrow, Mac."

Sienna looked around Mac's large, obstructing body and stared at the handsome man standing directly behind him.

"Kyle, Kyle Hanley. I'm Mac's partner."

"Hello, Mr. Hanley."

"You don't have to be formal with me, Ms. Featherstone. Kyle is fine," he said, reaching a hand out to shake hers, shoving Mac to the side.

When Mac barely moved, Sienna wasn't surprised. His body was a mirror of his bull-like personality.

"Call me Sienna," she said, smiling as she shook his hand.

"Look, I'd better go. Got a full day ahead, tomorrow," Kyle said, and turned to Mac. "You want me here tomorrow?"

"Yeah, I'll call you in the morning. You can go to the office first, pick up what you need. Meet me back here around nine or so."

Mac caught the way one of Sienna's eyebrows rose; yet she said nothing as they walked Kyle to the front door.

"It was nice meeting you, Sienna. I'll see you tomorrow, Mac," he said, and left.

After Kyle left, Mac turned to her. When he saw her staring up at him, one hand on her hip, he knew he was in trouble. He ran his hand down the back of his neck.

"So you wanna tell me what your friend was talking about. Since when did you decide that you were going to stay with me? Even if it's *nothing personal.*"

29

With satisfaction, she saw him flinch when she threw his words back at him.

"I think it's best until this is over for me to stay with you."

Sienna walked into the kitchen, leaving him to follow her. "Want something to drink?" she asked.

"There's more coffee in the pot."

"It's too early for me to drink coffee," she replied, opening the refrigerator door.

"No. I'm fine."

Mac leaned against the counter, warily watching her choose a dish, pour milk into a tumbler, grab a cookie from the jar, and sit down in one of the high-backed island chairs.

After dunking the Oreo, she delicately took a bite of the cookie, munching on it before taking a drink of milk.

Mac walked farther into the room and stopped in front of her. "I don't like that Marks hunted you out. Why the hell does he want you for this 'entertaining'? I'm sure he could find any number of women to do it."

"Hmmm" was all she said as she continued to munch on a cookie, never looking his way.

"You've dealt with the man, you should know that he's a snake. There's more to this than meets the eye. I don't think it's safe for you to be alone, until this is over."

She said nothing, again. Didn't even look his way.

"Are you okay with me staying?" he finally asked into the silence.

She placed her cookie down and gave him a *look*. One brow raised, head cocked to the side, hand on hip, "mouth pursed out" type of look.

The universal look women gave to men when they were thoroughly pissed.

"Oh! I have a say in this?"

"Come on, Sienna. Don't act like that. It's for the best, you know it. Who knows what else this guy has going on. And I'd bet money that he's not doing this alone. There's more to this."

She sighed and stood, dusting her fingers down her shirt, and picked up her plate and glass. Walking over to the sink, she rinsed them off and placed them in the strainer.

"Why don't we go back to bed. It's early."

"Think you can get me to have sex with you, and I'll melt in your arms, acknowledging your superior masculine thinking after you've sexed me up, good and proper?" she asked.

A raunchy grin split his face, his light eyes darkening as they slowly slid over her body. "Will it work?"

Sienna rolled her eyes, stomping out of the room, with Mac quickly following.

Sounded like a plan to him.

"I've been doing some thinking."

Sienna turned from the bathroom sink and stared at Mac expectantly. "Yes?"

"I don't want you to go to the yacht. I think we can handle this without putting you in danger."

She turned back to the sink and spit the wad of toothpaste out before rinsing her mouth.

"What? You don't like that?" he asked, leaning against her headboard, wearing nothing but the sheet partially covering his thick thighs.

"Don't get me wrong, Mac. I appreciate all you're doing for me—"

"But?" he asked, a frown settling across his handsome face as she walked into the bedroom.

She shed the light robe, laying it across the end of the bed, before she sat on the edge of the mattress, facing him.

"But, I'm not benching on this."

"Not benching?" he asked, running his hands over the silky material of her nightgown.

"Look, I've been running and hiding from men all of my life. I'm not running anymore. This ends now. I need to be a part of this. So, if you still want to help me, you're going to have to let me be in on ending this."

"No. It's not gonna happen. His harassing you is going to end. Now. Without your involvement. I don't want you coming into contact anymore with that son of a bitch," Mac bit out.

"Mac, how is that going to happen?"

"I told you about Runninghorse," he said, reminding her of their conversation earlier about one of his former military acquaintances who now worked for the government, who had agreed to help her and Mac.

When she asked why the man was helping, wondering what he was getting out of it, Mac hadn't gone into details, simply told her that it was a debt being paid, and left it at that.

She nodded her head and he continued, "We don't have all the details worked out yet, but that'll come. However, Runninghorse is calling in a favor from a female co-worker who can go in your place. We *will* work this out, Sienna," he promised grimly.

"Mac, he wants *me*. How are you going to get in there without me?" She kicked off her slippers and climbed into the bed.

"I woke up, thinking about this. *I've got to go.* Without me, you can't get in. There's no way around it."

"There's *going* to be a way around it, Sienna. Do you know how dangerous this could be?"

"No more so than any other dealings with Damian. Damn, Mac, I worked for the guy for years. I *know* him. I know what he's capable of. I also worked his private parties. I know the score," she reminded him, her hand on his arm.

"I know you whored for Marks. Don't remind me," he growled.

Sienna felt the blood rush from her face. "Screw you, Mac. Screw you!" She shoved him as hard as she could away from her and jumped out of the bed.

He leaped from the mattress less than a second after Sienna, grabbing her as she had her hand on the door, preventing her from leaving the room.

"I didn't mean that." He pulled her body back against his.

She kept her body stiff, immobile. "No. You meant it, don't lie." She pushed away from him, turning to face him. "Yes, I stripped for him, fine! Fine! But I didn't whore for him. I've *never* sold my body to any man, no matter how hard times got. But am I ashamed of what I did?" She felt the tears stream and wiped an angry arm over her face. "For a damn long time I was. Shamed as hell. But I did what I had to do, Mac. I did what I had to do to survive, to take care of my brother. And you know what?"

He was silent, his face tight, emotion swirling in his light gray eyes.

"I wouldn't take it back. None of it. It was all I could do at the time to survive, and it's made me a stronger woman. If you have a problem with that, then you need to reevaluate your motivation for helping me. I don't need to be 'taken care of.' I've been surviving, taking care of myself and my brother since I was a kid. And you know what? I'll keep right on doing it, with or without your damn help! Without anyone's help!" She cried and ran to the door once more, hand on doorknob, the need to get far away from him, paramount, in her mind.

He placed his hand on top of hers. "Don't. Don't go."

Sienna resisted, keeping her body stiff and away from him. She needed to get out of the room, needed to be by herself. She clenched her teeth and forced the tears to end.

"Christ, I'm sorry, Sienna. You didn't deserve that. You're not a whore. Forgive me, baby, please," he begged, his voice a hoarse whisper. "Let me help. I *need* to help. I care about you."

She closed her eyes.

No man had ever said he cared about her, with such emotion, such honesty, reflected in his eyes.

Never.

All the men who used her, men she was forced to be with, none had pretended to care. And caring was the motivating factor for her to share herself with them.

She faced him.

"If you care about me, then you should understand why I need to do this. Why I can't keep running." She stared into his face and saw the swirling contradicting emotions in his eyes. Frustration, anger, desire . . . concern.

He pulled her close, nearly crushing her. "I don't want you in this. If I could, I'd wrap you up in a big-ass wad of cotton and keep you hidden away in my bed until all this shit was over."

Sienna started to laugh, her face buried against his chest.

He soothed his hands over her head, down her back, holding her closer. "Don't cry, Sienna! Please. I'm sorry. You're right, you need closure with this. I just—"

"I'm not crying, Mac." She moved away, far enough to look into his face. "A big-ass wad of cotton?" she asked, choking on a strangled laugh.

His face flamed. "Hell, I never pretended to be a poet, Sienna," he said in a tone of self-mockery. He gave her a hard squeeze before freeing her.

"We'll work it out."

He leaned down and kissed her.

The kiss started out as a simple meeting of lips, but quickly turned heated.

With a growl, he covered her lips, pulling and sucking her fuller lower rim deep into his mouth. His tongue shoved deep, dueling with hers. He pulled away and leaned his forehead against hers.

"God, I love your mouth. Have I ever told you that?"

"You might have, a time or two." She laughed huskily, her breath coming out in gasps.

"There's nothing unappealing about you, Sienna," he said, capturing her lips again. When he released her, he palmed the sides of her face. "Damn, you're perfect."

When she cut her eyes away from him, he caressed her face, forcing her to look at him.

"What? You don't believe me?"

She was silent.

He'd hurt her, calling her a whore, he knew. He wanted to kick his own ass when he'd seen the stricken look in her eyes, despite the angry words she tossed back at him.

She wasn't a damn whore and he knew it. When she'd angrily told him off, defending herself, he'd felt like a pile of shit.

"I'm sorry for what I said to you. You didn't deserve that. I was pissed, thought you'd hooked up with Marks—again, I wasn't thinking."

"I didn't—"

He placed a finger against her lips. "Baby, I know that. You don't have to prove a thing. I was an ass. Forgive me, please," he begged.

He turned her to face the mirror on her vanity.

"You're a beautiful woman, Sienna. You don't need me to tell you that."

As they looked at their twin reflections, she watched with half-closed lids as he inserted a hand inside her negligee, palming one of her breasts, the contrast in their skin tones making the image that much hotter to her overstimulated nerves.

"But not just on the outside."

His other hand moved her straps down, rolled the gown down to her waist, and both hands cupped her breast, rolling and tugging on her long, chocolate-red-colored nipples. She leaned her body back against his, her hands coming up to rest on his, as they played with her tits.

"I know you're capable, Sienna. I know you don't *need* anyone to take care of you," he said, gliding one hand up her soft thigh, insinuating it beneath the silky gown.

His lips stretched in a satisfied, wide smile when he discovered she wasn't wearing any panties, giving him easy access to her.

He separated the lips of her pussy with two fingers; his middle finger he used to ease her juices over the hot nub of her clit. Sienna mewled, grinding back against his hard body as he fondled and teased her.

Slowly, at first, his fingers circled her distended clit, and then faster, creating an electric, hot friction that made her ache with wild desire.

As he fingered her, Mac grazed his teeth down the line of her neck and back up to the soft skin behind her ear, his teasing bites gentle against the sensitive flesh of her earlobe. He trailed kisses to the corner of her mouth, licking the edge, asking permission to enter.

Sienna shivered from his nips and caresses. She turned her head, giving him better access to her mouth, and opened her lips. At the same time that he plunged his tongue inside, one thick finger dove inside her creaming core.

His tongue swept over the roof of her mouth. With tongues swirling and playing, like two children spinning around a merry-go-round, they kissed.

He swallowed her cries as he pumped his fingers in and out of her wet heat. Her heart beat wildly from his drugging kisses, plunging fingers, and big hand palming her breast.

Her orgasm slammed into her.

Squirming around his hands and mouth, she bucked wildly against him, rolling her ass and pumping against his hands until she completed her release.

Moments later, before she'd caught her breath, he lifted her, carrying her over to the bed, and laid her in the center, on top of the soft down comforter.

"Lay down, baby. Let me take care of you."

30

Mac stared down at her as she lay with her legs splayed wide, her chest still heaving from her release. Reverently he brushed his hands over the springy, curly hairs covering her mound.

Her pretty, glistening pussy called to him. Her small bud of a clit, turgid from his earlier manipulations, poked out in invitation, begging for him to take a sample of its sweet honey.

He leaned down and dug his hands into the soft cheeks of her buttocks and dragged her down the bed.

He rubbed his face over her pussy before drawing back and gently flicking his tongue over her pulsing, turgid clit.

"Oh God, Mac, I don't think I can take that, right now." She laughed shakily.

He grinned against her mound and continued to lap at her gently, her honey covering his tongue lightly.

"All you have to do is lie there and enjoy what I'm doing to you." He mouthed the words against her cunt.

He twisted his torso and laid his upper body on the bed, knocked her legs farther apart, spreading her wide. He placed one hand on her thigh to steady her when she bucked against him, moaning and whimpering.

"Sssh, it's okay, baby," he murmured, and flicked her dripping seam with his tongue.

"Mac . . ." She sighed, and relaxed her body, allowing him to suckle on her.

Soft sighs escaped as he feasted on her. Taking two fingers, he separated her vaginal lips and tongued her, his mouth wide, tongue flat, capturing all of her essence.

He jerked when he felt her small hands grasp hold of his cock. When her warm lips fastened on him, it was his turn to buck against her.

"Baby . . . what are you doing?" He leaned on one elbow, so he could see her.

The sight of his dick cupped in her hands, and her tongue swirling around his tip, was as erotic as hell to him.

He flipped her body so that they weren't lying side by side, and her pussy was positioned directly in his face, her slight body draped over his.

"Mac!" she squeaked, and laughed. "What are you—" Her words were cut off when he grabbed the insides of her thighs, spread her apart, and delved his tongue deep into her streaming channel.

"Hmmm. Never mind," she moaned.

She grasped his dick again; this time, she engulfed as much of him into her mouth as she could. She slowly slid her tongue over and around him, swirling and licking him like he was her favorite lollipop.

She opened her thighs even wider, to give him better access to her. He continued to lick and stab his tongue deep into her core, loving her as hotly as she was loving him. There was no sound in the room except the heated moans of mutual pleasure, both received and given.

Her small hands clenched and squeezed his cock as she alternated between licking, stem to root, and deep-throating him. His dick brushed against the back of her throat with each bob of her head.

When she trailed her tongue down his shaft, licked the underside of his ball sac, the soft skin of his perineum, before taking each cum-filled sphere into her mouth, alternating, suckling gently on them, Mac groaned harshly against the lips of her vagina, feeling the cum in his balls heat, tingle.

The image of jetting deep into her warm, willing mouth was tantalizing.

In earnest, he stabbed his tongue deep into her creaming snatch, laving her lips, eating all her cream, ravenous, his head spinning, body straining, needing to release.

The taste, scent, and overall feel of housing him deep inside her mouth, along with the sinful things his mouth was doing to her, had Sienna, again, caught in the throes of an overwhelming orgasm.

Bubbling, gurgling up from her core, and sweeping through her body, she allowed the sensation to overtake her. Grinding herself against his mouth, and pumping her pussy against his thick, stabbing tongue, she shouted around his cock and came, just as his thick, tangy cum shot into her mouth. Greedily she accepted it.

She swallowed every bit of his seed, whimpering and crying, as he relentlessly held on to her, until she'd completed her orgasm.

Weak, depleted, she laid her head against one of his thighs; too tired to move, she closed her eyes.

She felt his hands at her waist, lifting her from his body, laying her back against the pillows.

He lay behind her, his chest moving in deep inhalations against her back, his breathing as ragged as hers.

"I know you don't need anyone to take care of you." He picked up the thread of their conversation before their earth-shattering orgasms.

Sienna nestled deeper into his embrace.

"You've done a damn good job of taking care of yourself

and your brother. *I* need to take care of you. *I* need to be a part of your life. And I want to be the one you know you can turn to in any situation."

Too tired and spent to say a word, she kept silent, listening to his heartfelt words.

"Please allow me that. I promise I'd never betray your trust. I'd never willingly hurt you. You have to know that, Sienna," he finished, his voice rough with need and some unknown emotion.

Sienna had relied on herself for so long, she didn't know if she had it in her to trust another completely.

"I don't know, Mac, I just don't know." She whispered the confession. "I've been dogged by men, life, so much . . . I just don't know. . . ."

"Please, baby. Give me a chance. Believe in me." He pulled her against him, holding her, sheltering her, in his arms.

Taking a deep breath, Sienna felt that small bit she'd been withholding from him release.

With it, came the knowledge that Mac would never abuse her in the way she'd come to expect from men. With that, came a burgeoning belief that she could completely trust him.

"I do," she agreed simply, before closing her eyes.

They both released sighs of contentment, and Sienna drifted off into a peaceful sleep, Mac's strong arms wrapped securely around her.

31

"This is cake. I can get in and out, bugs placed, in less than an hour."

"Time is short. How soon can you get in there?" Mac asked, peering at the assortment of gadgets and various electronic bugs strewn over the makeshift office he'd set up in Sienna's kitchen.

Jake Runninghorse's solemn face was thoughtful, his dark, watchful eyes squinted. "Tonight," he answered succinctly, and turned back to his work, carefully examining each piece.

Sienna had returned to work, despite Mac's insistence that she stay at home and call in sick for the week. He'd told her in no uncertain terms that he didn't want her to leave his sight, didn't want to chance Marks paying her another visit.

She'd then told *him* in no uncertain terms that she was a grown woman and able to take care of herself.

So much for laying down the law.

After a heated debate, he'd allowed her to go. Unknown to her, he'd asked Kyle to follow her and hang out around the school until she got off at three o'clock. There was always a way around a stubborn woman, he thought. He'd suffered through Kyle's mocking laughter that she had him whipped.

He could handle being whipped, *As long as my woman is safe from harm.*

His mental wording gave him pause. *My woman.*

Mac wasn't sure how true that was. Didn't know how much either she or he wanted it to be true.

"What about Sienna? What sort of bug can you place on her so that we can be in communication with her on the yacht?"

"Simple. Have her wear this." Runninghorse carefully opened a leather pouch and tipped out one diamond earring. He placed it in the palm of Mac's outstretched hand.

"Nice," Mac complimented, "but how is this going to protect her?" He turned the earring over in his hand. It had a diamond chip on both ends of a small, thin bar. "Other than it looking kinda strange, it's pretty. She'll love it."

"Pretty it may be, my friend, but it also serves a dual purpose. It has a micro–fiber-optic chip embedded within the diamond that serves as a communication device."

"Why not give her a bug she can wear inside her ear? Wouldn't anyone be able to hear the communication if they're within earshot if she wore this one?" Mac asked in doubt. "And where's the other one?"

"I see you know nothing about fashion. *Or* your woman." Runninghorse took the earring from Mac.

"What the hell is that supposed to mean?" Mac didn't like the man implying that he knew more about Sienna than Mac did.

"Take it easy. I make it a point to notice minute details. It's in my nature."

Mac grunted, but let it go. The man was a genius with spyware and COMMO. He needed Runninghorse on his side, to ensure not only the success of the mission, but also Sienna's safety.

"I believe Sienna has her tragus pierced, right?"

"Her what?"

Runninghorse flicked at the small cartilage projecting immediately in front of his ear canal to demonstrate.

"Oh yeah, *that* tragus," Mac mumbled.

He recalled that Sienna had both ears pierced, and also wore a small ring above her ear, in her—what he now knew was called—tragus.

"How did you know she wore that kind of ring?" Mac asked.

"I probably know more about her than you do," Runninghorse answered, carefully placing the earring back in the pouch before turning his unreadable gaze toward Mac.

Again, Mac felt unreasonable anger at his suggestion that he knew Sienna better than he did, but let it go. Runninghorse was doing him a favor, simply repaying an old debt.

"It's what I do for all my cases. This one is no different." He gave the slight amendment, amusement lurking in his eyes at Mac's obvious irritation.

"All she needs to do is wear the ring like she normally does her other one, both ends pick up sound, and she can communicate into it as well by speaking in a low voice. It'll pick up everything. This is all she needs to do," he said, and gave Mac a quick tutorial on how to work the device.

"Good enough. I'll show her how it works, and how to wear it."

Mac glanced over at the small clock mounted on the wall. "We've got an hour or so before she'll be home. You'll be gone by then." He plopped back down in the seat he'd vacated and rebooted his computer.

"I'll need to meet her."

Mac looked away from his monitor and back toward Runninghorse. "Why's that?"

Again, Runninghorse's dark eyes mirrored his humor, although his face remained bland. "You and Kyle will be parked outside in the van," he began, reminding Mac of the plan that he and his partner would be outside, waiting, a small distance away. "I will be on board, and a few of my men, among the crew. Sienna needs to know what I look like. I prefer she meet me, a photo won't do. She needs to know I'm one of the good guys."

Mac acknowledged the truth of his words, forcing his irrational anger to the side.

"I still think I need to get on board. I don't feel good about waiting outside. Something could go down—"

"I'll be there. You trusted me enough in Afghanistan, you can trust me now."

"Yeah, well, that involved the Taliban. Not my woman." He made the statement a warning.

"Yes. And just like then, you can count on me now. I'm more than able to do my duty. I would do no less with your woman," Runninghorse countered.

The two men stared at one another for long moments, memories of an earlier time—when they had no one but the small band of soldiers to rely on—flashed between them.

With a nod, Mac silently gave Runninghorse his trust.

The doorbell rang and Mac pushed away from the table. "I'll get that," he said, walking toward the door. His hand went to his side, on his holster, ready. After looking through the peephole, he slowly opened the door.

A uniformed man stood outside. "Package for Sienna Featherstone. Sign here, please." The courier pushed a clipboard toward him.

Mac took the clipboard, signed, and accepted the small box from the man. Grabbing his wallet, Mac withdrew two bills and handed them to the courier before he closed the door.

He turned and wasn't surprised when Runninghorse stood near the door, an expectant look on his face.

Because there was no return address, Mac opened the box carefully and withdrew a velvet-covered jewelry box. He opened it and nestled inside was a delicate diamond choker.

"What is it?"

"Some kind of necklace." Both men walked back to the kitchen to examine the necklace.

Mac withdrew the necklace from the box and held it up to the bright lights of the kitchen, peering close at it.

"Looks real. If not, a damn good knockoff," he commented.

"There's a note." Runninghorse went to his satchel next to his equipment and withdrew a pair of rubber gloves and pulled them onto his long fingers. He lifted the note from the box and read it out loud: *Make sure you wear this, Saturday.*

"It probably came from Marks." Mac glanced over at the note, written on expensive-looking stationery. There was a gold embossed *M* in the corner. "No return address," Mac said, turning the package over, searching for clues.

"Let me take this. Maybe I can lift a print from it."

"How will you do that?"

"I have a friend down at the local police station. I'll use one of his techs and see what we can come up with."

Runninghorse carefully took the note and folded it in a plastic bag before placing it in his tote. He turned back to Mac. "Let me look at the necklace again," he said, and held the necklace in his hand.

He ran his fingers gently over the diamond-studded choker. His expression thoughtful, he traced his fingers over the link between each fourth diamond.

"What is it?" Mac asked.

"The links have a sharp edge."

"And?"

"If pressed into the skin with the right pressure, they'd leave a mark. See this?" He held the necklace up so Mac could see better, his gloved forefinger rubbing the underside of the link.

"Yeah."

"Feel it."

Mac fingered the link, surprised that the delicate-looking link felt sharp against his skin.

"And take a look at the clasp," Runninghorse continued, turning the necklace around.

"Looks adjustable. Would fit any woman's neck."

"Yes, that, and it can tighten easily, without breaking the chain."

"Hmmm. Yeah, I see that."

Runninghorse ran his hands over the necklace once more before he deposited it back in Mac's hands. "As soon as you get her okay, I'd like to examine that, again, before she wears it."

"Is there something you're not telling me?"

"Nothing concrete, just a hunch" was all Runninghorse said, his expression closed.

"I'll get it to you tomorrow. Just let me get Sienna's permission."

"Good enough."

"Mac, could you give me a hand?" Both men turned when Sienna's voice called out.

"Damn, she's home. I'll be back, stay put," Mac said, ignoring Runninghorse's lifted brow and amused expression.

Mac strode from the room and reached Sienna, who was at the front door, carrying two filled paper bags.

"Let me take these." He leaned down and delivered a kiss to her soft lips before he grabbed the bags from her.

"Thanks," she said, allowing him to take the grocery bags away. She adjusted her bag over her shoulder.

"I have a friend here. He was in the service with Kyle and me. He's going to help us out with the case. He's in the kitchen."

"Oh? Is he going to follow me around all day like your other *friend*, your partner?" she asked, and Mac felt a schoolboy desire to blush at being busted.

"Uh, yeah, well, about that . . ."

They entered the room, and Runninghorse was gathering the last of his equipment into his leather tote. He turned to face them, a smile stretching his lips wide.

"Hello, Ms. Featherstone, I'm Jake Runninghorse. It's a pleasure to meet you."

Runninghorse stuck his hand out to shake Sienna's. Mac had never seen the man behave so friendly. Mac placed the bags on the counter and moved to stand in front of Sienna.

32

Sienna tried to move Mac's very large, unyielding body from her line of vision. "Move!" she hissed to no avail. This was becoming an ugly habit of his.

Shoving as hard as she could, she finally gave up and simply reached around him and accepted Jake's hand.

She stared into the darkest, sexiest eyes she'd ever seen in a man.

He and Mac were of the same height, both large men. But where Mac was heavily muscled, Jake was more streamlined, his lean body tightly muscled.

Her appreciative gaze ran over him. He was dressed in similar clothing to Mac's. Low-riding black jeans, hard-toed black boots, and a chest-hugging fitted black T-shirt.

Although he was leaner than Mac, Sienna could visibly see the outline of his chest muscles behind the formfitting T-shirt. Her eyes trailed down his chest to his flat belly and narrow waist.

His face had prominent cheekbones and a hawklike nose, which dominated his face, evidence of his Native American heritage. His deep-set eyes were sable brown and hinted at a tilt in the corners, surrounded by thick, dense lashes.

A small smile kicked up the corners of his full lips, and Sienna blushed. There was something about him that affected her on a basic female level.

Looking at him and the casual way his long body leaned against her counter—silently observing her as she looked him over—she experienced instant images of long nights of hot sex and tangled bodies.

Startled, Sienna jerked her head in surprise when Mac spun around and snatched her against him, the look in his eyes territorial. One arm lay low on her waist, the other tunneled in the back of her head. He brought her mouth to his, fully kissing her.

He slid his tongue inside the lower rim of her mouth, taking his time kissing her in slow, drugging caresses. Sienna wrapped her arms around his neck.

Finally he released her, and Sienna stumbled back, bit her bottom lip, and held on to the kitchen counter to steady herself.

She kept her smile from surfacing.

Definitely territorial.

Mac turned to the other man. "Jake, this is Sienna," he finished the introduction.

"It's nice to meet you, Mr. Runninghorse."

"Nice to meet you, too, ma'am. Please call me Jake."

Sienna grasped his hand. "Jake."

"I'll leave Mac to fill you in on the details of the plan for Saturday." He released her hand after holding it long enough to get Mac's blood boiling again.

"Why don't I see you out, Runninghorse. I'll be back in a sec, babe." Mac kissed her again; then he and Jake left the room.

Sienna took a breath, inhaling deeply, before blowing out the breath of air slowly.

That much testosterone in one room could be fatal to a

woman, she thought. Fanning herself, she set about putting away the groceries.

"I gather Runninghorse has your seal of approval?"

Sienna glanced over her shoulder when Mac entered the kitchen. She turned back to the pot in her hand, filled with water, and placed it on top of the stove, turning up the heat.

She circled around to face him with a stirring spoon in one hand and the other hand resting on her hip.

"He seems to be nice enough. Is there a problem?"

His face appeared neutral, but she'd gotten to know him. His eyes gave away his true feelings.

He was jealous as hell.

Sienna hid her smirk.

"No problem. Just want you to be comfortable around him. He's going to play a vital role in how all of this goes down."

As the water began to bubble in the pot, Sienna walked to the refrigerator and withdrew a package of chicken drumsticks. She reached up and drew down a skillet, pouring a generous amount of oil in the pan.

After she seasoned the drumsticks, she opened a cabinet drawer and withdrew a package of pasta. Opening the package, she withdrew the long noodles and placed them in the boiling water.

She jumped, nearly upsetting the pot, when Mac's arms wrapped around her.

"Mac!"

He pulled her away from the stove, moving with her to the middle of the kitchen. Sienna turned within his embrace. His hooded eyes stared moodily down at her.

"What?" she asked.

"Nothing. Just this," he said, and covered her mouth with his.

He pressed his lips against hers, his tongue licking at the seam of her lips, demanding entrance.

With a sigh, Sienna opened her mouth and he pressed his slick, moist tongue deep inside. Their tongues circled, dueled, and lapped at each other before he withdrew.

"You're mine, Sienna. Don't get too familiar with Running-horse."

She raised a brow at his demanding tone—ignoring her reaction to his hot kisses, her chest still heaving from the quick caresses. "What's that supposed to mean?"

"It means that I saw the way you were checking him out. Don't let that happen again."

"Since when did I give you permission to tell me who I could *check out?*"

"The first time you gave me access to your body."

Sienna licked her dry lips, staring into his face, trying to ascertain his mood, trying to figure out the message behind his words, *beyond* the words.

"When you gave me full entry into your life, your body, you gave me permission to take care of you. I take care of what's mine," he finished. "That means you, and whoever is important to you, are important to me. Jacob is my responsibility now. You don't have to shoulder the responsibility alone anymore. You have me now, baby."

"Oh God, Mac." Sienna felt tears sting the backs of her eyes.

That quick, he took her there. To that place where she felt he was the only man in the world who understood her. That he completed her on some level.

One minute, he pissed her off with his demanding, overbearing ways. The next minute, he had her hot, her body yearning, on fire for his.

And then he would claim he wanted to protect her, the promise in his eyes real, no subterfuge.

He tugged at her bottom lip, nibbling at the fuller rim, before releasing her again.

"Don't you think it's time I met your brother? Don't you trust me yet?"

Sienna stared into his eyes, torn. She did trust him. He'd proven that he was committed to her safety. She knew he'd extended her brother within his circle of those he protected, much as he had with his sister and her son. And now she and her brother.

She reached a hand up and stroked a caress down his rough-hewn cheek. He captured one of her fingers and suckled it.

"Yes. I think it is," she agreed, her voice soft.

Mac felt one corner of his mouth lift around the fingers he had in his mouth.

Sienna cared about him.

She may not have said the words, yet, but she did. Her love for her brother had been the motivating factor for the decisions she'd made most of her life. She'd never allow anyone within ten feet of him, if she didn't trust that person.

He'd had plans to go over the mission with Runninghorse, but he'd work around it. No way was he passing up an opportunity to meet her brother and show her that he wasn't all talk.

"Yeah, I think I can do that," he answered after pulling her finger from his mouth.

She smiled up at him. "Good. I think he'll like you," she said, pulling from his embrace. She turned to the stove and removed the pot from the fire, setting it on the back burner.

Mac felt nervousness settle in his gut. "Oh yeah? How's that? Has he ever met any of your other boyfriends?" he asked. Although he couldn't see Sienna allowing that to happen, he still felt jealousy rear at the thought that she had.

Sienna laughed. "No. I don't know that I've ever really *had* a boyfriend."

She bent over and opened the oven door, her short skirt hiked up higher, giving him a peek of her panties before she grabbed an oven mitt. Removing the sizzling pan of chicken from inside, she set it on the stove eyelet.

* * *

"And the only reason Jake has my approval is because you trust him. If you trust him, then I trust him," Sienna said simply.

Damn, the woman knew what to say to get inside his heart. She first trusted him with her body, nearly two years ago. Now she was showing him that she trusted him to take care of her.

It was only a matter of time before she completely trusted him with her heart.

He walked over and kissed the back of her neck as she finished preparing dinner. When she turned to him in question, he shot her a quick grin and set about taking out plates and silverware. He placed them on her small dinette table.

With a curious grin on her face, she shrugged, turned away, and they worked in companionable silence.

Sienna withdrew a pitcher of tea from the refrigerator before placing the chicken on a platter, the spaghetti noodles and sauce in separate containers, and placed all of it on the table.

Mac sat down, inhaling deeply. The tantalizing aroma from the food made his stomach growl in anticipation. "This looks delicious! I'm starved."

She grinned. "Dig in!"

They ate and Mac asked her about her day at school.

As he sat and listened to her tell him about her day, pride in her voice, he realized how much he enjoyed sharing even the small things with her—sharing aspects of their lives beyond the physical.

He didn't know if he'd be able to willingly go back to a life without Sienna being a daily part of it.

33

"I came up with something," Runninghorse said into the phone.

"What's that?"

Jake Runninghorse examined the necklace he held in his hand, turning it over in his palm, his fingers caressing the diamonds.

"Looks like the diamonds are real, not fake."

"Oh really?"

With Sienna's agreement, Mac had allowed Runninghorse to take the necklace to examine it further.

"Yeah. Also looks like the links between the diamonds are made of platinum and not silver. The edges are smooth, not sharp. They were designed so that when lying flat against the throat, they're harmless. But if pressed against the skin, the edges could cut as sharp as any knife into the tender skin of a woman's neck."

Mac felt dread clench his gut, tying it in a knot at Runninghorse's disclosure.

"What else?"

"I did some digging. Something about this necklace jarred a memory, reminded me of one of the cases in our closed files. A woman named Karen Hughes was murdered six months ago, strangled. Official autopsy report was death by asphyxiation from her own blood."

"What's that got to do with the necklace?" Mac asked. The dread he felt increased.

He'd spent most of his time working out of Sienna's home and this was the first time he'd come into his office. Although she wasn't there, was at school, he felt uneasy leaving her house.

Runninghorse placed the necklace down gently on top of its velvet case, returning it to Mac, and picked up two of the autopsy photos of the dead woman from Mac's desk.

One was a close-up of her neck, magnifying the deep gash marks into her throat. He placed the necklace below the distinct imprint along the woman's neck. It was a perfect match.

He described the photos to Mac, and how the necklace fit as the method of murder.

"Christ," Mac murmured.

"Yeah, and it's not the only one. This may not have been the first time this happened. Did some more digging. She was the third woman found, dead, with the same MO. Never connected them all, until now."

"Fill me in," Mac said grimly.

"Looks like the first victim fitting the MO, same method of murder, similar history, was murdered five years ago. Was a skin worker in one of the seedier downtown strip joints in DC. Her death hadn't caused much in the way of a blip on the radar."

"No family?"

"No family or close friends ever filed a missing persons report. No real manpower given to finding the perp."

"Surprising if there would be."

In Mac's line of work, he knew it was a harsh fact of life that little police power was given for men and women who worked in the sex trade industry. Especially if she had no family or friends to report her missing.

"Her autopsy pictures were cataloged and stored away in the unsolved-murder files and sent to us."

Runninghorse went on to fill Mac in on the other cases.

The second woman had been a prostitute, and would have gone by unmarked—except that she'd been the runaway daughter of a woman who *refused* to allow her death to go by unnoticed.

There'd been a bit of a stir surrounding her death when the mother had gone on one of the local DC news shows, begging for information on the death of her only child.

"It was Karen Hughes's death that caught the media's attention. She'd been living a double life."

"How's that?"

"Recently divorced from one of the city's power players. She'd disclosed to a best friend what she did at night. It was the reason her husband divorced her. He tried to keep it quiet, the reasons for divorcing his young wife. Once she was identified, it was all over the news. No hiding it, even if her family wanted. When it had been found out who she was, it had caused a sensation in all the papers."

Runninghorse's team had been assigned the case, and he'd been in the process of unearthing information linking Carlos Medeiros to the women.

Carlos had been under close scrutiny from various government agencies. He'd exploded on the crime radar screen, after evading a drug-related charge and link to several money-laundering operations.

But the man was smart.

He'd carefully covered his tracks with various front men. He used local drug lords and hustlers to do his dirty work. His own identity and involvement were carefully guarded so well, none of the charges stuck—the men protecting him to the point of conviction. To inspire that type of loyalty was a shield hard to penetrate.

Rather than risk the wrath of Medeiros, every one of them had clammed up, more afraid of Medeiros's reprisal than spending time in federal prison.

One of the caught men *had* been willing to talk. The paperwork had been started to get him quickly into witness protection, but not soon enough. Both the criminal and his police guard were found dead in his hotel room within days.

It had sent out a blood message like no other. Going to the pen was preferable to a bullet in the head.

The FBI went back to square one, trying to arrest the elusive man heading the operation. Carlos Medeiros.

"We've been watching Medeiros. We knew he was somehow involved with the women."

"How's that?"

"Each woman had either stripped or was a prostitute for men known to have association with the Dominican."

"I wondered why you were willing to come so quickly," Mac said.

"Is there a problem with that?"

"No. I don't give a shit for your reasons. Just glad you're willing to help."

"We think Medeiros may also be supplying women to act as sex slaves for wealthy men. Nothing concrete, but we have a list of men known to have dealings with Medeiros."

When Runninghorse had gotten the call from Kyle, along with the facts of the case, his interest had been stirred. When Carlos Medeiros's name had been mentioned, that was all it had taken for Jake to cut his leave time short and fly to the Coast.

"This time, we'll get the son of a bitch."

34

As Sienna went about her nightly ritual that evening, in the adjoining bathroom, Mac lounged on the bed. With his back propped up against pillows, he watched her clean her face, brush and floss her teeth, and begin to braid her long hair.

"Don't braid it tonight. Leave it down," he told her.

Sienna turned to face him, brush in hand. "But I always braid it at night, you know that. It'll be all over my head in the morning if I don't."

"I like you looking all tousled. It's sexy."

"Yeah, well, there's a difference between casual messy and a rat's nest." She laughed when he gave a pathetic attempt at pouting. "Okay, fine! I'll leave it down."

"Good. Now come to bed. I miss you."

He watched her with half-closed eyes. She wore nothing but his old ratty T-shirt, her face scrubbed free of makeup. Still, she was the most beautiful woman he'd ever seen.

Damn, I have it bad for her, Mac thought.

Sienna placed the brush back down on the counter and turned back to the mirror, finishing her ritual. Standing on tiptoe, the shirt rising and showing a hint of one round creamy-brown cheek, she opened the mirror cabinet.

She didn't see him leap from the bed.

She had no time to think when he turned her around to face him.

"Mac, what are you doing? I said I was coming—" Her protest was cut off by his mouth on hers.

As he kissed her, he shoved one hand up her shirt, deliberately rough, and yanked her panties down her legs with the other. "Lift your feet," he demanded. She obliged him, allowing him to shed her panties completely off her body.

His rough handling excited Sienna.

He aroused her even more when he ripped the panties off her body. When he took possession of her mouth again, pulling her naked body tight against his, she moaned into his mouth.

She ground her pelvis against him, impatient when he opened the medicine cabinet to retrieve a condom.

Sienna wanted to feel him, only him, desperately. She bit her bottom lip until she felt the tangy taste of her own blood, anxious to feel him slide into her.

"I need it now, Mac. I need you," she begged, greedy for him.

Her breath came out in gasps of heated anticipation when he finally sheathed himself, knocked her thighs farther apart, and targeted his shaft at her core.

When she felt the knob of his shaft begin to press into her, Sienna almost sobbed. The relief was so strong, so overwhelming, it bordered pain.

She met his eyes as he pushed inside her. Unable to resist, she feathered her fingers over his face. His skin was stretched taut; the masculine lines etched in his forehead and lean cheeks appealing. His eyes reflected his deep desire for her.

And something more.

Something she'd wanted to see in a man's eyes for longer than she cared to admit.

Sienna closed her eyes, swallowed deeply, and shuddered with pleasure from every plunge and retreat of his shaft inside her body. The pleasure built until she felt delirious. On and on, he dragged his penis in and out of her core; her head lolled to the side, her eyes tightly clenched.

"Open your eyes and look at me," he whispered hoarsely, increasing the tempo of his thrust.

The look in his eyes and the demanding way he was working her body sent her over the edge. She clutched his thick fore-arms as he jostled her body, pounding into her slick flesh without mercy. The pleasure crashed over her in waves—hot, hard, and exquisite.

She came in shaking quakes, her body pulsing as the orgasm slammed into her.

He completely lifted her off the counter and flipped her so that her back was rammed tight against the wall. He continued thrusting in long, hot strokes. She wrapped her legs around his lean waist and screamed when the second, unexpected orgasm broke.

"Mac," she whispered, unable to say more.

Just the sound of his name on her lips as he gave her satisfaction sent the lust and love Mac felt for her building like a volcano until he erupted.

His fingers dug into her soft skin, her walls tightening on his cock like a silken fist, gripping him with friction so hot that his body felt on fire.

His head fell back and he yelled, his body and mind shattering as her muscles convulsed around him in powerful contractions, milking him until he had nothing more to give.

Mac's legs felt weak, shaky, as he allowed her legs to fall from his waist.

He rested his forehead against hers, briefly, before he could gather the strength to lift her and carry her to the bed.

After pulling down the sheets, he laid her down and turned off the lamp and lay down beside her.

She rolled over to face him and he pulled her so that she was resting on top of him.

He pushed the hair away from her face. "Why do you wear my T-shirts to bed?" he asked after kissing her on the forehead.

"They feel good," she said, snuggling her body closer against his. "Why? Don't you like the way I look in them?"

"Yes. But you look good in anything you wear. T-shirt, negligee, or preferably butt-naked," he said, nuzzling the side of her neck, making her squirm.

"Hmmm," she moaned when his hands warmed her cheeks.

"Sometimes I get carried away with you," he murmured against the top of her head.

"What do you mean?"

"I wanted to make long, sweet love to you, not take you like an animal in heat. Like I did in the bathroom," he admitted, his voice hoarse.

She leaned up and held his face between her hands. "Mac, I've told you before, I love everything you do to my body. Tender and sweet or wild and hot. You do it for me, no matter what. You take me there." Her smile was breathtaking and his heart seemed to pause before it stuttered back to its normal cadence.

"Can I make love to you now, the way I wanted, before I lost my mind?"

"That sounds good to me," she whispered, raising her body. She placed her hands on his thick shaft, angling it toward her opening.

"Wait, baby." He leaned over to the side drawer, where he kept some condoms, and her hand stilled him.

"No," she said, and he looked at her, frowning.

"What? You don't want to make love?" Mac felt sharp, stabbing disappointment. She'd never refused him before.

"No. I mean, yes, I want you to make love to me. I don't want you to use a condom," she whispered, her gaze locked with his.

"What are you saying?"

"I want to feel you. Nothing but you this time, Mac. I want to feel you loving me, completely, no barriers."

Mac's heart slammed against his chest.

What she was saying had more meaning than his mind could wrap around at the present. His erection beat heavily against them, his desire to make love to her painful.

"Are you sure about this?" he asked, wanting to make sure she would have no regrets.

In his mind, there would be no turning back after this. If she allowed him to love her without protection, to chance bringing a child into the world, she was his.

Lock, stock, and barrel.

"Yes," she cried out when he lifted her and impaled her on his shaft. He felt his cock bump the tip of her womb and his ball sac tap against her seam, he was so deep.

"Yes, this is good, Sienna. It's so good, *so* good, baby."

Planting his feet on the mattress and raising his knees, he grasped her by the waist and drove her body up and down, gliding her over his shaft, her inner muscles clenching on his naked cock.

"Yes, Mac, this *is* good. Oh God, oh God," she whispered over and over, scrunching her thighs close to his, her hands clenching the tops of his knees as she rode him.

He held on to her hips, watching her ride him, her face washed with pleasure. Mac was determined to maintain control this time. He wasn't going to go caveman on her. As she rode him, he shifted a hand toward her breast, palming the small, warm mound and fingering the tight cherry nipple.

He shifted her body so that her clit was exposed, providing easier access. He pressed a hand against her pelvic bone, one finger fingering her clit. Propping himself partially against the headboard, he was able to bring their bodies into perfect alignment. He separated her folds, allowing her pink clit to peek out.

She rode him as he rubbed his finger over her distended nub, his naked cock sliding in and out of her creaming core.

Sienna's eyes were closed as she uttered soft sighs and breathless gasps of pleasure as she rode him. Her body was hot silk, her channel tightening on his shaft, throbbing.

He set a smooth rhythm, easing in and out of her warmth, his hands pleasuring her as his shaft rocked her. The seesawing, back and forth, built until Mac felt ready to explode. He gritted his teeth and held on, determined not to rush her into orgasm.

"Mac," she whispered, opening her eyes and staring into his. She paused, nostrils flaring, before she spoke again. "I need to come. I need to come now!"

With a harsh groan of relief, Mac grabbed her by the hips and surged her against his body, rocking into her twice before she screamed out her release. He then came, the blood rushing to his head as his semen gushed from his body.

He flipped her so that he lay on top of her and shoved his cock as far as he could into her pussy, an instinctual need to fill her with his cum.

Sienna opened dazed eyes, just as Mac was coming, deep, inside her. The veins on the side of his neck stood out in stark relief, his face flushed a deep red as he held on to her tightly. He pushed his dick into her until her head bumped the back of her headboard, his thrust was so powerful.

When he completed his orgasm, he buried his face in her throat for long minutes, his breath coming out in harsh gasps, his lips pressed in the hollow of her throat.

He finally lifted his head and softly placed a kiss on her mouth; then he repositioned their bodies so that she lay in front of him.

Sienna felt the cool air chill her and shivered. Mac threw the sheets over her body before nestling her against his body.

Exhausted and content, despite the nervous rumblings in her stomach, worries of what tomorrow would bring, Sienna fell asleep.

35

"I want to make love to you."

Sienna laughed and groaned at the same time. Mac had woken her, his hands roaming over her body, his shaft, hard, pushing against her buttocks.

When he bounded from the bed, her drowsy eyes watched the muscles in his buttocks bunch and flex as he strode to the adjoining bathroom.

"I thought that's what you've been doing to me, for the last—" She glanced at the clock on her mantel. "God, Mac! It's almost one o'clock in the morning."

She heard him muttering, and the sound of cabinets opening, before he said "yes" in satisfaction.

"What are you doing?" she asked warily.

He walked out of the bathroom, his beautiful, sculpted body highlighted from the small light streaming in. Her eyes fell to his member, long and thick, jutting out from the nestle of sable curls on his groin.

He sat on the edge of the mattress, uncapped the tube, and squeezed out a liberal amount of cream on his fingers. He placed the tube of ointment on the nightstand.

With a wicked gleam in his eyes, he turned back to face her. Her avid eyes watched as he grasped his shaft in his hand, smearing the thick, white cream over the bulbous knob and down his cock.

"Mac . . ." She moaned when he leaned down and lapped his tongue between the tender folds of her labia, his tongue darting around her clit, gently circling it, pulling it into his mouth, before releasing it.

"Sssh, it's okay," he said, lifting his head from her mound.

"Baby, I don't think I can take any more."

Despite her protests, she was creaming for him within minutes, and Mac laughed roughly.

He picked up the discarded cream and moved behind her. She felt his dick press close against her buttocks, his engorged length nestling in her crease.

"I'll be easy on you. You'll like it," he murmured against the back of her neck.

"Yeah, that's what you always say." Her breath caught when he ringed a finger around her opening, the smooth oily cream from his fingers lubricating her hole.

"Yeah, and I always make good on it, don't I?" he asked, and bit lightly down on her neck.

He reached a hand around her body and began fingering her clit, dipping his fingers inside her pussy and smearing her essence over the tight bud. His other fingers continued to massage the cream over her hole. He felt her tense when he pressed one of his creamed fingers, and then a second, into her ass.

"I need you to relax. I want to make love to you this way. With my cock. But you need to relax your muscles or it'll hurt, baby."

"Mac, no—" she cried out, clamping down harder when he inserted a second finger inside her tight ass. He ignored her whimpering cries and rotated his fingers inside her, loosening her. He kept her body close to his, plying both ends. His fingers dipped into her vagina, rubbing her clit, while the fingers on the other hand pressed farther inside her ass.

She bucked back against him, trying to dislodge him until her distressful cry turned to moans of pleasure once he'd reached deep enough inside her anus to tap the erotic spot buried deep.

"Ohhh—"

"Yes, baby, just like that." He laughed low, in triumph, when she ground back against his fingers, lodging him farther inside. "I told you I'll take care of you."

As she rolled against him, the thought of how it would feel to have her tight ass clench his dick sent blood racing to his head, until he was damn near dizzy.

Mac removed his fingers from inside both openings and separated her butt cheeks. Squeezing the tube, he allowed the thick cream to flow, drizzling down onto the smooth S curve in her spine.

He rubbed the cream over each plump cheek and farther separated the brown globes to massage the cream directly on her puckered hole. Pressing more of the cream inside, he readied her for his invasion.

Grasping his shaft with his free hand, he rubbed his dick back and forth, pressing it against the tight rosette. When she twisted her body, trying to move away, he gripped her hips, tighter, to keep her steady.

Although he'd played with her this way before, fingering her tight anus while he plunged inside her vagina, he'd never made love to her this way, with his cock. And neither had it been after a round of marathon sex. He knew he had to be careful with her. Despite preparing her, he was introducing her to an extreme way of lovemaking.

"You call this taking it easy on me?" Sienna choked out, her laugh strangled, reminding him of his earlier words.

"It'll be good," he murmured. "I'll always make it good for you."

Once he'd gotten the knob of his shaft inside, he moved his hand around and plunged two fingers deep into her vagina. His thumb rubbed hard against her rigid clit; the other hand molded around her breast.

As he toyed with her clit, pumped his fingers in and out of her core, he pressed more of himself inside her ass. Unrelenting, he nudged her body with his, until she lay flat on the bed, and then fed her more of his dick.

Once she was wet, her cream running freely down his hand, he removed his fingers.

He moved so that he was straddling her back, and then pressed her flat on the mattress, continuing to push past her tight opening until half of his cock was deep inside her ass.

He spread her legs farther apart, centered himself between her thighs, and placed each one of his hands on one of her tight butt cheeks.

The mangled cry she released was one of pleasure mixed with pain as he rocked completely into her. Mac knew it would be all pleasure, once her body relaxed around his shaft, accepting him.

"You're perfect. So fucking perfect," he growled, his eyes trained on the smooth lines of her back, her beautiful, creamy brown skin, where the light of the moon both shadowed and silhouetted her flawless backside. "Let me ride this perfect ass, baby."

She lay on the bed, her head to the side, half of her face masked by her wild tangle of curls. Taking frantic breaths, she cried as her moans grew.

Agitated, she fisted the sheets, pushing against him.

He pressed her deep into the mattress, forcing her to grind her vagina against the bed while he penetrated her deeply.

"God, Mac!" she cried out, and Mac knew the pain was easing. Soon she'd feel nothing but pleasure.

"Relax, baby. Relax." His breath mirrored hers, coming out in gasps, harsh as hers, while he filled her. "This pleasure is for you, for us. Let go. It's just you and me. Whatever we do is good. It's all good, baby. There's no shame in taking your pleasure this way."

Spreading her legs even wider, he pushed through, until he

was embedded all the way. His balls slammed against her ass and he started fucking her in slow, long, dragging strokes.

One hand grabbed the headboard as he pushed against her, as far as he could go, and then dragged his cock out until he nearly stroked out of her, only to slam back in.

"Damn, *damn*, baby, you feel so fucking good on my dick." The exquisite feel of her tight ass gripping his cock forced the stark words from his tightly clenched lips.

She bucked against him while rolling her pussy on the sheets, moaning out her pleasure.

"Is it good yet, Sienna? Tell me it feels good to you. Talk to me."

He'd said dirty things, raunchy things, to her often. When in the heat of the moment, her pussy milked him, or her sweet mouth was wrapped around his shaft. But she'd never reciprocated.

He wanted to hear it.

He wanted her to tell him, in graphic detail, how good he was making her feel. He wanted her to scream out to him how much she needed this feeling he gave her.

That she needed *him*.

"Mac—I can't! I—I can barely breathe. . . ." She panted out the words.

"Why? Why can't you breathe?"

"It feels so good. God, it's good!"

"Yes, baby, just like that. Keep riding me. Keep talking to me. What do you want? Tell me!"

"I—hmmm." She paused, moaning, taking deep breaths when he grabbed her hips and pulled.

"Oh God," she shouted when his thrusts became deeper, stronger. "I want you to play with my pussy while you—"

"While I stroke this pretty ass?" He lifted her buttocks higher so he could reach a hand between them and stroke her. "Like this, Sienna? Is this what you want?"

"God, yes! Just like that." She rolled her vagina against his hand, while grinding back against his penis. Mac leaned down and moved her hair, fanning it to the side, so he could see her face as he rocked into her.

"I need this, Mac!" she cried out. "*I need you!*"

Watching her moan and grind against him, he felt his balls tighten, swollen with cum, and draw close to his body as his dick thickened within her tight anus.

When she cried out her need for him, it sent him over the edge. Blood filled his head. His body grew taut to the point of pain.

He threw back his head, snatched her ass tight against his groin, and yelled as the cum burst free, jetting deep inside her. "I'm coming, baby!"

"Yes!" she wailed in reply, arching her back. Head thrown back, she came, her body shaking, her cream rushing down the sides of her thighs.

Mac ran his hands down her thighs, catching her essence, and brought his fingers to his mouth. His nostrils flared as he licked her juices from his hand, his body still plowing in and out of her clenching anus.

Once he'd filled her, once his body calmed from the raging release, he gathered enough energy to pull out.

He rolled away and lay behind her, nestling her soft backside against his body.

Nothing but gasps and calming breaths were heard in the room for long moments.

He felt her soft breath fan the hair on his forearm and knew she'd fallen asleep.

"I love you, Sienna," he whispered behind her, his voice barely audible even to his own ears. "God, I love you, woman."

36

Sienna woke up early, Saturday morning. Not that she'd gotten much sleep the night before, she thought, then eased her leg from beneath Mac's heavy thigh pressed over hers.

She slipped out of bed and reached for her robe, which lay over the foot rail.

She grimaced when she began to walk out of the room.

Last night, Mac had been alternately tender and sensually dominating with her.

God, the things he'd done to her body, the way he'd made her feel, forced a groan from her lips. Her mind shied away from the last words he'd murmured before sleep overtook them.

"Sienna?" Mac murmured from across the room.

"It's okay, honey. I'm just getting up to make coffee." She glanced over at the bedside alarm clock, noting the time. "It's early still. Go back to sleep." She smiled when he murmured what sounded like an assent before going back to sleep.

Closing the door gently behind her, she left the room and went downstairs.

She needed time to herself. Before the day began and the house filled with Mac's partners, and final preparations were made, she needed to be alone.

After filling the coffeepot with water, she set it on the stove to heat.

This was it.

If all went well, according to the plans the men had set up, this would be the end of a journey she'd started over ten years ago. She'd finally be free of Damian Marks and Carlos Medeiros, and could put her past behind her. It would be the end of a past that had brought her as much pain as it had . . . enlightenment.

Sienna released a small, pain-filled laugh.

She'd grown so much from that young girl she'd been, running away with her brother to a city she didn't know anything about. Getting caught up in a world that she knew nothing about.

And surviving.

Her only thought then, and until recently, had been to survive.

When Mac entered her life the first time, she'd known he was different. Known he was not like the other men who frequented the club.

She vividly recalled how he'd stood up for her, asking her to go with him, to leave the Sweet Kitty, when Damian had tried to hit her.

She'd been afraid to leave then. In part, because of the fear for her brother's life, of what she knew Damian was capable of doing. Also, because she was afraid, didn't trust herself or Mac enough to break the bonds keeping her tied to a life she abhorred.

Now things were different. She'd proven to herself that she had what it took to leave Damian, damn the fear. She'd also proven that she could do it on her own, and not rely on a man to help her.

Because of that, she knew she was a strong woman. Strong enough to accept the assistance of another, and trust her instincts.

Her instincts told her then, as they did now, that Mac was a man she could rely on. His actions over the course of the last week had proven her instincts were correct.

"Why don't you come back to bed? We have a few hours before we need to get up."

Sienna turned her head when Mac entered the room and smiled, reaching a hand out toward him.

"Hmmm. Can't really sleep."

He lightly grasped her hand in his, pulling her close. He cupped her face within his big, warm palms, his expression intent as his eyes roamed her face.

"It's all going to be okay, baby. You know that, right?" he asked, and pulled her close, covering her mouth with his.

Sienna sighed into his kiss.

His lips began a leisurely exploration over hers. Taking his time, he nibbled the corner of her lips, licking the seam of her lips, asking for entry; gladly she allowed him access.

For long moments, he kissed her, his tongue lazily laving hers before he reluctantly withdrew from her mouth.

He kissed each of her eyelids, her nose, and gave her one final, sweet kiss, to the lips.

"It's going to be fine, baby. This will all be over, and you won't have to worry about Damian Marks—or anything associated with him—ever again."

She sighed heavily and pulled away from him. "I know. I'll just be glad when it's over. God, I'll be glad when all of this is over."

Sienna laid her head on his chest, allowing the steady, strong beat of his heart to reassure her that she could finally escape. She would finally have a real life, without looking over her shoulder, waiting for the other shoe to drop.

* * *

Mac watched Sienna as she methodically dressed. His brow creased in worry over how quiet she'd been.

She'd been too wound up to go back to sleep earlier that morning, so they'd spent the time talking about anything and everything, except what she would face later in the evening.

He hadn't slept much himself.

He'd wanted to make love to her, needed to fill her with himself, reassuring them both that what they had was real. Reassuring her that he would take care of her now, and forever.

After their lovemaking, when he'd told her that he loved her, the final barrier had been removed. He had wanted to mark her as his.

He laughed ruefully. He'd once called himself an animal. When making love to her, she seemed to bring that out in him. Yeah, well, after last night, there was no question about it. The woman brought out the beast in him. His only thought had been that she was his, finally, completely. And no one was going to hurt or threaten what was his.

"Help me with this?" she asked, holding out the diamond choker.

Mac nodded his head and stood from the bed. He strode over to where she stood in front of her mirror and then stopped behind her. Taking the necklace from her hands, he placed the cool gems against her warm skin. She released a small shudder.

"God, I don't like wearing this thing. Especially after what Jake said."

Sienna released a small shudder, reminding him of Jake's belief that the necklace had been associated with several murders that had gone unsolved.

He'd given Sienna an abbreviated version of what Jake had told him about Medeiros. He was certain that Medeiros was not only involved in various underground crime activities, but was also responsible for the death of at least three women, each strangled by the diamond-studded choker Sienna was now placing around her neck.

He'd told Mac the information when Sienna had been at work. The two men had detailed the way the operation would unfold on Saturday, when Sienna went to the yacht. The plan was that Jake would be on board, working as wait staff, along with several of his men. Mac and Kyle would be stationed in a surveillance van, waiting.

Sienna would be bait, Jake told him.

Mac's instant response had been to reject the plan. He didn't want Sienna anywhere near the yacht, or the murdering son of a bitch. No way in hell did he want her to be in the line of danger. It had taken both Jake and Kyle to convince him it was the only way to free her from the man's stalking of her.

It was the only way to free her from certain death.

"You're not going to have to worry about that, Sienna. Nothing's going to happen to you."

After he secured the clasp, he placed a kiss alongside her neck. Her wide, beautiful lips stretched into a small, lopsided grin, her eyes slowly drifting closed.

"It's all going to be okay, Sienna."

"I know. Just looking forward to this all really being over," she said, and he moved away from her.

"Well, how do I look?" she asked, her voice filled with nervousness as she smoothed the feathers attached to the skin-toned thong.

"You look beautiful. All eyes will be on you." The admission was torn from him, from behind his tightly clenched teeth. She placed her hand in the crook of his arm as he tried to turn away. Her eyes were pleading in the mirror's reflection.

"I'm not concerned with anyone's eyes on me, but yours, Mac. I just want this over with." Her eyes pleaded for his understanding.

He felt the surge of anger recede and pulled her roughly into his arms.

No words were exchanged; they simply held on to each other tightly. Mac finally eased her away, lifting her chin between two of his fingers.

"Yeah, baby, I know. I wish I could be there with you."

"You'll be outside. And if this thing works, you're just a call away, right?" Sienna picked up the small earring, fingering it, before she carefully removed the backing and inserted it.

They'd practiced using the device until she and Mac were both confident it worked out of visual range from one another.

She was on edge. They both were. The tension had escalated over the course of the last hour, the closer they came to go time.

"Just a call away." Mac forced his lips to stretch into what he hoped was a reassuring smile.

She stood back and examined herself one final time before turning back to face Mac, her expression determined. "Let's get this over with."

37

Sienna killed the engine to her Honda, withdrew the keys, and tucked them into her small, beaded purse.

She released a long breath and tried to calm her racing heart. She opened the door of her car, and after adjusting the trench coat she wore over her skimpy outfit, closed the door and glanced toward the brightly lit anchored yacht.

Her stomach churned with nervousness. She swallowed down the bile rising in her mouth. She had an overwhelming need to find the nearest bush and hurl. "Baby, are you okay?"

Mac's reassuring voice filled her ear, low and intimate. She barely stopped herself from looking around. She surreptitiously glanced over her shoulder as she clicked the button on her car's remote to lock the door. She could just barely make out the surveillance van in the dark, parked several hundred feet behind her, where she knew Mac and Kyle were watching.

"I'm—I'm fine," she whispered.

"You're doing great, Sienna. I just had contact with Running-horse. Everything is in place. He's set up and so are his men. All you have to do is go in and pretend like everything is normal. Can you do that?"

Sienna wanted to laugh out loud. "Oh yeah, sure. No problem. Just walk in, strip for a few gangsters, try and forget the whole thing about the leader of the pack and his link to a slew of women found strangled. Try and get him to confess something to me, so the FBI can get information to nab his ass—" Sienna broke off, giving a choked laugh. "Yeah, sure, piece of cake," she finished, laughing humorlessly.

"We're here, nothing's going to happen to you."

Sienna nodded her head and took a deep breath before she began to walk toward the long dock. The clipping sound of her heels against the pavement was the only sound she heard—that and her racing heart.

The closer she came to the dock and the brightly lit yacht, the harder her heart thudded against her chest.

"Baby, you've gotta calm down. Take deep breaths." Sienna jumped and dropped her small purse in her nervousness.

"You can't go scared now. This is it. I thought you said you could handle this. If you can't, if you need to pull out, turn around now! Come back to—"

"No! I *can* handle this, Mac. My nerves are just a little taut, that's all. I can handle it."

With determination, and fear, Sienna stared at the large, looming yacht anchored to the pier. The massive, gleaming white yacht was as beautiful as it was intimidating.

Three-tiered, each of its levels was brightly lit, and even from the distance she currently was from the yacht, she could hear the music and laughter pouring out to greet her.

"Good. You aren't going to be alone." Mac spoke into her ear at the same moment Sienna reached the small steps to the dock that would lead her to the yacht.

Out of nowhere, a man appeared to her left. Startled, Sienna glanced up at him.

"Let me help you," he said, and grasped her elbow, guiding her onto the dock.

With a murmured "thank you," Sienna accepted his hand as he assisted her.

"Right this way, Ms. Featherstone."

Surprised, Sienna glanced up at the man, wondering how he knew her name. "How did you know—" She stopped when recognition dawned.

It was Jake Runninghorse.

Although the large Native American man's presence was reassuring, Sienna would have preferred it was Mac's warmth she was leaning into.

As she stared into his dark, unfathomable eyes, a chill ran down her arms—not because of the brevity of her clothes, but because of the look in his eyes. Although his face was a mask, no emotion shown, his dark eyes seemed to soften.

Looking into his deep eyes, Sienna knew that if Mac didn't have her heart completely wrapped, this man would be one she would have to be careful around.

He wore the same hard masculinity that Mac did. The type where a woman knew she'd be safe around him. That he'd protect her to the end. Yet, that safety would only go so far.

He'd keep her safe from anyone he deemed harmful to her. How safe would a woman's heart be around him? Sienna knew that like Mac, Jake would be hell on wheels with a woman he claimed as his own.

Another shiver of pure feminine awareness raced over her. She glanced up at him and caught the corner of his wide mouth pull up in a small grin, as though he *knew* what she was thinking. Then his expression settled back to its normal look of placidity.

"Here you are. They're waiting for you here, Ms. Featherstone." With his words, Sienna felt like the proverbial sacrificial lamb.

They stood before closed double glass doors, and inside, Sienna could see the party had definitely started. Women, in various stages of undress, were either dancing solo or with a partner. From what Sienna could see, one or two were sitting on the laps of men, who were scattered throughout the room.

It was showtime, Sienna thought with a disgusted sigh.

With a silent nod, she reached for the doorknob. Before she could twist it open, Runninghorse placed his hand over hers. She brought her gaze to his.

"You won't be here long, and I have my men here as well. Nothing, and no one, will harm you, Ms. Featherstone. I promise you that."

With a shaky indrawn breath, she nodded her head.

"You get in, do what you're supposed to do, get next to Medeiros, follow the plan, and we'll take care of the rest. Remember, we know that he wants you—particularly you—so he'll find you as soon as you enter. Do what he says, play the game, and we'll take care of the rest."

With that, he removed his hand from hers, opened the door for her, and ushered her inside. Moments later, he'd melted into the crowd.

Sienna glanced around the large, opulent room. She'd never been inside a tugboat, much less a yacht as glamorous as this one.

To say she was out of her league was the understatement of the year.

"Lord, what have I gotten myself into?" she murmured to herself, under her breath.

38

"Is she here?"

Damian watched Carlos, nervously, as the other man's dark eyes scanned the crowd.

"Yes, she's here. One of my men brought her onto the main floor, just now."

A satisfied smile spread across Carlos's face and he clapped a hand over Damian's shoulder.

"Good, now go and bring her to me. I want her to give me a private dance. I've been waiting a long time to see her. Way too long. And when you bring her to me, make sure no one bothers us. We're overdue for a nice, long reunion."

"Yeah, sure. I'll go and get her."

Damian was careful not to allow his anger to show. The fact that Carlos was so caught up in Sienna—had been since he'd first met her—pissed him off completely. He touched the side of his face, where the scar remained.

She was the reason for the scar. When she'd left DC, with no trace, and he'd told Carlos, he had no idea the man would react the way he had. Damian considered himself lucky he'd escaped with only one lifelong scar, a reminder of the man he was dealing with, and what could happen if he ever angered the Dominican again.

As he went in search of Sienna, he hoped the dumb bitch went along with what Carlos wanted from her. Better to be alive and whoring than dead and noble.

39

Sienna slowly made her way through the small crowd on the main deck, the variety of perfumes from the women assaulting her nostrils. She smiled and avoided outstretched hands, reaching for her. She knew it was only a matter of time before she'd have to start entertaining.

She'd gone to several private parties that Damian had sponsored when she stripped for the lounge, but none had been like this one. There were uniformed wait staff circulating the room, carrying trays of food and drinks on platters, as they weaved throughout the room.

The women were dressed in sexy clothes—yet none were dressed like she was. She had expected they would be dressed in skimpy outfits designed for stripping. Also, she didn't recognize anyone.

True, it had been nearly two years since she'd danced, but she thought she'd see a familiar face or two. Not only did these women not look familiar—although they were here for the same reason she was—none of them had the hard-eyed look of a seasoned pro. She walked along, giving a hesitant smile to a woman whose eyes she caught.

The woman was sitting in a man's lap, her hand rubbing over his crotch, his hand embedded inside her blouse, fingering her breasts as she swirled her tongue around the outside shell of his ear. The woman gave Sienna a wink and continued to lick and nibble on the man's ear, laughing and squealing around his probing hands.

Sienna heard the man rumble a suggestion for somewhere else he'd like the woman to lick him.

Sienna shook her head—different, more sophisticated operation, but it was no better than what took place in the upper rooms at the Sweet Kitty.

She swiftly turned away, and into the arms of another party-goer.

"I'm sorry, ex-excuse me—I was, uh, trying—" she stuttered, panicked when the man wrapped his arms around her.

"Hey, what's the rush, beautiful lady? Come on out here with me and we can get to know each other," he said, guiding her out of the room and onto the deck. He brought them to the railing, keeping his arms tight around her body.

She ran her gaze over him. He was wearing a large Stetson, black slacks, and a Western dress shirt, complete with a thin leather string tie and pearl buttons. On his feet, he wore a pair of black shiny ostrich-skin leather boots, giving him an overall appearance of exactly what he was: a wealthy cowboy. Sienna remembered seeing his face in one of the photographs that Jake had shown her of men to look out for at the party.

This one was a Texan cattle rancher, who was looking to get in on rustling more than animals in his next business venture. He was one of four other men she'd seen in the photographs Jake had shown them of men looking to get into Carlos's high-end prostitution ring.

Sienna knew she had to play her part, she had to go along with the game, until they could get enough information to incriminate the men involved.

She also knew that most men like this one discounted a woman's worth—particularly women who performed as strippers, dancers, or prostitutes. In this man's eyes, women were like the custom suit he was wearing, or the gold diamond-studded Rolex on his wrist. Beautiful, something to flaunt around, to show he was a man of means, and the women were nothing more than eye candy and outlets for mindless sex.

Expendable and inferior.

She forced a smile on her face and released from her lips what she hoped was a girlish giggle.

"Okay, wait a minute, can't I get to know a little about you first?" she said, licking her lips and slanting a smile his way.

"Sure thing, sugar, what ya wanna know?"

"How about giving me your name first, big daddy? I like to know a first name of the men I play with before the games begin," she said, grinning. The music changed from an upbeat rhythm to a slower beat.

Sienna began to slowly dance in front of him, trailing her fingertips down his leather thong tie, over the bulge of his belly, skimming her fingers over the thick, hard ridge behind his zipper.

She didn't linger, just feathered enough to get him even more excited.

She rolled her hips, smiling, lightly touching his body as she did so.

"What's your name, big boy?" she asked again, her voice husky with promise of what he'd get if he answered.

"Uh, yeah, sure. My name. Roy. Roy Fender," he said, and grabbed her taunting finger, capturing and holding her small hand within his large, meaty one.

He was one of the men.

"What do I get for telling you my name?"

Sienna laughed. She swallowed the bile in her throat and took his hand, and placed it on her breast. "I'm here to please you, whatever you want . . . within reason." She laughed. "You give me what I want, I'll give you what you want. . . . That's a nice exchange, don't you think?" She stood on tiptoe and whispered in his ear, hoping he'd give her more information.

This was more difficult than Sienna thought it'd be. She swallowed down the rising bile in her throat and kept her smile fixed on her face, pouting her lips, playing the game. . . . It all came back so easily, she thought in shame.

"Why don't we take this somewhere more . . . private?" Sienna panicked when Roy grasped her hand and turned with her in tow.

As they turned to leave, a uniformed waiter stepped into their path. "Ms. Feathers, your party is waiting for you. I'm to escort you to see Mr. Medeiros. Please follow me." Sienna gratefully sidestepped from underneath Roy's thick, meaty fingers grasping her upper arms, pinning her to his side.

"Now wait a minute here! You tell that damn Medeiros this one is taken! He can damn well find his own—"

The waiter turned to stare down at the Texan. Although the rancher was easily six feet tall, the waiter topped him by several inches. Sienna carefully looked at the waiter, and knew this was not the average wait staff. The muscles in his chest and abdomen bulged beneath the crisp white uniform dress shirt. She trailed her eyes down the length of his fitted tuxedoed pants, and saw the rope of corded muscles bunch beneath the fabric.

She looked into his eyes and caught the flash of warning in their dark blue depths.

This was one of Runninghorse's men.

Sienna breathed a sigh of relief.

"If you go back into the party room, sir, I'm sure we can find another lady to accommodate you."

The big Texan bristled, but allowed the *waiter* to steer him away. "You stay right here, ma'am . . . I'll be back," he said to her before he walked the man back into the room.

Sienna swallowed nervously, sure she'd jumped from the frying pan into the fire.

She wanted so bad to see Mac, to speak to him, but she knew she had to be careful. Any wrong move at this point could not only mess up the plans, but could land her in a situation worse than the one she was in.

Moments later, she was rejoined by the waiter and he grasped her elbow, leading her away.

"Mr. Medeiros is waiting for you in his suite, Ms. Feathers. His room is located on the top deck. I'll take you there."

"Thank you for—" Sienna winced in pain, and stopped talking. She'd been about to thank the man for his intervention, and then he'd tightened his hand on her arm in warning.

She felt foolish and nodded her head in understanding. The yacht was crowded, and there was no telling who was around, and could overhear what she said.

She quietly followed the agent along the passageway leading to Carlos's suite.

40

Sienna rapped her knuckles softly on a glass-paned door and stepped back.

The door opened and she was surprised to look up to see Damian.

"Come in, Sin, we've been waiting for you."

Sienna walked inside and closed the door, rubbing her hands over her arms. When she entered the room, her stilettos sank into the plush forest-green carpet.

"I thought I was supposed to be meeting with Carlos. Alone," she added, cutting her eyes in Damian's direction.

A sneer stretched Damian's thin lips wide. "What? I'm not good enough? Used to be a time when you couldn't wait to . . . dance . . . for me."

Sienna caught Carlos in her peripheral vision, near the bar. She turned her eyes toward Damian. "I don't think so. You've got it twisted. I think you've got me confused with someone else. You *never* had it like that with me, Damian." When Damian blushed, his lips tightened angrily. She knew she'd scored a direct hit.

She knew she came off hard—harder than Damian was used

to—but she wanted to present an image of a woman who was unafraid, one who knew the score. She had to show confidence in order to get Carlos to open up to her.

Maybe he'd open up enough that he'd spill some small information the men could use to get his ass behind bars for any of the many charges Runninghorse said Medeiros was guilty of committing.

"Damian, you can go now. I believe Ms. Feathers and I can handle it from here out."

With an insincere smile plastered across his lips, Damian inclined his head toward Carlos. He shot Sienna a malevolent glare before turning on his heels and leaving the room, closing the door behind him.

"Hmmm . . . I'm gathering there is no love lost between you two, no?"

Sienna turned to face Carlos fully. "No, I suppose not," she replied.

Although she hadn't seen him in a long time, nothing had changed about him: The suit he wore would probably cost her a year's salary. The cut of his expensive clothes, the Rolex, the diamond cuffs, and handmade Italian leather loafers on his long, thin feet smacked of wealth.

Glancing back at his face, she noticed that nothing had changed there, either. He stared back at her with the same cold, calculating stare she remembered from when he'd watch her dance, his lust-filled yet cold stare unwavering on her.

His gaze fell to the necklace she wore. One corner of his mouth lifted, the look on his face, satisfied.

"Are you cold, *mi belleza?*"

"No . . . no, I'm fine."

"Come farther in, I won't hurt you. In fact, you might like what I have planned for us."

"I'm sure I will," she murmured, moving farther into the room.

"Can I get you something to drink? A martini? Scotch? Anything?"

"I don't drink. A Coke is fine, if you've got it," she murmured.

"Why don't you have a seat while I fix us something to drink."

When he gestured with one manicured hand toward the living area of the large suite, Sienna's gaze followed.

In the center of the room, a king-sized bed dominated, set up on a high platform. The bed was canopied, the head swathed in sheer fabrics, and the bed itself covered in a spotlight of recessed lighting.

Behind the headboard, extending the length of the wall, was a dark, smoky-tinted mirror, which instantly reminded Sienna of the mirrored walls in the Sweet Kitty.

Just like back then, the feeling of being watched sent goose bumps down her arms.

She turned her gaze away from the mirror and toward the cream-colored suede settee and matching chairs.

"Let me turn on music for us. Would you like that?" he asked, and didn't wait for a response. He picked up a small remote and pressed a button and the suite was filled with soft music.

"A bit different than the type of music you are used to, but it is nice, *si*?" He walked toward her as she sat on the edge of her seat and handed her a drink.

She carefully took a sip and raised accusing eyes to Carlos. "I told you I wanted a Coke—"

"You need to relax, loosen up. It's not much alcohol, just enough to relax you, *hermosa*."

"I'm fine, Carlos. What makes you think I need to relax?" she said, carefully placing the beverage on the glass table in front of her. She pushed back into her chair, crossing her legs in front of her.

He followed the motion of her legs as she swung one back and forth, rubbing it against the other.

"So what do you want me for, Carlos? What made you have Damian seek me out? Like you said . . . it's been a while."

"You've grown up since I last saw you."

She lifted a brow in question. "I've been grown for a long time, Carlos."

Carlos sat down next to her, close, without touching. Sienna kept the sultry look on her face, despite her need to jump up and move away.

"Hmm. Maybe mature is a better word," he replied.

"We all have to grow up one day," she quietly uttered.

"Yes, and you've *matured* into such a beautiful woman."

He trailed his fingertips around her neck, skimming over the necklace, before dipping his fingers between her cleavage. He boldly spun his finger around the thin material covering her nipples.

When her nipples beaded against his fingers, he smiled.

"I always knew beneath that cool veneer, you were hot. I knew you were just waiting for the right man, a man who knew how to take care of a woman, to tap that ice shield you put up."

He leaned close and began nuzzling her flesh, rubbing his nose down her neck. The goose bumps that slithered along her skin weren't due to arousal, but disgust.

Sienna felt the light dinner she and Mac had eaten rise, clogging her throat.

Wanting his hands off her body, Sienna moved slightly away and lifted her glass from the table and took a sip.

Carlos gave her a knowing smile and lifted his own drink, staring at her intently over the rim of the glass. After taking a healthy swallow of the dark whisky, he set the glass back on the table.

"What do I want from you?" He turned back to her and took her glass from her hands, and placed it on the table next to his.

Sienna remained silent, projecting an air of confidence she

was far from feeling. "Yes. What do you want from me, Carlos? What made you send Damian after me? It can't be for a piece of ass. A man like you could get that anywhere, from any number of beautiful women. Why me?"

His expression showed his surprise at her words, but also at the confidence she showed. She waited, carefully keeping her expression bland, neutral.

He ran a long finger down the side of her face and she forced herself not to flinch.

"Yes, you're right. A piece of ass, I can get anytime, anyplace, *mi querida.* But you're not just any piece of ass."

He lifted the diamond necklace from around her neck with one long finger, caressing the cold diamonds, feathering his fingers along the column of her neck.

"I'm glad you wore the necklace I sent," he murmured.

Sienna widened her eyes, feigning surprise at his disclosure.

Carlos smiled, laughing low. "Yes, I was the one who gave this to you. When you worked at the Sweet Kitty, I had Damian give it to you after the first time I saw you dance. Do you remember that, Sin?"

One hand wrapped around her neck gently, while the fingers on his other hand trailed down her throat, between her cleavage.

"Yes, I do," she whispered, unable to look away from his mesmerizing stare. Her chest swelled, her breath coming out in small pants of air, her gaze locked with his.

"You looked so small, so delicate, so beautiful, dancing with your eyes closed. Dancing for no one but you, *mi peacock hermosa,*" he murmured.

As he spoke, he moved behind her, close, and stroked her breasts through her clothes. He moved the small strip of fabric to the side and cupped one of her breasts, nestling it within the palm of his hand, his thumb toying with her nipple.

"I never realized you watched me so intently."

"I was the one who brought you to that simpleton Marks's attention." He laughed again when she inhaled sharply. His thumb continued to pluck at her nipple as he spoke.

"Damian found me at the diner I worked. He used to come in—"

"At two P.M., every Monday," he finished.

"How did you know that?" Sienna swallowed nervously when he lifted the necklace again, his hand cupping her throat, while the other played with her breast.

"I was the one to discover you. I knew you would be perfect."

"To dance at the club?"

"No," he laughed. "That was for me to 'audition' you. To keep you within easy access. When I needed you, I would have you. *Tú sabes?*" he whispered, before he placed kisses down her neck.

The chills that ran down her body weren't from sexual excitement, but fear. Cold fear.

"No, I don't understand." Sienna struggled to keep her voice from trembling, from letting him know of her fear.

"I wasn't *in need* of a woman at the time, but I knew it wouldn't be long before I would be. When I saw you dance, saw this beautiful body move for me on the stage, I was so excited. I could barely wait to get my hands on you." He laughed again, and the cruel-sounding laugh sent fear racing through Sienna.

"And then you left." The smooth, easygoing flow of his voice changed, the hand he had on her neck moved to the necklace, pulling at the jewelry wrapped around her neck.

"I wanted to rip someone apart when I found out you left after I'd treated you so well."

Sienna's throat began to close, tears stinging her eyes when he pulled the necklace tight against her throat, cutting off her breath.

"I didn't know it was you!" Sienna choked the words out,

desperate. "I didn't know you were the one taking such good care of me or I wouldn't have left."

His hands hesitated, until he finally released the choking hold.

"If I had known it was you, I wouldn't have left, Carlos." She took deep, gasping breaths, her chest heaving, tears running down her face.

He turned her around to face him, staring down at her; his hands on her upper arms, punishing in their tight grip. He assessed her with his dead eyes.

Sienna fought to keep her revulsion and fear at bay. Showing fear was something she knew better than to do around him. Like any addict, he fed off fear. The results could turn disastrous, Sienna knew this.

"What about your new man?"

Sienna felt a renewed dread. She shouldn't be surprised that he knew about Mac. If he was the one who found her again, he no doubt knew everything that was going on in her life.

She had to do something to throw him off. If she could keep him calm until Mac showed up, if she could just do that, she'd be okay. She took a deep breath and smiled up at him.

"Who, Mac? He doesn't mean anything to me. Just another man. No one special," she said, giving him a purely feminine smile. "Someone to warm the pillow. That's it."

He studied her carefully, and Sienna studiously maintained a look of nonchalance on her face.

"You and I might be more alike than I thought," he murmured, stroking his hand down her cheek.

"Would you like to be my special *mujer?*"

"It might be something I'd consider."

His grin widened, and, laughing, he said, "Yes, *mi hermosa*, you and I will be good together. You will need to come with me, right away. Tonight. Now." He moved her hair to the side and placed moist kisses along her neck. He pushed away to look at her again. "*Esta bien?*"

41

"Damn it!" Runninghorse cursed.

"Sir, we've lost communication with Ms. Featherstone," one of his agents, who'd accompanied him on the yacht, said into his earpiece. "What do we do?"

"Just hold off. I'm going to the suite," he muttered.

He looked around the crowded room and spotted another uniformed man who worked as wait staff. He walked over and handed him a silver platter filled with crystal goblets of champagne.

"Going to take a piss. Take this," he said, handing the man the tray. Without waiting to hear a reply, he swiftly left the room.

"Do you need us to meet you there, sir?"

"No. Stay put. I'll contact you if I need assistance," Runninghorse replied quietly.

"What about the detective and his partner? Do I let them know that—"

"No," Jake interrupted. "I don't want him busting in here, fucking up any chance to catch Medeiros."

Jake briskly pushed past a couple, his attention focused on getting upstairs to Medeiros's suite.

"Yes, sir," the agent replied, and Jake cut communication.

Jake's attention was so focused on getting to Medeiros and Sienna that he didn't see the uniformed man watching him from the opposite side of the room, quietly following.

42

Sienna's eyes widened with panic. "Now?"

"*Sí.* I have my man waiting to take us. He is in my helicopter. It is on the yacht." When he saw her eyes widen, he continued. "Wealth has many privileges, this is but one. To be able to leave at a given notice is necessary, in my line of work.

"You will not have to work anymore, *querida.* You will have whatever your heart desires. Your only job will be to please me." His lust-filled eyes darkened. "No one else will dare touch you."

"Special?" she asked, stalling his hands by placing her shaky hands on top of his, trying her best to get his mind away from his obvious desire to strip her clothes.

"Just like the others. Just like the one you are replacing. You will be mine, to service only me. You will want for nothing. All of your desires will be fulfilled. Clothes, diamonds, jewels, cars, more wealth than you could dream of."

"The others? You've had other special women?" she asked, moving away from him, casually making her way toward the door.

He stopped her, pulling her roughly into contact with his

chest. Placing one long finger under her chin, he lifted her face, forcing her to look at him.

"None of them were the right one. None of them *appreciated* me. They didn't deserve the things I gave them. Took them off the streets, and tried to make ladies out of them." He brushed kisses alongside her jaw.

"You can take a whore out of the streets, but you can't take the streets out of the whore." He laughed at his own crude joke. "I gave them so much, but in the end, none of them were worthy."

As he nuzzled her neck, Sienna forced herself to remain calm, to try and lull him into a false sense of compliance.

"What happened to them? I can't imagine a woman not wanting to be with you. Who wouldn't want to be pampered, *loved*, by a powerful man like you?" she asked.

He leaned back and narrowed his eyes, staring at her from his dark, soulless eyes. He studied her for so long, Sienna was afraid that she'd overplayed the part.

Fear beat strongly in her, but she hid it.

She needed him to believe she was on board with his plans, that she felt disgust at the women he'd gotten rid of for not satisfying him.

When his lips stretched into a lazy half smile, she breathed an inward sigh of relief.

"What would you say if I told you they are no longer anyone's concern? That they got exactly what they deserved?"

Sienna's heart thudded, heavily, against her chest.

Dear God, he was going to admit what he'd done to them. She didn't want to hear it.

She knew she should encourage him to continue, to tell her what he did so that the man could get his confession taped. But at the moment, she desperately wanted to get away from the monster in front of her. No amount of wealth or expensive, tailor-made clothing could hide the sick monster he was.

"They called me an animal. Said I was sick when I requested

them to perform certain acts for me." He was no longer look-ing at her, but instead his eyes were glazed. He was staring off into space, thinking of God only knew what, Sienna thought, shuddering.

"What—" Sienna stopped, but forced the question out. "What did you want them to do?" she finished, pushing past the repugnance and fear.

Her question brought his attention back to her.

"I showed them the beauty and pleasure of a woman giving her man what he needs. Pain, when given in measure, results in the ultimate pleasure."

Sienna didn't, *couldn't,* say anything. There would be no de-ceiving him if she tried to fake her way through a semblance of a response.

"Sometimes I'd tie them up and eat them out, not allowing them to touch me as I pleasured them. They seemed to enjoy that." He laughed. "I shoved my cock in their seeping cunts and fucked their tight little asses with a dildo, until they begged to come. But it was too soon. And none of them could wait, the whores." He laughed, his mind far away, remembering his ex-ploits with the women. "*I* wasn't ready. It took more than what they gave for me to come. I'd keep them tied up in my bed for hours, and give them what they wanted. Too soon they would cry and beg me to finish it, to let them go. They did not care that I had not felt satisfaction. It took so much more than a wet pussy or tight ass to satisfy me."

He tunneled his hand through her hair, his fingers tightening painfully, pulling her close to his body. As he spoke, the bulge in his pants grew as he ground his cock against her mound. Si-enna bit back a cry and closed her eyes, forced to listen.

"I'd fuck them the way they were used to being fucked. But never did *I* come. Not until I realized what I needed. Can you give me what I need, sweet Sin?" He stared down at her, his eyes unfocused.

"Wha-what do you need?" Spellbound, Sienna stared in helpless fascination as his face twisted. A sneer crossed his wide lips.

"I need complete trust. Can you trust me, my sinful beauty?" The sneer stretched his lips wide.

"I—I don't know," Sienna whispered, and gritted her teeth when he pulled on her hair. Pain slammed into her when she felt her hair being ripped from her scalp.

"I require that. I cannot settle for anything else. Not anymore. None of the others would allow me to give them *true* pleasure."

His hands released their punishing grasp on her hair, only to return to the necklace that now felt like a noose. He circled his long, lean fingers around her neck, his thumb at the hollow of her throat, thumbing a rough caress back and forth.

"When I would try and show them, wanting to gift them with pleasure, they'd fight me. Right before unconsciousness, the incredible orgasm, the high is unbearably sweet. Life and death in the balance, the pain and pleasure blending, until one is indistinguishable from the other." He stopped speaking, closing his eyes.

His eyes dead, not looking at her, he recounted the horrid acts he performed on his "special" women. How he'd strangled them until he came. But first, he desecrated them, showering them in his urine, marking them as his. Then, and only then, would he come.

"The last one did not trust me. In her mistrust, she died." He finally said the words she dreaded hearing.

He pulled Sienna unbearably close.

"Carlos, please—let me go!" Sienna choked the words out behind the tightening constriction of the necklace, desperate to break him out of his self-induced trance.

She wildly pushed against his chest. Finally he opened his eyes, loosening the strangulating hold.

He was speaking to her, looking at her, but his eyes appeared glazed. His face twisted as he recounted the horrid sexual acts he forced the poor woman to perform.

"It was inevitable. As it was with all of them, eventually. She, like all the others, was no more good to me." The left side of his wide mouth hitched in a sneer.

"But this will not happen with us. You are no longer afraid, hmmm? You trust me, *sí?*"

As he spoke, he completely loosened his punishing hold and returned to delivering caressing touches to her neck, down her throat. He eased all but two more fingers from beneath the necklace and her neck.

"They didn't understand a man with your passions," Sienna answered, licking her dry lips, her breath now coming out in fast gasps.

He focused his attention on her, the glazed look easing from his eyes, and smiled.

"*Sí, querida,* this is what makes you special. I knew I was right about you. You share my passions. A woman who knows what she wants. Who is not afraid of the power and excitement, the true passion of life. I cannot tell you how happy I was when my men found you, my sneaky little beauty." He scolded her as though she were a wayward child, and Sienna felt like throwing up.

She wasn't about to smile for him. She couldn't fake it even if she tried.

It was all she could do to keep it together around his crazy ass.

He was a bona fide madman. To think she'd been close to death for so long and hadn't known it.

When she'd left the Sweet Kitty, she thought that all she left behind had been stripping for nameless horny men who paid to see her nearly nude body gyrate and grind on stage.

Instead, she'd barely escaped the clutches of the demonic man in front of her.

She inclined her head in response, saying nothing.

In her mind, she knew she had to convince him to feel comfortable with her. Despite the heart-pounding fear she felt, she *had* to present an image of a woman who knew the score, and show him she wasn't the scared little girl he once thought her to be.

She moved closer to him, ran a caressing hand down his chest, her hand stopping mere inches from the bulge straining his pants.

"What makes you think I was once frightened?" She returned the conversation to his earlier question.

Carlos's dark eyes glittered with desire, mingled with some other frightening emotion, one that made Sienna cringe. She had to divert him from what his lust-filled eyes told her was dominating his thoughts.

He wanted to fuck her . . . and hurt her. His ideal way to have sex with a woman.

She allowed her hands to drift closer to his thick erection.

"Do not take it as an insult. It is what drew me to you. Your innocence and your passionate nature at war with one another." He moved closer, so that her hand was flush against his cock.

"No one understands you, do they, *querida*?"

"I don't know what you mean." Sienna barely choked out the words. Her heart was beating fast, her skin felt itchy, and she felt perspiration bead her forehead.

She was overwhelmed and felt completely out of control.

"Yes, you do," he countered.

He held her hand over his crotch, guiding it, forcing her to massage his thick, bulging cock beneath his pants.

His words crashed over her; the intimate gesture he was forcing her to perform filled her with revulsion and shame. The type of shame she hadn't felt since she'd left her days of stripping.

Unable to hold his gaze, she turned away. Carlos grasped her by the chin, forcing her to look at him.

"With me, you are free to be who you are. No pretenses. Sienna Featherstone, or Sinful Feathers. Quiet schoolmarm, or the sensual woman who enjoys exposing her body for scores of men."

He brought her resistant face closer. Sienna's jaw tightened in anger and denial of the words he uttered.

She was *not* that woman. There was *no* duality in her nature. She'd stripped because she'd *had* to. She did what she needed to do, to survive.

That was all there was to it.

Yet, his words beat at her, relentless, echoing in her mind.

His tongue struck out, licking the corner of her lips. "A woman who enjoys making me fantasize what it would be like to make incredibly passionate love to her."

"Carlos—no—" He slammed his mouth against hers in a punishing clash of lips and teeth.

Forcing her lips to part, he then shoved his thick tongue deep inside her mouth. For long moments, his mouth assaulted hers, and he ground his cock against her groin. His groans were harsh and labored as he sucked and pulled at her lips.

Sienna struggled against Carlos's hold, pounding her fist against his chest, shoving with all her might against his body, trying to get away.

He laughed against her mouth, continuing to plunge his tongue inside it, his lips bruising hers.

Sienna renewed her struggles, shoving him away with all her strength. Finally she pushed him away, stumbling back against a table. "Stop it, damn it! What are you doing?"

"What do you mean, what am I doing? I'm taking what's mine!"

"When did I give you permission to manhandle me?" she cried out, her chest heaving with her exertions.

He grabbed her by the hair and hauled her close, whispering, "You gave me permission when you agreed to be *mi mujer.*" He laughed, his hot breath fanning the hair at her temple.

43

Sienna flinched when she heard a popping sound in her ear. Something had gone wrong with the communication device and her fear turned to stone-cold dread.

Sienna knew that she had to tread lightly with him. She had no idea where Mac or Runninghorse was, or if they'd get to her before he hurt her.

She hoped to God the men knew she was in trouble and were on their way. The demented, crazed look in Carlos's eyes told her he was teetering on the edge.

When he released her, she stumbled back, watching him warily. He pulled her with him, dragging her to the large desk in the corner of the room.

"What are you doing?" She cringed when he yanked harder on her hair, dragging her to the desk in the corner of the room.

He laughed harshly before replying. "Come now, *mi belleza*, you did not really think I thought your boyfriend would allow you to come here, without accompanying you, did you?"

"Wha . . ." Her voice faltered when he turned his dark eyes in her direction.

"Surely, you do not believe I am so stupid. I would not have been able to stay on the top, if I were that ignorant."

He wrenched a drawer open in the desk and withdrew a gun. With his hold on her tight, he reached inside his suit jacket and withdrew a small phone.

His eyes trained on her, he pressed a button.

"It is time to go. My guest and I will be on deck within five minutes. Be ready to leave," he said, and pressed another button, ending the call.

"Where are we going?"

"You will know when it is time. Come on," he said, dragging her resisting body along with his, toward the door.

She had to take care of herself, she had to get away from him before he took her wherever he planned to go. She knew it was somewhere no one would be able to find her.

Her eyes darted around the room, looking for something she could grab and use as a weapon. If she didn't locate something, there was no telling what the hell would happen to her.

As usual, she had to rely on her own wits to save herself, she thought. There was no time to fear, no time to allow this asshole to dominate her.

She had to take care of herself.

44

"What the fuck is going on? Why have we lost communication with her?" Mac yelled into the small microphone headpiece. "This wasn't part of the plan. She wasn't supposed to be alone with that motherfucker!"

"There's some type of interference, but we got what we need in order to bring Carlos in," Runninghorse spoke calmly.

"I don't give a shit about that! Sienna could be in danger—I'm coming in!" Mac barked, angrily.

"She's safe. My men and I will get her out. Just stay calm and *stay put*. You charging in won't—"

Mac ripped the headpiece off and slammed out of the chair.

"Man, where the hell are you going?" Kyle asked, turning his body around to face Mac as he opened the passenger side of the van.

"I'm not sitting around here waiting for Runninghorse to give me permission. Sienna needs me." He jumped out of the van and turned to Kyle. "You coming?"

"Shit! Wait up!"

Kyle heard the distinct sound of the charging handle on Mac's 9mm pulled. Before he could close his door, Mac was already sprinting toward the brightly lit dock, heading toward the yacht.

Kyle caught up with Mac as he sprinted across the empty, darkened street, the moon's light streaking across his dark-clad body.

Mac raced along the walkway, toward the yacht, with Kyle close behind. He yanked open the door and raced inside. The main room was crowded with the partygoers, the music loud, the smell of marijuana thick in the air.

He glanced around, looking for Runninghorse or any signs of his men, past the partyers lounging, women in men's laps, lines of cocaine openly on tables.

"Damn it, we'll never find her this way!"

Kyle turned to Mac as both of their eyes darted over the crowd, past the women sitting in laps, all but fucking in public, past the couples huddled in corners, men with their pants shoved down enough to expose their cocks, pressing against their naked partners, grinding their bodies against the wall. His glance then went over the handful of guards that casually strolled through the throng, easily identifying them as Medeiros's men, before he spotted one he recognized.

"There's one of Runninghorse's men!" Mac spotted one of the men Runninghorse had introduced him to earlier in the week. The man was dressed as a waiter and was making his way toward them.

"Follow me! Agent Runninghorse is out," he said, and the two men raced along with the agent, taking the stairs two at a time toward the second floor.

"What the hell do you mean, he's out?"

"He was stopped by Medeiros's men. It was a setup. They knew we were here."

"What the fuck?" Mac's gut clenched in fear with the information that Runninghorse had been discovered and could be dead.

"He'll be fine, sir. We have to get to Ms. Featherstone!"

All three men raced along the passageway. When there were no guards standing outside the door, he turned to the agent.

He kept his weapon ready, in case he and Kyle were headed into an ambush.

"You sure this is the right suite? Where the hell are the guards?" he asked in suspicion. He subtly gave Kyle a nod, to make sure he was prepared for potential ambush.

"Yes, sir, this is it. Agent Runninghorse was able to disable one of the guards before he was taken. Communication with him was cut right before you came."

The young agent's earnest face sought to reassure Mac. When Mac heard a gunshot from within the cabin split the air, he didn't care if it was an ambush or not.

"Let's go!" he yelled.

With the amount of adrenaline rushing through his body, Mac easily broke through the door, the power of his kick splitting the wood into fragments as he ran into the room.

He came to a stumbling halt, once inside, surveying the room.

45

As Carlos dragged her along, toward the door, Sienna's eyes darted around the room until they lit upon a crystal vase that was filled with flowers.

She allowed him to continue to pull at her, and when they reached the vase, she twisted her body away from his, grabbed it with both hands and slammed the vase over his head.

The crystal shattered into a thousand pieces, raining down over him.

"You goddamn bitch!" he howled in pain. He released her and grabbed his head, blood trickling down from the gash in his temple.

Sienna wasted no time, and began to run toward the door. The heel of one stiletto caught in the rug, and with a cry, she went down, landing on her knees.

She glanced over her shoulder in time to see Carlos's looming body moments before he tackled her, crashing down on her back, her body slamming into the floor, facedown.

"You are going to pay for that, bitch!" he threatened.

He rolled with her on the carpet, until he was straddling her, then slapped her so hard, her head snapped viciously to the side. With a cry of pain, she turned her face and bit down with all her might on the fleshy underside of his shoulder.

"Yes, fight me! It will make the pleasure so much better. You'll forget any other man was ever in this cunt!"

"Fuck you, Carlos!" she shouted, leaning up far enough to spit into his face.

He grinned, his eyes glistening with a combination of lust and rage. His hands tore at her clothes, ripping them away from her.

"Yes, I will. And when I get through fucking that pussy, that tight little ass is next." He grunted, shoving her back down on the carpet, ramming his arm under her throat.

He flipped her body so that her face was once again smashed into the carpet.

Grabbing both of her arms, he held them tight in one hand, pressing them into the small of her back. Sienna heard the rustle of clothing, and then the cool leather of his belt wrapping around her wrist, binding her tight. She bucked against the hold . . . to no avail.

"Maybe I'll fuck this pretty little hole first." He laughed. She heard him shove his pants down and seconds later felt the knob of his shaft poking against her anus.

With a cry of denial, Sienna redoubled her efforts and fought him, kicking her legs and bucking her body to get him off. There was no way in hell she was going to let him rape and sodomize her.

He grabbed her by the back of the head, fisting her hair, and slammed her face into the carpet.

The pain was so intense, she was dizzy and nearly blacked out, seeing stars as the coppery taste of blood filled her mouth.

But Sienna had to ignore the pain—to give in to the pain at this point meant possible death.

"I'm going to give you what you've always wanted. Fight me, *sí*, fight me! It will only make it better. Pain and pleasure."

His dick began to press painfully into her, tearing into her tender flesh until she cried out in agony.

"No!" she screamed, tears streaming down her face, mingling with the blood, rendering her nearly blind.

She rubbed her face back and forth along the carpet, to clear her vision. She had to do something! *Please don't let this happen, God,* please! She screamed the desperate prayer in her mind.

As the pain filled her, her eyes lit on his jacket, which had been torn from his body during their struggle.

She could barely make out the shiny handle of the .45 as it lay outside the pocket of his jacket.

As he began to drag his cock in and out of her, his moans and grunts filling the room, she frantically fought the binds. With a superhuman effort, one born of desperation and unbridled fear, she wrenched free of the binds and shoved him off her body.

Before he could react, she clawed her way to the jacket and grabbed the gun.

She scrambled backward, and despite hands trembling so badly she was in jeopardy of dropping the gun, she held on to the cool chrome handle. Her body was weakened, racked with pain, yet her resolve strengthened.

Blinded by the blood streaming down her face, Sienna knew she only had one shot.

She gripped the gun with both hands, steadied her shaking hands.

46

"No!" Mac bellowed in a primal yell of denial.

Sienna was lying still, head to the side, eyes closed, with blood oozing down her face, trapped beneath Carlos Medeiros's prone body.

The sight of her unmoving body propelled Mac into action. His long strides took him to Sienna's side and he roughly shoved the man's body away from hers. He spared only a passing glance at Medeiros's still body before squatting down to Sienna's side.

He lifted her body and pulled it into the cradle of his arms, thumbing the hair away from her face.

He placed two fingers at her pulse point under her chin, and the reassuring, steady thud filled him with overwhelming relief.

Her eyes fluttered open, a moan escaping from her lips, and he crushed her to his body.

"Oh God, baby, please be okay!" he said, and felt his eyes burn with the sting of tears.

Her swollen, bruised lips moved and she whispered something inaudible.

"What is it, Sienna? Baby, are you okay?" he asked tenderly.

"Ummm," she groaned, clenching her eyes tight. "Yes. I'd be better if you stopped crushing me, Mac," she said, and allowed her eyes to shutter closed.

Mac released a sound, a cross between a sigh of relief and laughter. He pulled back, loosening his hold.

He forced himself to remain calm as he moved the hair at her temple, sticky with blood, away from her forehead. A small gash in her head was responsible for the blood, but he didn't see anything deep, just superficial.

"Where are you hurt, baby?"

Mac began to run his hands gently over her nude body. She groaned when his fingers grazed the exposed skin under her breasts.

"My ribs," she hissed, and he moved his hands away.

He ran assessing eyes over the bruised skin near her rib cage, as well as her body. When he saw no gunshot wounds or anything beyond the horrific, darkening bruises, he sighed a silent breath of relief.

Carefully he pulled her tighter into his embrace, leaning his head on top of hers. Mac kissed her soft hair and allowed the tears to stream down his face.

Kyle rushed inside, followed closely by the young agent, along with two more of Runninghorse's men and two paramedics.

"I called for backup and an ambulance. They're rounding up as many of the men downstairs as they can."

"Most of them got away. Most of the ones we got up are the women. We'll take them in for questioning," the agent explained.

Mac covered her with his jacket, shielding her nude body.

"Sienna okay?" Kyle asked, running his eyes over Sienna, who was held close in Mac's embrace.

"Yeah, she's fine."

"What about him?" Agent Smith asked as Kyle hunkered down to the unconscious man. He felt for his pulse; then he moved Medeiros's body, searching for injury. When Kyle moved Carlos's arm to the side, he saw the blood oozing down his shoulder, his arm dangling at an odd angle.

"He'll live. His shoulder is shot to hell, but he'll live."

Mac turned to one of the paramedics. "Take her first. She needs medical attention," he said, and stood with Sienna in his arms.

"Yes, sir. We'll come back for him as soon as we get her into the ambulance." The men placed her on the stretcher.

"Mac—" Sienna opened her eyes and searched for him.

"I'll be right behind you, baby," he reassured her, clasping her small hand within his. With a soft sigh, she closed her eyes and Mac allowed them to take her away.

He turned back to Kyle and Agent Randolph.

"Can you handle this?"

"Yeah, man, go on. I'll catch up with you at the hospital," Kyle reassured him.

Mac nodded his head and turned to leave.

At the door, he turned back. "What about Runninghorse? Have your men found him yet?" he asked the agent.

"No reports back yet, sir. If he's still on the yacht, we'll find him," he said. Mac nodded his head and followed the paramedics out of the room, leaving Kyle and the agent to deal with the police.

47

"Mac, I'm fine. I can walk!" Sienna protested when Mac opened the car door and lifted her into his arms.

"Hush up and enjoy the ride, woman."

Sienna gave up protesting and linked her arms around his neck. Although she had only an overnight stay—at Mac's insistence—Sienna was more than ready to come home.

When they reached her door, he looked at her expectantly. With a sigh, she handed him her key and allowed him to unlock it and walk inside with her in his arms.

Once inside, he turned on the lights and walked with her over to her small living room. After gently depositing her on the sofa, he turned on a small lamp.

"I'll go make you something to eat." He lifted the small blanket on the sofa and covered her, tucking the ends around her. Sienna hid her grin. Over the last twenty-four hours, he'd been treating her as though she would break.

"I'm not really hungry," she said, nestling into the sofa.

"You need to eat something, baby."

"I'm fine, Mac," she told his retreating back.

She sighed and settled into the sofa, listening to him in her kitchen, opening cabinets and drawers.

"Maybe some soup and tea. That's about all I can handle. There's canned soup in the side cabinet, next to the fridge."

"Okay. After that, we'll get you to bed."

Sienna lay against the cushions and fell into a light doze. She didn't know how long she had slept, when she was awakened by the smell of the aromatic soup, and Mac's large frame sitting next to her on the sofa.

"I have your soup, sweetheart." He set the wicker tray with the small bowl of soup and crackers on the table next to her.

"Thank you," she murmured, pushing the hair out of her eyes and sitting up. She groaned from the pain in her ribs, and Mac quickly set her steaming tea down and steadied her.

"Damn, be careful, Sienna!" he admonished her, helping her to sit up.

"I'm okay." She smiled past the momentary pain. "I'm doped up enough that I don't even feel my own toes." She gave a small laugh.

"Speaking of that—" He jumped up and grabbed the brown bag he'd brought inside. He withdrew the small bottle and shook out two pills.

"Open up," he said, and Sienna smiled. With mock docility, she opened her mouth and swallowed the pills after she took a sip of her tea.

"A girl could get used to all this attention," she said after placing the steaming mug back down on the tray.

"I wouldn't back away from that." His eyes bore into hers, his expression intense. Sienna was at a loss for words, so she said nothing. Unable to hold his gaze, she looked away.

"Have you heard from Jake?" Sienna asked, changing the subject.

"Kyle got a call from his men. He's okay."

Sienna heard the hesitancy in his voice and knew he was holding back information.

"And?"

"And what?"

"What happened to him? Where is he now?"

Mac debated how much to tell her. After making sure Sienna was okay, he'd gone back to the yacht, to go over the details with the local cops of what had transpired. The yacht had been teeming with police and he'd finally found Kyle and Agent Randolph.

When he'd questioned the agent on Runninghorse's whereabouts, he'd gotten the runaround. They'd located Runninghorse, but that was all the agent would tell him.

Mac had cornered him, away from everyone else, demanding to know what had happened to his friend.

Intimidated, the agent had given Mac more details, telling him that Runninghorse had gone underground, that it had something to do with the case.

Pressed for more details, he'd told Mac that Carlos hadn't been alone in his operation. He'd chosen Sienna to be his latest submissive, and that it wasn't something he did only for himself. Carlos was a supplier. Supplying women no one would miss, to act as concubines for hundreds of wealthy men.

Runninghorse had given Smith permission to disclose to Mac that he was on a quest to root out the man at the pinnacle of the operation.

Satisfied that Runninghorse was alive, Mac hadn't pressed for further details.

"He's fine. You don't need to worry about him. You need to concentrate on getting better," Mac told Sienna, taking the tea from her hands when he noticed the fine trembling in them.

"God, Mac, I could have died," she said, her voice breaking.

The drama over the last week, ending with a near-death experience, finally caught up with her. Mac had been carefully watching her, waiting for it to happen.

She stared up into his face, her face losing its creamy brown color, becoming ashen in appearance. Her brown eyes appeared larger, her pupils dilated. One by one, fat dollops of tears began to flow down her face.

Soon she was crying deep, racking tears. His heart broke as he looked at her. She was huddled, appearing so small, relief and fear of what could have happened were stark in her eyes.

"It's okay, Sienna, baby, you're safe. No one will hurt you again." He soothed her, wrapping her in his arms.

As she cried, he knew she was releasing pain, fear, and hopelessness that she'd suffered from for years. This last, dramatic ending allowed her to finally let go.

He ran his hands over her back, murmuring soothing words, wanting her to get it out.

"It's okay, you're safe now, Sienna," he repeated, not knowing what else to say as he held her close, careful not to touch her sore ribs.

Once her tears had eased, her broken sobs turning to an occasional hiccup, he gently lifted her up and carried her to the bed. In the dark room, he lay her down on the bed, carefully removing her clothing.

He quickly shucked his own clothes and lay down behind her.

He turned her around and placed kisses over her face, over her closed eyelids, down her tearstained cheeks, a small moan of pleasure escaping her lips.

He didn't want to hurt her, but he had to make love to her, had to feel her body wrapped around his, feel the reassuring warmth of her feminine sheath gripping his as he rocked into her body.

He moved their bodies so they were facing each other and gathered her closer to kiss her, his mouth moving over hers, capturing her moan of desire.

"I love you, Sienna. I love you so much." He whispered the words past the constriction in his throat and the desperate kisses he was placing around her mouth.

His hand traveled over the length of her body, past the in-dent of her waist, over the curvature of her hips, and crossed over to the small strip of curls protecting the triangle juncture at the apex of her thighs.

He ferreted out the small nub, dipping one finger inside her well, and withdrew his finger, covered in her sweet juices.

He placed his finger in his mouth.

"So good. So damn good." He rubbed his finger over her turgid peak and stroked her.

"What we have is real, Sienna. I don't want to imagine my life without you. Wherever you are, I want to be." He captured her lips.

She tasted herself as he kissed her for long moments, before releasing her. "Tell me you want the same," he begged, his voice breaking.

Sienna stared into his handsome face and wanted to weep when she saw the tears and love shining brightly in their light gray depths.

She placed her hands on each side of his face and kissed him. She couldn't say anything. She couldn't think past the tangle of emotions beating down on her, clouding her mind, her thoughts in a chaotic whirl.

"God, baby, you've got to want me. Want us."

She said nothing, her mind and emotions all over the place.

"I couldn't imagine my life without you." The words rushed out of him. In the dark room, Sienna felt, more than saw, the deep breath he took. His frustration and fear were layered thick, the tension in the room, visible.

"I want you to marry me. Live with me. Let me take care of you for the rest of your life. Let me be the one to help you shoulder the responsibility of your brother. Let me in, Sienna. Baby, let me in."

Sienna felt as though someone was literally pulling her heart out of her body. Exposed and afraid, she felt overwhelmed with his love for her. Love he'd shown her in ways that mere words failed to convey.

"Mac, I know you love me. Baby, I know that. And I love you, too. God, how I love you."

In the semidarkness, she saw relief spread over his face, his eyes lightening in relief. She ran a hand down over the scratchy roughness of hair covering his cheek.

"But I don't know that I'm ready for that yet."

The beginnings of his smile began to fade, and his hand on her waist tightened. "Why? What else do I need to do to prove how much you mean to me?"

"You don't have to prove anything to me, Mac. I know you love me. More than I ever thought any man would. And I love you with everything I have inside me." Her words seemed to reassure him.

He continued his slow caresses, forcing her to think past the surge of desire sweeping through her.

"I've run for so long. It feels good to finally have peace. My brother is safe now. I have a career I love. And most important, I have a man I love by my side. One I trust. I'm not going anywhere. My running days are over."

"So what does that mean for us?"

Sienna smiled. "It means that I want to enjoy my newfound happiness. I want to enjoy the blessing of you. *Of us.* Of happiness. I'm at peace. And I'm not going anywhere. I'm yours."

She held her breath, hoping her words would assure him that she loved him. That she didn't want anyone else but him. "Is that okay with you? Being stuck with me?"

A smile lifted the corner of his sensual mouth before it blossomed into a full-out grin. "Yeah, I think that'll work fine. I'll work on convincing you to agree to the picket fence and 2.5 kids later. Right now, I want my woman," he said, and she laughed out loud as he gripped the swell of her hips and surged into her tight, moist sheath.

He gently stroked into her once, twice, and on the last thrust, he came, holding her body tightly against his as his cum rushed deep inside her. He held her close so that she felt every hot splash of his cum against her womb.

"I love you, Sienna. Forever mine," he covered her cries of release with his mouth. Their tears of joy, acceptance, and contentment mingled as their kisses sealed their comittment.

Epilogue

"Why does he insist on putting things so high and out of reach that I need a stepladder to get them?" Sienna groused, standing on tiptoe, staring up into her kitchen cabinets.

She turned away in disgust, absentmindedly rubbing her aching lower back.

"So you won't try and lift anything too heavy and possibly hurt yourself?"

Sienna turned and raised her eyebrows, exclaiming, "A jar of mayonnaise? How is *that* too heavy?"

Chrissy, Mac's sister, laughed. "To my brother, any and every thing is a potential danger for you, particularly now that you're pregnant. Let me get it for you." She easily reached over a much shorter and very heavily pregnant Sienna to pull the jar down. After opening it, she handed the jar to Sienna.

"Thanks," Sienna said, smiling at her sister-in-law.

The two women were in Sienna's kitchen in the new home she and Mac had recently purchased, finishing the last of the food preparations for the afternoon Sunday picnic.

The last year had brought about changes—good ones—for

her, Sienna thought, as she glanced out of one of the large kitchen windows, putting the finishing touches on the potato salad she was making. One amazing change had been the one in her brother, Jacob.

The wooden spoon she was stirring with stilled, and a small smile of happiness lifted her lips as she gazed out of the window that overlooked their backyard.

Mac, his nephew Daniel, and her brother Jacob were playing a game of flag football and even from a distance she could see her brother's face set in serious lines as he ran the length of the yard, heading toward the goal. When he made it to the end, he turned around, his chest heaving with exertion as he faced Daniel and Mac, in hot pursuit.

She saw a wide smile break out on Jacob's normally somber face when Mac congratulated him. Mac raised his hand and Sienna inhaled a sharp breath, wondering what Jacob would do.

She blew out the anxious breath in a sigh of relief when her brother slapped his hand, returning the universal high-five. Sienna bit back the tears that burned the back of her throat.

"He's good with them, isn't he?"

Sienna turned slightly and looked into her sister-in-law's face. The understanding and love she saw made her own smile widen as broadly as her brother's.

"He is. It's really amazing," she murmured. "This is like a dream come true. One I'd never thought I'd see."

Chrissy smiled at her.

"The addition of you *and* your brother to my family has been a gift to us," she said, and gave Sienna a brief hug.

"I feel the same way. The way you all have welcomed me and my brother into your lives is truly a gift to us, as well." Sienna returned her hug, and allowed the tears to fall.

"Hey, what's all this?" The two women pulled apart when the patio door opened and Mac walked inside, followed by an out-of-breath Daniel, and Jacob.

Mac walked over to Sienna and wrapped his arms around her rotund belly, kissing her on the neck.

Sienna leaned back into his embrace, moving her head to the side to allow him better access.

"Awww, come on! We don't wanna see all that kissing stuff, we wanna eat!" Daniel groaned. "Don't we, Jacob?" he asked, turning to the man at his side.

Jacob's dark brows met in the middle, his expression similar to his sister's, as he tilted his head to the side, considering Daniel's question.

"I think I like it. I don't ever want her to be the way she used to be. I like my sister happy," he replied simply. Sienna felt Mac's arms tighten around her.

"I guess." Daniel shrugged. "Hey Jacob, let's play a game until dinner's ready!" Daniel tugged on Jacob's arm. Jacob allowed Daniel to pull him down until he was sitting next to him, and within moments the two were engrossed in the video game.

Sienna didn't think she'd ever get over the sight of her brother not only allowing someone to touch him, but seeming to enjoy the contact.

Over the last year as he'd come to know Mac and his family, Mac's careful attention to him and Daniel treating him like an older brother had amazed Sienna, but nothing had prepared her for the way her brother had taken to them all.

He now spent his weekends away from the residential home with both her and Mac, or occasionally with Chrissy and Daniel. The change that had come over her brother had been nothing short of miraculous.

Fresh tears slipped down her cheeks, and Mac turned her around in his arms, pulling her as close as he could.

Sienna returned his embrace and mumbled into his shirt.

"What, baby?" he asked, pulling her away so he could see and hear her. "Are you okay?" he asked, concern in his eyes as he thumbed away the tears staining her cheeks.

"I'm fine," she hiccupped and laughingly tried to dismiss her obvious emotions. "These pregnancy hormones are rendering me a complete and utter crybaby."

"That explains it! I must be having that sympathy pregnancy we've been learning about in our Lamaze classes. Thank God! If word got around how emotional *I've* been lately, I don't think I'd ever hear the end of it from Kyle," he replied. Sienna grinned up at him.

"I won't tell a soul, even Kyle. Your secret's safe with me," Sienna promised. "I love you so much," she said, softly, her heart overflowing.

"Good, because now that I've convinced you to agree to the white picket fence, all I have left is one point five children—" he rubbed a hand over her belly—"and I will have everything I need," he said and pulled her close to give her a tender kiss.

Sienna laughed lightly, remembering his promise over a year ago. Then he slanted his lips over her mouth, their kisses sealing their commitment and love . . . forever this time.

Turn the page
for a preview of
Delta Dupree's STRIP!

Coming soon from Aphrodisia!

1

―――――――

"Ooh-*ooh*. Girl, I'll need to change my panties when this is over. He chose the perfect tune to turn us out. "Jamaica Funk" was the baddest hit on record," Galaxeé said. She swayed to the hip-hop song's downbeat, snapping her fingers as loudly as she popped gum. "He's hot, isn't he?"

"No doubt." Rio Saunders shifted, sat straighter on the bar stool at Killer Bods. The male strip club she and Galaxeé Barnett owned wasn't open for business until eight tonight, but the current dance applicant . . . mercy.

For a youngster he was a prime specimen, one of Denver, Colorado's finest. With a sable mane hanging well down his thick neck and a startling pair of slate-gray eyes, this tall honey paraded his attributes. He was God's blessed gift to women.

He swaggered toward the stage's edge. Under bright spotlights in the darkened theater, his view was nowhere near as good as hers. He flaunted all his finery. With broad shoulders, acutely defined pecs with just enough dark hair and a rippling six-pack, his body was a temple built for some lucky girl's loving.

"Mm, mm, mm," Rio purred quietly. And he had rhythm. Hiding a smile, she sipped from the glass of lemon water the bartender had set down.

"What do you think? Yes? Can't imagine otherwise," Galaxeé insisted.

They'd judged all sorts of wannabes for three hours—lean, stout, cute, plus a few sure-goners. Bryce Sullivan was the last performer applying for one soon-to-be vacant position.

No one else had danced so well. No one else had boasted his hard-body physique.

No one else looked this darn good.

Except Dallas Cooper, a.k.a. Panther Man. He—rather, his twenty-two-year-old hussy, Shannon Fields—decided to hang up his G-string for marriage. Dallas was Killer Bods' shining star. At twenty-eight, with smooth skin blacker than obsidian, he moved effortlessly during his performances, flexing his bulging muscles. Had he been a dozen years older, closer to Rio's age, she'd gladly let him turn her inside out. Welcome it.

"Let's think about it a couple days," she finally replied. "This is an African American revue."

Galaxeé's huffs would deflate most people's lungs. "Girl, time is running out. Panther's last night is next week. So what if this guy's white? As good as he looks, not to mention how well he boogies, he'll draw more chicks to the club. From Silk's."

Killer's dancers loved their sistahs, although a variety of women, single and married, looking for outstanding action frequented the nightclub. Quality advertisement was a must in this business. "White women."

"Blacks, too. And Latinas, Thais, hell, Egyptians. He is fine. You know it. I know it. Why wait? He could start tomorrow night. We can break him in for the Christmas rush, ready by . . ."

"Slow—" Rio clamped her mouth shut, shaking her head. Galaxeé talked faster than any auctioneer's banter during a hot sale.

"... We've booked four private parties so far, all between now and New Year's. He could work them. Shit, he'd clean up and so would we. Think of how much money we'd have coming in for only three real working days a week."

She shook her head again. "I don't think so."

Two deep frown lines creased Galaxeé's forehead and her lips thinned flatter than the straw Rio had chewed on. "Why not?"

"You know the sisters hosting these parties. They want chocolate, not vanilla."

She stared at Sullivan as he moved across the stage. He halted, struck a sexy pose. Every lean muscle rippled.

Jesus.

He unzipped his pants, stroked the length of his ... Rio sucked in a tank full of air, held it.

Slowly, sensuously, the denim slid down narrow hips, displaying powerful thighs and strong calves. When he kicked the garments aside, Sullivan straightened to his full height—a towering statue of regal flair fit for any queen's fantasy.

Breathing again, Rio lowered her gaze.

Good night!

Brazilian G-string. Miniature. Bulging flame-red against bronzed skin. Unblinking as he gyrated, she wasn't sure the fabric would hold together or hold all it carried inside the thin material. Barely enough to cover ... She drew in the next breath between her teeth and sat straighter on the stool.

"Ooh, gir-irl," Galaxeé breathed, fanning her face twice as fast as the music's rhythm. "He's exactly what you need."

Air flowed from Rio's lungs in a long, unsteady rush. "You mean us. Killer Bods."

"I mean *you*," her partner qualified. "You need a good fucking by a young buck just like him to fry your brains senseless. You've been going without way too long."

"Shut up."

Water and ice spilled over her hand as she set the glass down, splashing on the wooden bar top. An instant later, Luanne the bartender wiped away the puddle and handed Rio a fresh white towel.

"You do. That's why you've been so evil." Smoothing her hand down the length of her auburn dreadlocks, threaded beads clicked together. Galaxeé flicked the thick mass over her shoulder, still staring at Sullivan, mesmerized.

Rio tsked. The nerve of this woman. She folded the towel neatly into quarters and laid it across the curved bar. Yeah, maybe she had been evil, but she'd never shown bad manners to anyone other than her best friend and, of course, her ex-husband Devon, the midlife-crisis hound.

Arching one eyebrow a fraction, Galaxeé said, "You're getting another pimple, too, right there in the center of your forehead. At your age, any fuckable age, lack of weenie action always launches a round of zits."

"Shut up. Where do you come up with this mess?" She stole another glance at Sullivan. This man wasn't lacking anything from what she could tell.

Galaxeé leaned back, dangling her arms behind the chair, cackling. "It's true, especially after wrestling the monthly blues. I used to get them." She'd hooked up with a new honey, an older man who, after four months, still lavished her with expensive gifts, bombarding her with boyish love. "Besides, I can tell you really like the way this guy looks, the way he moves. Your aura's melting, on the verge of disintegrating. And it's the first time I've seen your eyes glaze over in almost two decades."

Aura. And glaze? She tsked again. Sometimes Galaxeé talked too much smack. No one caused Rio Saunders to glaze over, especially youngsters. "Bar lights, disco lights—"

"Bullshit. Admit it. He's hot."

He was hot—*is* hot—and far too young for her. Plus, he was nowhere near *right* for her. "Why do you think he came here for a job? Why not apply at Silk's?"

Smoothly Silk, Killer's sole competition, employed two African American dancers Rio and Galaxeé had disqualified from their league of performers a month before their own club opened. The guys were physically unsuitable for near-naked entertainment.

"Maybe he did," Galaxeé replied as the music died away. "We need to interview him anyway. Ask him."

Bryce collected his clothes and went backstage. After stripping out of the G-string, he struggled into a pair of tight stonewashed jeans. Luckily, his navy knit pullover soaked up sweat. It was freezing outside.

Snow—big flakes—had begun to fall by the time he'd arrived here. Winter had settled on Denver on Halloween night as usual, and continued a blustery rampage.

This was the stupidest plan on record. Galaxeé and whoever the hell this Rio broad is will never hire me. Should've come up with a better scheme and left Dallas out of the mix. If he ever finds out, our friendship is history.

His half sister, Angelina Berardi, owned Killer's competition and Bryce was her silent partner. Silk's was headed straight to hell as long as Killer Bods kept its doors open.

The club's downward spiral had stretched his cash thinner than ice after a first hard freeze, compounded by Thorobred Computers lacking a new contract over the last seven months. Banking on a few still in the till, he hadn't exactly wanted to strip to please a bunch of frenzied chicks. But, he also had a second working program: boxing in Jason Simmons, one of Killer's dancers, who needed somebody to knock the arrogant chip off his shoulders. Simmons dated Angelina—as in, walked all over her.

Armed with a fail-safe plot backed by his computer exper-
tise, Bryce had pretended he'd met Rio Saunders. Dallas had
fallen for the in-lust ruse.

"If you want her," Coop had said, "you got to get close to
her. I'll tell you what, my man. She is not easy meat. The
woman's got soul and determination, along with much class.
This club means everything to her. Everything, dude. Nothing
and nobody gets in her way when it comes to Killer Bods. As
for Galaxeé Barnett, don't try to get slick—nothing gets by her.
Some of the guys nicknamed her 'Loose Lips' for good reason,
and she knows everything that goes on, somehow. But the
owners are professionals, all business."

At the time, Bryce needed Dallas's foot-in-the-door help.
"She must have an old man or sugar daddy." Not many chicks
had their own business without financial help—like Angelina.

"Not. Unless she's got him under lock and key, hogtied and
gagged. She dates. Saw her with a couple older dudes, fifty-ish
maybe. I've never seen her with a youngster like you, and never
any guy tinted on the color scale's lighter side, especially one
with hair longer than Cher's. I'll get you an application, drop a
heads-up, but you gotta lose those damned Coke-bottle
glasses. Makes your eyes look bigger than E.T.'s peepers. Might
want to think about waxing, too." Laughing, Dallas said,
"Hurts like hell."

Testily conforming, Bryce permitted a beautician to chop
off his locks to near-respectable length. Lasik surgery corrected
the crappy vision he'd had since childhood. Horn-rimmed
glasses had been a pain in his . . . on the bridge of his nose. Fuck
waxing.

The new look had earned him lots more attention when he
had little time for play. Work kept him busy, kept his libido in
check most of the time.

He tucked the pullover inside his jeans, slung his black
leather jacket over his shoulder and went out the dressing

room's door. Unfamiliar with Killer's layout, he strode back across the stage and down the stairs, his gaze directed at the floor. Through a collection of tables stacked with hardwood chairs, he wove his way to the bar where Killer's owners sat. Dancing was the easy part.

"Very nice."

He recognized Galaxeé's business tone from the call for try-outs.

"Exceptionally provocative."

That sultry voice, chilly as a winter pond, floated through his senses, heating his skin unnaturally. Bryce looked up. The partner?

Exotic features fit her—coppery skin coloring, short-cropped platinum-blond hair lengthening to a shag that framed an oval face. Penetrating catlike hazel eyes held his gaze. When was the last time his heart stuttered and pounded like a damn kettle-drum? He wiped away the cool trickle of sweat from his fore-head.

"Thanks."

"Better than nice." Galaxeé tipped her martini glass toward him. "Sheer perfection."

Encouraged, Bryce nodded, smiled. One point for his side.

"This is my partner Rio Saunders."

"Tell us something," she said. "Why aren't you dancing at Silk's?"

Busted. Ears on fire, his face surely flushed five different shades of crimson. "They aren't hiring." God, he hoped not. He'd forgotten to ask his sister. "And Killer Bods is better known, hiring the best of the best."

"Bravo. Smart reply for someone so young."

At least she flashed a brilliant smile. More encouragement, except that degrading "young" crap declared like a long-lost aunt.

Scooting up on her barstool, Galaxeé said, "Grab a seat.

Would you care for a cocktail while we discuss business?" The offer earned a flat-out frown from her partner.

Bryce declined anyway, needing to get back to the office clearheaded. Building and selling desktop computers killed off brain cells the same as man's favorite poison, not to mention the headaches software development induced. If he nailed this gig at Killer's, his work schedule would turn crazier than it already was. After laying his eyes on luscious Rio Saunders, he thought dancing here might be well worth a pounding migraine.

"How long have you been shaking?" the woman of his super-erotic dreams asked.

He dragged a stool across the floor, placed it directly in front of her and said, "Years, but not professionally."

Truthfully, dancing ran a close second to skiing, third to computer work. Dallas had worked with him, claiming he had no rhythm or soul. Lacked funk. He'd laid down the law of the club.

Jam well, if he wanted to get next to Rio. Seductive moves earned the right to get close to her. Above all, he'd better know where to start.

Bryce knew exactly where to begin.

Even now, he imagined her skin felt soft as cotton. Nothing could be finer, except the blond hair framing her face. Would the tuft of hair between her legs feel as silky? He intended to find out one day. Slide his hand up her thigh, part her soft flesh, teasing her relentlessly.

"You do very well for a . . . a baby," she said.

He raked his fingers through his hair, his sensuous thoughts frozen in one brutal second. "I'm pushing twenty-nine. I'm not a damn newborn."

"Ooh, with a temper."

Bryce yanked his head around at Galaxeé's gum-popping explosion.

"Sorry," she said, but the disapproving sideways glare she gave her partner meant otherwise.

She'd sided with him. Add another point for the one-man team.

Sliding down on the stool, he spread his legs wider, nearly made contact with Rio, but she twisted in her seat, crossing a pair of lengthy, stunning limbs. "Am I at least in the running?"

"You most—" Galaxeé began.

"We like to discuss each applicant before we make a final decision," Rio interrupted, which earned another narrow-eyed glare from Galaxeé. She patted the stack of applications. "Everything on your résumé is current? Phone numbers, addresses, etcetera?"

Eyes locked on hers, he nodded. "Email, too." When she didn't deny having Internet access, he mentally ticked off an important item on his agenda.

"Well, Mr. Sullivan." She stuck her hand out. "We'll be in touch one way or the other."

What? The interview was over too damn quick—completely illogical. He'd interviewed potential technician applicants, at minimum, for an hour. And this was what, three minutes? Four? Two-hundred-forty stinking, chitchat seconds? How could she learn anything about him in so little time? Granted, he had abbreviated his account of the duties at his day job for good reason, but hell.

Bryce leaned forward and clasped her delicate hand. Long and slender, nails well manicured, her fingers curled around his with softness enough to caress a man into delirium while she kept him under the spell of her eyes—eyes he could drown in. He really wanted to drown.

He held on longer than he should have, but for a shorter time than he would've liked, without resistance, until Galaxeé cleared her throat.

"Thank you for your time," he said.

When their palms slid slowly apart, Bryce got to his feet. Galaxeé added a sly wink to her handshake. He slung his jacket over his shoulder and started toward the front door, telling himself not to look back, not to appear too eager or too arrogant. Step two now completed.

A blast of bitter-cold air and snow flurries whirlwinded into the club before the heavy door slammed shut.

"He likes you," Galaxeé said. "And he's got a penetrating pair of gray bullets that were fixed on you every second. When he arrived here, I was concerned, ready to boot the boy out. His aura was dark, murky. It glows now. Maybe it was fear, trepidation."

Rio rolled her eyes.

"Did you notice how he opened for you?"

"Stop," she said flatly.

"He did! An open invitation only for you. He's well hung too. Majestically." She grinned, winked. "You couldn't hide your attraction either. Your tits swelled."

"Stop it, Galaxeé." She had to admit, her lacy bra still felt uncomfortably binding.

"I saw your nipples perk up under the silk. Bet Bryce saw them. Stood out like cat's-eye marbles. Bet it made your tattoo spread with bigger, pink ears."

Rio hated the sound of a cackling witch, but she agreed with Galaxeé on one item. Bryce Sullivan was very well endowed.

She'd felt the first signs of pleasurable interest: nipples tightening, quivering between her legs when she'd glanced down at the bulging thickness nestled inside tight jeans. Lots of inches. Lord. What would it look like during an erection, a big oak tree? She shuddered.

Why couldn't he have a tenor or sissy voice instead of an I-can-make-you-come-multiple-times bass? God, she loved hearing a seductive, low-pitched rumbler, whispering, promising a thoroughly carnal interlude. A tenor would've made it so much easier to forget Sullivan and file his application at the back of the folder. Or in the circular file.

Still, at her age, any twenty-eight-year-old was too young, too inexperienced; she would consider it robbing the cradle.

Uh-uh. No way.

Anger crept under her skin for thinking of the sinful images, if a liaison ever happened. It never would, not in this lifetime. She had more important issues on her mind, like Killer Bods and her future. Denver's metro area had plenty of room for another women's club to strip Killer's of its dancers and clientele.

"I bet he's got a hundred young chickies chasing after him. Besides, I don't like men who flaunt their meat and put it on display like a hot item on a smorgasbord. Especially rookies." Temper had crept into her tone.

"He can't help it. It's part of him. What do you want him to do, cut it off? Is that why you like Dallas—Dickless?" Galaxeé laughed hard, mouth wide open, head falling back.

"You drink too much," Rio said. She meant it to sound snappish and snatched up the applications. "I'll make copies for you. When you're sober we'll discuss them."

Rio stomped toward their office above the club. Four-inch stilettos clicked noisily on the wooden stairs as she planted each foot, climbing each riser. She might hide her innermost feelings, but they never slipped by Galaxeé. The woman had an impossible perception, able to see through her, see inside her brain, read her thoughts. Ever since childhood, darn her.

Galaxeé had the nerve to call herself a fortune-teller and worked as one for a year, back in the good old days. She'd changed her first name from Cecilia for that reason alone and legally processed the paperwork. Astrology, palm readings and dreams were her best games. She'd said it was all in the hands and mind.

Two weeks ago, Rio had had a nightmare involving snakes. She should've known better than to tell her partner, who explained any visions about snakes meant a good "fucking" encounter and, if the dream included an anaconda, a big cock.

Rio chastised her for using foul language and laughed off the prediction, even when the dream featured one very large, very stout serpent chasing after her. She'd awakened startled, drenched in a sweat when it wrapped around her body.

Yeah, so she was afraid of too much meat. Too much meant pain and no enjoyment. Good old Devon had cured her.

But she was also aware of how her body had responded seeing Sullivan leisurely sprawled out like a sultan deciding on his daily choice from an ever-ready harem, displaying every thick, tempting inch of his staggering . . . Her mouth had watered and something else had shimmered from within. Something maddeningly metaphysical swept through her on one long wave from pinky toes to the roots of her hair, like the hot flashes she'd begun having recently. A sudden fire searing her flesh.

Even now, heat flooded her insides as she recognized the tingling of erotic sensations. Excitement coursed through her body, though Bryce Sullivan had already left the club with his fine self.

He did it on purpose, damn him. Just like a man. Baby! He's a baby!

She slammed the office door. These thoughts were absurd. Why hadn't she listened to Galaxeé and bought a vibrator for all the cold, lonely nights she spent without companionship in her downtown loft, for any time when horniness riled her libido and fantasies ruled her dreams?

"There're always the personal digits," Galaxeé had hinted.

"Forget that. If I ever decide to have sex again, I want the real thing, not fingers, not toys." She had avoided adult stores for good reason, still unable to defy her staid upbringing with too much change at once. Hopefully, one day she'd have another chance at a sexual encounter before she was too darned old to enjoy it.

By the time she finished work today, all of these flaming thoughts should melt the frost on the skylight, break the glass and fly away. They'd better fly somewhere. She had no insane reason to entertain them or Mr. Too-Young, Mr. Too-Hot Sullivan.